Tart

The Fluffy Cupcake Book 2

Katie Mettner

Katie Mettner

Tart

For the real Amber.
When I think about writing a funny best friend, you're always the gal to pop into my head. Thanks for always making me laugh!

Katie Mettner

One

My name is Amber Phyllis Larson, and my dirty little secret is that I'm terrified of thunderstorms. Embarrassing for a woman of thirty to admit, but there it is in a nutshell. At three a.m. on a Wednesday morning in late May, it was dark, the skies were heavy with rain, and thunder rumbled in the distance over Lake Pendle. We shouldn't have to deal with thunderstorms this early in the season in Minnesota, but someone forgot to tell Mother Nature that.

I popped a pod of coffee into the machine and waited while it spit the rich, black coffee into my travel mug. Whoever said the early bird gets the worm had never worked in a bakery for almost ten years. I didn't just work in a bakery for nearly ten years, though. I'd been the co-owner of The Fluffy Cupcake with my best friend, Haylee, for all ten of those bliss-filled years. She was recently married to Brady Pearson, her partner in crime at the baker's bench and now in life. That left me, the only one of the dynamic duo to remain single, much to my mother's chagrin. Unlike Haylee or my mother, I didn't see being single at thirty as the end of the world.

I chuckled to myself when I snapped the lid on my travel mug and turned off the kitchen light. Last year, Haylee decided she had to be in a committed relationship before she turned thirty. She made that resolution on New Year's Eve, which only gave her seven months and thirteen days to find Mr. Wonderful. Haylee was so focused on her goal that she was too obtuse to see that the perfect guy was already right in front of her face. So, I set her up with every guy I knew she wouldn't be able to tolerate for more than an hour, much less forever. I'm happy to report my plan worked. If she ever found out I tortured her on purpose, she wouldn't be amused, but sometimes, we need a little help to see what is directly in front of our face.

I grabbed my purse and slung it over my shoulder, taking a deep breath before I opened the door to my apartment. With any luck, I'd make it to the bakery before it started to storm any harder. I hated driving in lightning and thunder. Childish, I know, but if you'd lived my life the last seventeen years, you'd understand. I stuffed my thin athletic frame inside the car and slammed the door. Haylee was always jealous of the fact that I could eat anything I wanted from the bakery case without gaining a pound. I was always jealous of the fact that she had curves. What she saw as a negative feature, I would kill to have. Women are funny that way, I guess.

I shut off the engine in front of the bakery as the first drop of rain hit the windshield of my Subaru. I grabbed my purse and mug, limped to the door, and made it under the awning as the skies opened up and the rain sluiced down. When I unlocked the door and stepped inside, the smell of fresh bread and cakes hit me straight in the face. The scent was always like coming home. I loved that I worked in a place that brought so many people joy day after day, but I loved the people I worked with even more.

"Hey, Amber!" Brady yelled from the back of the bakery. "Glad you beat the rain in."

"Barely," I said as the first bolt of lightning lit up the sky. I darted away from the window and to the back of the bakery where I couldn't see it. I never said I wasn't a chicken. "Where's Hay-Hay?" I asked, grabbing my apron off the hook after I put my purse in the office.

"In the cooler. We have cupcakes coming out of our ears and no place to put them."

I pointed at him. "That's why I came in early. I figured you guys were going to be scrambling to get the order ready for the school this morning."

Tart

Brady laughed and went back to his bread kneading. "Scrambling is an understatement. I'm sure she would appreciate the help. I have to finish the standing bread and bun orders."

Brady had become a master baker last summer and was now in charge of all the bread baking for The Fluffy Cupcake. Haylee was in charge of the pastries, cakes, and cupcakes, which meant with an order the size she had today, she was going to need help, or our bakery case would be empty this morning.

A clap of thunder boomed overhead, and I darted for the cooler, glad Brady had his back to me. Did I mention that I hate storms? I grabbed a jacket off the hook and slipped it on, then opened the cooler door and stepped in. I wasn't upset to be in the cooler. It was our safe place for severe weather, and you couldn't see the lightning inside.

"Hey, cupcake," I said, gazing at the scene before me. "It looks like a cupcake apocalypse in here."

Haylee stood up and blew out a breath, and it rustled the hair that had fallen over her forehead. "Why did I think this was a good idea?"

"I don't know what the problem is, Hay-Hay. I mean, forty-one dozen cupcakes are like no big deal," I said, flipping my hand around while I imitated her. "That's what you told me when I asked if I should take the order this year."

She rolled her eyes and went back to her cupcake counting. "It's not a big deal when I thought I was going to make generic cupcakes. When I found out they wanted the school logo on each one, then it became a big deal."

I peeked at the tray of cupcakes closest to me and grinned. "They look great, though! Look at the cute penguins." We were called the Lake Pendle Penguins, and even growing up here, I never entirely understood it. We don't have penguins in Minnesota.

"They're cute, but they're a pain in my gigantic ass," she muttered, putting together another cake box to start packing cupcakes. At this rate, it will only take nine hundred boxes to transport them all to the school. Okay, that was dramatic. It will only take thirteen. I started putting together another box and helped her move all of the cupcakes from pans to boxes.

"I know the kids at the elementary school are going to love them, Hay-Hay. They're cute, and we all know they're going to be delicious." Another boom of thunder shook the cooler, and I leaned back against the shelf, covering my ears and waiting for it to pass before I started packing again. I didn't want to drop a cupcake and get in trouble with the baker.

Haylee came over and rubbed my back a couple of times. "You're okay. The weatherman said it's just passing showers and storms today. Nothing severe."

I nodded and let out the breath I'd been holding. "You know I'm a chickenshit, but I'll be fine."

She started on the next box of cupcakes. "You're not a chickenshit. You went through a lot, and you're entitled to carry scars because of it."

We packed the next four boxes of cupcakes in silence, my fingers able to count the forty-eight cupcakes for each box without even having to think about it. When most of them were packed, I glanced around the almost empty cooler.

"There's not much product here for the case," I observed.

Haylee pointed out the door of the cooler. "Able Baker Brady is baking off all the cupcakes and cakes we need for today. They should be cooling on the racks by now. I'll decorate everything when I finish here. I kept it simple for today since we had all of these cupcakes going out the door. It's Tuesday, so three flavors of cupcakes will be enough."

"I should have known you had it under control," I said on a head shake. "You've never not had it under control."

She frowned, and her eyes clouded for a moment. "Well, there was that one time."

My arms went around her for a gentle hug. "And that one time wasn't your fault."

Tart

It was just a few days before Haylee's birthday last July when Darla McFinkle attacked her. She thought Haylee had cost her the title of Strawberry Fest Princess, but at nearly thirty, it was pathetic that Darla was even running for the crown. Darla always did what Darla wanted to do, though. She'd bullied Haylee her entire life, and it culminated with Darla trying to kill my best friend behind our bakery. If Brady hadn't found her when he did, Darla might have succeeded. I was so glad she was still here with me every day.

"Have you heard anything about the trial?" I asked, sliding the last box onto the rack we'd push out to the delivery van later.

She grimaced, and her eyes went to the ceiling. "Jury selection starts next week. She's hired the best attorney in the state, so she'll probably walk."

"Where does she get the money to pay for that?" I asked, stymied. "She hasn't worked a day in her pathetic thirty years of life."

"Daddy," Haylee said, her eyes rolling. "Daddy has always spoiled her. He's the reason she's the way she is now."

"A murderer," I muttered, shaking my head.

"Innocent until proven guilty, Amber," she reminded me, and we both broke down into a fit of giggles.

"Hard to pretend you're innocent when you leave the knife you stabbed someone with in your bathtub, and your DNA all over their body."

"I'm sure she will find a way to twist it in her favor. She always does. Anyway, I think we're done here." She pointed at the cupcakes, but I knew she was talking about the discussion regarding Darla. She didn't like to talk about it, not that I could blame her, so I nodded my head in agreement.

"We're ready. Once Taylor comes in, I'll have Brady help me load these, and I'll deliver them. That way, you can finish your work."

9

She slung her arm over my shoulders and squeezed me. "Thanks, bestie. I appreciate it. You're better at schmoozing with people than I am anyway."

"That's what makes us a great team," I said, throwing her a wink and heading to the front of the bakery to start the day.

The Lake Pendle School District consisted of three schools in different areas of the town. Lake Pendle Elementary sat near the lake in a sprawling brick building that had been around for only a few decades. It was built new in the nineties to replace an old building past its prime and fire codes. The new building was a source of pride for the community, with windows in all the classrooms, interior computer labs, and a beautiful gymnasium. There was no doubt that the Lake Pendle Littles, as they're referred to, get a state-of-the-art education. I don't have kids, but I do know technology is more important than anything now that our world runs on it.

Today's event was for the Lake Pendle Littles and their Bigs. The elementary and high school partner together in a program to offer mentoring, support, friendship, and encouragement between schools. A high school freshman is paired with a first-grader, and they spend the next four years together, culminating in a graduation ceremony at the elementary for the fourth graders going to the middle school and the high schoolers moving on to college or transitioning to work life. It was a favorite event of the community, and in a few more hours, this place was going to be packed. Luckily for me, at just a little past seven, it was quiet, other than staff preparing for the day. Thankfully, the storms had petered out and left us with just a few rain showers on this Friday morning. Delivering thirteen giant boxes of cupcakes was easier when it wasn't raining, for obvious reasons.

I slammed the doors shut on the van and pushed the cart toward the side door of the elementary school, where deliveries were made to Cook Cramer. I swear Mrs. Cramer was timeless. She'd been cooking here since I was a kid, and since I'm thirty, that's a lot of years. In truth, I went to school with her kids, so she's not that old, but she is one of the most beloved figures in this school for both her fantastic food and her sweet nature. She didn't have time to make forty dozen cupcakes, though.

"Oaf," I said, nearly coming to a complete halt and grabbing boxes of cupcakes as they started to slide off the cart. "What the hell?" I exclaimed, standing with the last box before it hit the ground.

I stared into a face that was as surprised as mine was. "Sorry," the guy said, taking the box from my shaking hands and sliding it back onto the cart. "I had my back turned and didn't know you were coming."

"You couldn't hear the cart with the one rattling wheel coming up behind you?" I asked hotly. "I don't think the kids are going to appreciate smashed cupcakes for graduation. You were probably on your phone."

He held it up sheepishly, and I huffed. "I was, but in my defense, I was arguing with a teenager." Before I could answer, he stuck his hand out. "Bishop Halla."

I reluctantly shook his hand but didn't smile. "Amber Larson. Halla. That's?"

"Finnish," he answered, hitting the doorbell by the kitchen door so Mrs. Cramer knew someone was waiting.

"I should have known since we are in Minnesota," I said, chuckling. Another crack of thunder filled the air, and I jumped, sliding under the awning over the door while silently begging Cook Cramer to hurry up.

"That's a long way away," he said casually.

"I know. Are you here for a reason?" I asked, wondering why he was hanging around.

He pointed at the door. "I'm a teacher. I'll go in this way, too."

"If you're a teacher here, don't you have a key?"

The door opened, and Mrs. Cramer peeked her head out. "Oh, Amber!"

"Hi, Mrs. Cramer. The Fluffy Cupcake has arrived with your, well, fluffy cupcakes."

She clapped excitedly and propped the door open. "You know it's graduation day when the cupcakes show up! Hey, good morning, Mr. Halla," she said, acknowledging the man standing next to me as she peered into a box. Her grin grew when she spotted all the penguins in their cuteness. "Adorable as always. Haylee is a cupcake goddess."

"You know it! I have thirteen of these boxes."

"I already made space. I'll unload this cart while you get the next load. There's another cart over there," she said, pointing to a metal cart by the wall. "You have about twenty minutes before the buses arrive and the kids start streaming in."

"I better move then," I said, heading to the door. "I don't want to be accosted by three-foot-tall cupcake thieves."

The man who I had forgotten was still standing there laughed heartily. "You've got them pegged. How about if I help you with the other boxes, and we'll make quick work of it?"

"Oh, you don't have to do that," I said instantly, grabbing the cart after swapping mine out with Mrs. Cramer. "You have work to do, I'm sure."

He set his bag and coffee mug down just inside the door of the kitchen and shrugged. "I can't do much until the kids arrive. Maybe if I help you bring the rest in, I'll feel less guilty about almost ruining the cupcakes."

I eyed him up and down then. He was ridiculously handsome standing there in his button-up dress shirt and tie. The pink pinstriped shirt was tucked into his dress slacks, and his feet were adorned in a pair of Hush Puppies. The look was trendy and hip, but that wasn't what sucked me in. His face did that all by itself. His eyes were a luscious garnet green that drew you in and held you in his atmosphere whenever he spoke. Dammit. I was a

12

sucker for green eyes. I could feel my resolve weakening about letting him help. He wore a beard tightly clipped to his skin, his hair slicked back and blended in to meet the beard, and a pair of lips that could kiss the heck out of you without breaking a sweat. Where the heck did that come from, Amber?

I realized I was staring at him, so I shrugged nonchalantly—so as not to look like I cared what he did—and started pushing the cart toward the van. "Suit yourself," I said as he walked beside me.

"I haven't seen you around before, Amber," he said, making conversation as we loaded the cart up with boxes.

"Then you must be new here. I've lived in Lake Pendle my entire life, and I run the bakery on Main Street. You don't have to look hard to find me."

He rose to his full height of over six feet, and I whimpered a little. He was good enough to eat. I loved a tall, handsome man with a pair of eyes to lose myself in at the end of the day. He was all of that and then some, which meant he had to be taken. Also, I'd sworn off men after the last debacle I'd dealt with over the winter.

He brushed off his hands and smiled. If possible, his smile made him even more handsome, and his straight white teeth weren't creepy when they peeked out from between his lips. Cripes. I desperately need to get laid. I was ogling this guy like he was a fine cut of meat from Butcher Don's shop.

"I'm new here and haven't had time to investigate the bakery. You're always closed when I'm done with work, and I've been so busy setting up house on the weekends I keep forgetting to take a break."

"I see," I said, just as a bolt of lightning lit up the sky and the thunder followed almost instantly. I screamed and jumped into the back of the van, huddled there until the last of the thunder rumbled overhead.

"Hey, Amber, it's okay," he said softly.

I glanced up to see him kneeling on the floor of the van with one knee, his hands out to me to keep me calm. "Just a spring storm. It's not going to hurt you, but if we don't get these boxes inside, the rain is going to ruin them."

I was shaking, and my heart was pounding when I lowered my arms from over my head. I had to swallow around the lump in my throat before I could speak. "Sor— sorry. I overreacted. It took me by surprise." I stiffened my shoulders and climbed out of the van, slamming the doors closed again and grabbing the handle of the cart. He was carrying the sheet cake while I pushed the cart, and we hurried toward the entrance of the school to get inside before the rain started in earnest. We dodged inside just as the skies opened and the rain poured down again.

"Wow, just made it," he said, lowering the giant cake box to the counter before he grabbed his bag.

"Thanks for helping," I said, closing the door against the rain. I would have to wait out the storm before I headed back to the bakery.

"Anytime," he said, offering a wave before he disappeared through the door of the cafeteria.

That left me standing there staring after him, wishing I knew a whole hell of a lot more about Bishop Halla, but knowing that was never going to happen.

Girls like me don't end up with guys like him.

Two

The bell rang over the door of the bakery, and I stood up from where I was packaging bread to see a woman walk through the door.

"Momma!" I exclaimed, limping around the counter to hug her.

She chuckled while she hugged me tightly. "Hi, baby girl. I wanted to stop in and say goodbye."

My parents were heading down to Florida to see my sister and her family. They would drive their RV down and camp out in my sister's backyard. You were never going to find me in an RV in Florida, but my parents loved going down to visit the grandkids.

"Did you get everything packed?" I asked, handing her a pastry from the case to snack on while we visited.

She took a bite, and her eyes rolled back in her head. "Damn, Haylee sure knows how to make a cream cheese Danish."

"Mrs. Larson!" said baker said from the doorway as she came bustling into the room. "I'm so happy I got to see you before you left." Haylee hugged my mom just as hard as I did. My parents had practically raised her, and even in her formalness, Haylee considers my mom her mom.

"Girl, you've known me for twenty-five years. Call me Phyllis, or better yet, Mom," she scolded, hugging my best friend. "What are you going to do, introduce me to your children as Mrs. Larson?"

15

"Wait, I'm having children now?" Haylee asked with laughter in her voice.

"Yes, lots of them. Little mini-bakers to keep this town in cupcakes for generations. I miss seeing you. How's that man of yours?" she whispered in Haylee's ear. "Is he treating you right?"

"You don't have to worry, Mrs. Larson," Brady said from the doorway of the bakery with a huge grin on his face. "No one is going to hurt her ever again."

"Especially not him," I added, my eyes rolling. "Haylee can't sneeze without him taking her to the doctor."

"Ha-ha," he said from the doorway, but his smile was sheepish because I wasn't that far off. "I love her. What can I say?"

"You can keep saying that," my mom said as she patted Haylee's face. She then held up the pastry. "I'll keep saying these are amazing. I need some to take with us for the trip. It's going to be a long summer without any cupcakes from The Fluffy Cupcake."

"You'll be too busy to care," I promised, boxing up some of their favorite treats to take along on the trip.

"Well, I just wanted to stop in and let you know we were leaving, so keep an eye on the house," Mom said when she took the box from me and offered a second hug. "Your dad is in the RV by the lake, or he would have come in, too."

"I saw him last night, but hug him for me and tell him I love him. Keep me posted on your whereabouts as you go."

"Always do," she promised, kissing Haylee's cheek again on her way to the door. "I put the rest of our milk and juice in your fridge to finish up. There's plenty of meat in the freezer for you."

What? I live with my parents, okay? It's not like I live-live with my parents. I have my own apartment and rarely see them since they are always running around the country.

"Thanks, Mom, but I know where the grocery store is. I'm not going to eat your food."

"You most certainly will!" she scolded. "If you don't, it will be freezer burnt, and I'll have to toss it when I get back. Have Haylee and Brady over for a cookout and go wild."

I chuckled and shook my head. "Okay, momma," I promised.

Brady walked around the store and stopped next to her, holding out his arms while wearing a smile. "You might need some of Able Baker Brady's bread for the trip, too," he said, handing her two artisan loaves wrapped and ready for her.

She hugged it to her chest and purred. "Thank you, Brady. There has to be some perk to having two girls who own a bakery, right?" she asked with a wink. "Bye, my girls. Love you, see you in August!"

She waved after another hug, and I closed the door behind her, a smile on my face. When I turned around, Haylee and Brady were stripping off their aprons.

"We're going home. You got the cleanup?" Hay-Hay asked, throwing the apron in the dirty laundry as I followed them to the back.

"Sure, I'm going to start closing up. I'll deliver the day-old goods to the soup kitchen and head home. I'll see you tomorrow," I said on a wave as I grabbed a basket to put all the day-old goods into as I went through the shelves. If we have product left at the end of the day, we mark them down for the second day, and at the end of the second day, whatever is left goes to the soup kitchen or food pantry. During the winter, we always have a lot left, but not in the summer. Brady always made sure to provide them with whatever they needed for their meals at the soup kitchen during the summer, so their patrons could take the day-old items home with them.

I was checking dates on the bread when the bell over the door dinged again. "I'll be right with you," I said without turning, wanting to finish the shelf I was on so I didn't have to start over.

"You betcha," a voice said from behind me. "I'll stand here and admire the goods."

I spun around when I realized the voice was vaguely familiar. My gasp was audible when I saw Bishop standing in front of me. Or was he behind me? I shook my head at myself but resisted the eye roll waiting in the wings. I didn't want him to think I was rolling them at him.

"Hey," I said lamely, wishing I was way less socially awkward around men. "Welcome to The Fluffy Cupcake. I guess you finally found time to stop in."

He smiled and stuck his hands in his pockets, bouncing up on his toes. "Today was only a half-day of school, so I thought maybe I'd celebrate the end of the year with a cupcake. The ones we had last week at the graduation ceremony were addicting."

"You've come to the right place," I said, plastering a smile on my face as I walked by him. "We still have a few in the case, which is unusual for this time of day. If you're a serious connoisseur, you're here before prime cupcake hour."

"Prime cupcake hour?" he asked, perplexed, while he stared into the case.

"It's a thing," I promised, leaning on the counter with my hip. "If you don't believe me, stop by between the hours of ten-thirty and noon."

He pointed at me and smiled. "I just might do that. I'm always into new adventures, and since school is out for the summer, I'll have lots of time on my hands."

The way he said *new adventures* sent a shiver down my spine. The look on his face when I glanced up made me swallow hard around the lump in my throat. He was making conversation, but he was eyeing me like a lion eyes its prey.

I cleared my throat and plastered on the smile I use for little, sweet old ladies and incorrigible elderly gentlemen. "Maybe I can interest you in a new flavor of cupcake." I motioned to the case. "I have some Berry Sinful, and some Raspberry Delights left."

"What are those?" he asked, pointing at a pan below the cupcakes.

"Miniature raspberry lemonade tarts," I answered.

"Tarts," he said with a question in his tone.

"You know, a pastry crust filled with, in this case, lemon cream cheese, and topped with fresh raspberries and powdered sugar. It's very tempting, a little sassy, a little sweet, and a lot yummy."

When his eyes met mine in the next moment, I wanted to whimper at the look they held. If eyes could lick their lips, his would, and they were looking at me like I'd be their next meal. "That could be your nickname," he said, his eyes never straying from mine. "Tart."

I put my hand on my hip and huffed. "I am not promiscuous!"

He waved his hand in the air. "Not that definition of the word. Rather the one you just described. You're very tempting, a little sassy, a lot sweet, and probably even more yummy. Anyway, I will definitely take one of those and also a Berry Sinful. I see cream cheese stuffed in the middle of that strawberry, and I'm all about stuffed strawberries dipped in chocolate."

I was trying to make my brain work again after his little declaration. Those things he said about me were so far from the truth that they were laughable. At the same time, the way he said them raced a shiver up my spine. What should have been an easy transaction had become dangerously flirty and out of my comfort zone. I cleared my throat before I spoke to avoid my voice sounding like a whimper. "Excellent choice," I said as I started packaging them up. "The Berry Sinful cupcake was last year's Lake Pendle Cupcake Bake-off champion. Haylee competes every year."

He held up his finger. "And wins every year?" I nodded, and he grasped his wallet from his back pocket. "Odd that they'd let a professional compete."

"You don't know the half of it," I said, leaning on the counter with my palms. "Oh, that's right. You're new here. I'll have to tell you the story someday."

"I'd like that, Amber."

The way he said my name made me swallow hard around the desire that filled me. I wanted him to leave immediately and stay forever. The fact that I had to war with those two emotions told me I needed to get him gone now.

"What do I owe you?" he asked, motioning at the box.

I thrust it toward him and waved away his money. "Consider it your welcome to Lake Pendle. Thanks for stopping by The Fluffy Cupcake."

He accepted the box and smiled. I hated how much I liked the way it made his green eyes light up like a Christmas tree. "Thank you. A tart from a tart," he said, holding up the box and winking. I swear I whimpered when his lashes brushed his cheek—men with lashes that long should be outlawed.

What is wrong with you, woman? Get a grip.

"Are you busy later?" he asked as he backed up toward the door.

"No, why?" I asked before I stopped long enough to think about it. Crap.

"I was hoping you could tell me the rest of the cupcake story," he said, lifting the box in the air.

What do I do now? I just told him I didn't have any plans, so I can't pretend that changed in the last two seconds.

"Oh, I don't want to bore you with all of that," I squeaked, brushing my hand at him.

"You couldn't possibly bore me. You have to eat, and I have to eat, so we could eat together while you tell me the story. I would love to make some friends in Lake Pendle that don't work at the school. It's boring talking about the same stuff with the same people all the time."

"Okay, sure," I said before I could stop myself. "I know what it's like to see the same people all the time. I work here with my best friend, and I get tired of talking about cupcakes and bread all the time."

"I knew you'd understand," he said on a grin. "How about seven? I can pick you up if you'd like."

I waved my hand at my neck. "I'll probably still be here."

I wouldn't be, but I didn't want him to know where I lived just yet.

"I'll pick you up here then? I thought we could check out The Modern Goat. I hear they have great food."

"They do," I finally agreed. "I'll see you here at seven."

"I'm looking forward to it, Amber. See you then." He waved, opened the door, and headed down the street with a spring in his step.

I lowered myself to a chair and put my head in my hands. What did I just do?

I set the phone on the dresser and waited for it to be answered. When my best friend's face filled the screen, I leaned in to see her better.

"I need help," I said before she could say hello. "Major help."

"Hello, Amber," Haylee said with laughter in her voice. "I already know you need major help. Was this just a reminder call?"

I tossed my head back and laughed hysterically with heavy sarcasm. "You're hilarious. I have a new problem."

"I'll try to help," she said, turning serious. "What's the problem."

"I don't know what to wear tonight."

"Uh," she said, her head tipped to the right. "Pajamas?"

"I have to be ready for dinner at seven!" I exclaimed, letting my arms fall to my sides.

"That's a new development," Hay-Hay said, checking her watch. "I just left the bakery a few hours ago."

I rubbed my forehead and sighed. I was standing in my sports bra in front of my best friend while freaking out. "I agreed to dinner with this guy. I don't know if it's a date or just a friend thing, so I don't know what to wear."

"Whoa, back up the bakery wagon," she said, leaning into the phone. "You agreed to go somewhere with a guy?

21

You? Amber Larson? Miss I Am Never Trusting A Man Again?"

"Ha-ha," I said, rolling my eyes. "He's new in town, and he's looking for friends. He stopped into the bakery earlier and bought a Berry Sinful. I mentioned that I'd have to tell him the story behind them someday since he was new to town. That's when he asked me to dinner."

"Wait," she said, drawing out the T. "Are you talking about the new teacher you met when delivering cupcakes?"

I rubbed my temple and bit my lip. "Bishop Halla. That's him. I don't think it's a date-date, though. I think it's like a friend date."

My best friend whistled and shook her head, a giant smile on her face. "I would bet my bakery that it's a date-date."

"Hey!" I exclaimed with fierceness. "That's half of my bakery, too! Don't go betting it on anything."

"Geez, relax," she said, the smile still on her face. "I'm not going to bet the bakery. I am going to bet that if you wear that long sundress you have, Bishop won't be able to take his eyes off you."

I waved my finger around at her on the screen. "I don't know if that's what I want. I don't even know why I agreed to this date!"

"Because as much as you don't want to admit it, you're lonely, Amber."

"I am not!" I exclaimed.

"You are, and we can all see it. There's nothing wrong with it, sis. You told me last year when I was dating all those hideous frogs that you were happy where you were. That's changed over the last six months, or at least something has changed."

I shrugged and lowered myself to the bed. "We need to talk about some stuff, but right now, I need to figure out what to wear to this date."

Haylee tipped her head even more to the right. "Did I do something wrong? Are you upset with me? I'll come over there right now if you don't tell me what's going on."

I waved my hand at my throat. "No, you haven't done anything wrong. It's not a big deal. Things have changed with my health, and I have to stop pretending it hasn't."

"I know," she whispered. "I can see it. Brady can see it. We want to help, but we can't if you won't let us."

"Then you understand why going on this date is a terrible idea."

She swung her head back and forth while her hair bounced against her shoulders. "No, it's not. It's okay to go out and have fun sometimes. You aren't marrying the guy. You're just meeting him for dinner."

I stood up and sighed. "That's true. Long sundress? Which one? I have thirty."

Haylee chuckled and pointed at me. "You might have too many sundresses, but I meant the black one with the cap sleeves and the sunflowers. It's gorgeous, and you always look super sassy when you wear it."

"Super sassy?" I asked with a brow up in the air. "Is that a good thing or a bad thing?"

Her finger came out to point at the screen. "An excellent thing. He will see that you can hold your own, and you aren't going to take crap from anybody."

I tossed my head back and forth a couple of times while I thought about it. "Not untrue. Okay, sunflowers it is. Thanks, Hay-Hay."

"You're welcome. Have fun, okay? You don't have to be petrified. It's just a date."

I rolled my eyes all the way to the back of my head. "I'm not petrified. I think it was a bad idea to agree, but since I did, I have to go. I mean, he's a teacher, and I work in a bakery."

She shook her finger at the screen. "No, you own a bakery, there is a huge difference. Do not start playing the inferiority card to keep this guy at arm's length. It's not like you didn't go to school and get a degree, too. Relax and let things happen naturally. Maybe you'll end up despising the guy. Maybe you'll end up finding a friend or something more, but don't be resistant to the idea that he's the one you've waited for."

"That's rich coming from you."

She shrugged her shoulder with a grin on her face. "I kissed a lot of frogs to get my prince, and you know it. I know now that I wouldn't have had to, but they taught me that when you do find the right guy, you hold on tight."

"Now I'm holding on tight?" I asked, dropping the sundress over my head.

"No, now you're about to apply the lessons you learned watching me kiss those hideous frogs."

"I'll let you know how it went in the morning," I said, reaching out to end the video call.

"No, you'll let me know that you made it back safely. I'm your text out if you need it. I'll stay by the phone."

"Okay, thanks, Hay-Hay. Love you."

"Love you, too. Now, get out there and have some fun!"

The screen went blank, and I shook my head at her silliness while I fastened a necklace around my neck and fixed my hair back in a long braid. I smoothed the dress down over my barely-there hips and frowned. The hitch in my left hip was so much more noticeable than it was last month. My heart started to pound in my chest, and I fought back the rising panic at the idea I was about to put myself in another dangerous situation.

"It's dinner with a friend, Amber," I said to the woman in the mirror. "No big deal. Don't make it something it isn't."

I inhaled deeply and let it out before I grabbed my phone and purse then headed out the door. I was going to drive back to the bakery rather than walk the few short blocks. My leg was sore after working all day, and I was afraid I'd get halfway there and fall. I thought about my crutches sitting in the corner of the apartment, but shook it away.

Forget it. You don't need the crutches. Toughen up, Amber.

I locked the apartment and followed the path around the front of the house to the sidewalk. A shooting pain jabbed me in the thigh, and I whimpered, grasping the edge of the old wooden fence to keep from falling. I bent over, dragging air into my lungs to keep from vomiting until the pain passed. This was a mistake. I should go back to the apartment and go to bed. Then I remembered I didn't have Bishop's number, so I couldn't cancel the date. It would be rude to stand him up, and I refused to do that. It would only reflect poorly on my business if word got out that I had, regardless of my reasons.

I righted myself and shook out the leg the best I could inside the brace, determined to make the most of the evening. I would have to keep it short, though. The last thing I wanted was for Bishop to see me fall or worse yet, have the leg spasm so I couldn't walk. I heard a noise and turned my head, my gasp loud enough that the man shutting his front door heard it, too.

"Bishop?" I asked, releasing the fence and limping around it to the driveway. "Why are you at Tyler's place?"

He jogged down the stairs and stopped by his driveway, pointing behind him. "I live here. I bought the place from Tyler when he moved to Wisconsin."

"And you just forgot to mention that you're living next to me."

He swung his head immediately and pointed at my house. "I didn't know you lived there. Mrs. Larson mentioned that she had daughters, but she never told me who they were. She said they were going off to visit a daughter in Florida, so I thought all their kids had moved away."

"Sure," I said, my eyes rolling. "You've lived in Lake Pendle for three months and didn't know I was your neighbor."

He held up his hands in defense. "I'm telling you the truth. I bought the house from Tyler sight unseen and lived in a long-term rental cabin on the lake for the first four months. The house needed so much work that I just moved in last weekend. Phyllis mentioned she had, and this is a quote, a gaggle of girls, but I didn't know you were one of them."

I looked to the sky and laughed at his explanation. "That sounds like my mom. There's my oldest sister,

Jenika, who lives in Florida, which is where they headed today. My middle sister Kailey lives in St. Paul with her husband and kids. I'm the baby of the family, and they consider their foster daughter Haylee, my twin. Haylee and I own The Fluffy Cupcake together. I'm the only one who still lives here," I explained, pointing behind me at the house.

Another stabbing pain hit me right at that moment, and I grabbed for the fence to hold me up. Instantly, I wished like hell that I hadn't. The old rotten wood gave way, and I ended up on the ground with both hands full of splinters and my leg in an agonizing spasm. A word not fit for a lady tore from my lips as he knelt next to me, his eyes worried while he freed me from the fence.

"Are you okay?" he asked, but all I could do was moan to hold back the rest of the cuss words waiting to spill out.

Before I could blink, he scooped me up and strode toward his house. "Please put me down," I cried, the pain in my leg agonizing where he held it against his arm.

"Two seconds," he promised, turning the handle on his front door and then lowering me to the couch.

I grabbed my thigh, only to hiss when I remembered the pieces of wood in my hands. "Fuck my life," I moaned, my hands shaking as I held them out. My jumbled brain couldn't decide what to do, so I just sat there, my entire body shaking and a tear falling down my cheek.

"We're going to fix this," Bishop said as he inspected my hands. "Damn, these are some big splinters, but at least I can pull them with a tweezer. Hang tight."

He disappeared into the kitchen, and I moaned again, my leg absolutely done for the day. I knew this was a bad idea. I should have listened to my body. Instead, I'm going to die of embarrassment on my neighbor's couch. I was going to swing my legs down off the couch and leave, but I couldn't decide if I'd even make it to the door, much less to my apartment. Bishop strode back into the room, his muscular thighs carrying him without a second thought, which made me jealous. The way the muscles bunched beneath his pants made me hot and bothered, but I wasn't going to think too much about that.

"Just relax. I'll have you fixed up in no time," he promised, going to work on the splinters with the tweezer from the first aid kit. "I was going to ask your mom about that fence. I realized what bad shape it was in, but I wasn't sure which one of us owned it."

He pulled a particularly stubborn splinter, and I inhaled sharply, his head coming up immediately. "I'm sorry. I'm trying to be as careful as I can be."

"It's okay," I answered, wishing I could fall through the couch and melt away into the ground. "It was dumb to grab the fence."

He lowered my right hand to the couch and reached across me for my left, his arm brushing my belly and leaving a trail of blazing heat across my skin. I swallowed around the lump in my throat when he rested his arm on my hip bone with his head bowed to finish the splinter removal. It hurt so much I bit my lip to keep from crying out. "It's human nature to try to catch yourself when you start to fall. I should have asked about that fence sooner."

I squeaked, and he glanced up when I started breathing staccato to kill the pain.

"What?"

"Hip," I forced out. "Arm on hip."

His arm came up instantly, and he grasped my face, forcing me to hold his gaze. "Breathe in slowly. You have to breathe slowly, or you're going to pass out."

I followed his directions until the pain passed. "That's better," I promised, offering him a weak smile.

He released my face and went back to my hand, making sure his arm didn't touch me anywhere. "We're almost done here. Do you know who owns the fence?"

I knew he was trying to take my mind off the pain, so I nodded and took another deep breath. "We own it. Dad and I talked about that fence about a week ago, and he agreed it needs to come down. He planned to remove it when he got back and mark the property at the front and the back. It looks like I just accelerated that plan. I'll ask

Brady to help me pull the rest of it out, so it's not an eyesore."

"Who's Brady?" he asked, his brow going down toward his nose.

"He's a baker at The Fluffy Cupcake. He's married to my best friend, who is the other baker."

"Haylee, right? Your sister from another mister?" he asked, grasping the last splinter.

"Darla McFinkle," I spat. No matter how hard I tried, I couldn't keep the venom from my voice whenever I said her name. "She deserves to rot in jail for trying to kill Haylee."

"I can't disagree," he said, setting the tweezer down before he handed me an antiseptic wipe. "I'll let you do this part. I don't like hurting beautiful women."

I smiled weakly and accepted the wipe from him. "Thanks for the help with the splinters. That will save me some pain tomorrow when I have to pan all those cupcakes." I swiped at my hands with the wipe, biting my lip to keep from grimacing at the stinging sensation. I scrubbed at them until the dirt was gone, and all that was left were little red dots.

He grabbed a tube of ointment and squirted some on his finger, gently rubbing it into my palms while he spoke. "I have a lot of experience pulling out splinters. As a teacher, I'm always playing doctor. I have to say that you're about two decades older than most of my patients and a hell of a lot easier on the eyes, though."

I chuckled while he wrapped gauze around my hands. "Thanks, I think. I don't even know what you teach."

"Physical education and English," he said, glancing up when I laughed aloud.

"That's," I paused, searching for the right word, "different."

"It's unusual, I know, but hear me out. I love teaching physical education, but there aren't always a lot of job openings. I got a minor in English so I could teach both. That way, if I ever needed a job—"

"You had a fallback plan," I finished, and he pointed at me from where he sat on the coffee table.

"Bingo. I'm only teaching one unit of English at the high school here. The rest of the day, I teach elementary physical education."

"Best of both worlds?" I asked, my hands wanting to grab my aching leg, but my steel willpower held onto my pride. I didn't want him to see that I was still in pain. Who was I kidding? I just didn't want to look weak in front of him, or anyone, for that matter.

"In this case, yes. I love the little kids, but it's not exciting to teach them English, at least in my opinion. I prefer teaching them how to be physically active and healthy, while I save discussions about literature for the high schoolers."

"Hmm," I said, nodding my head to block out the pain in my leg and hands, "I see your point. Book discussions about Ramona Quimby wouldn't be nearly as exciting as book discussions about Don Quixote."

"Not even close," he agreed, a smile pulling his lips upward. "The arrangement makes me appreciate the mentorship program that Lake Pendle has. I get to see my fourth graders interacting with my seniors in positive ways. If you think the fourth graders are the only ones who get anything out of the deal, as I did at first, you'd be wrong."

I chuckled and tried to straighten out my leg without it spasming again. "I'm a Lake Pendle graduate. I was part of the program as a first and fourth-grader and again as a freshman and senior. I know exactly what you mean. I got more out of it in high school than I did in elementary school. I loved coming back in as an upperclassman and participating in the program from a different standpoint."

"Everything had changed over those years, right?" he asked on a chuckle.

"Not everything," I corrected, "but a lot of things, yeah. Anyway, thanks for helping with my hands. I should go."

He frowned and motioned to the kitchen. "Why don't I order in for dinner? I'm sure you don't feel like going out, but The Modern Goat delivers."

I swung my legs down and sat up, waiting to see if my leg was going to behave long enough to get me home. "Thanks, but I kind of just want to go home. I'm not feeling that great. I'm sorry."

He pushed himself up off the coffee table and helped me up, his smile kind when he spoke. "I understand, Amber, you don't have to apologize. Let me help you back to your apartment."

I took a step, relieved when my leg held me up with no problem other than the constant ache. "I appreciate it, but I'm fine," I promised, walking to the door with as much dignity as I could muster after the last thirty minutes of moaning on his couch—and not the right kind of moaning.

Bishop held my elbow all the way to the door and then opened it for me, without relinquishing my arm. He helped me down the stairs and to the edge of the driveway, where he finally dropped his hand. "If you think your dad would be okay with it, I'm happy to pull this fence down—no sense in bothering Brady when I'm off for the next three months. I'll get rid of the debris and just leave a marker at the front, middle and back. Not that I care about the property line, I'm not about owning every last inch of my land, but I know the county cares."

I nodded and smiled at his offer. "I appreciate that. I'm sure Brady and my dad will, too." My mom's comment about the meat in the freezer ran through my head, so I paused by the sidewalk. "Since I owe you a mulligan on dinner, if you want to wait until Saturday afternoon, I'd be happy to help you and then grill some steaks or burgers to make up for tonight."

He bounced up on his toes and smiled. "I'd like that, Amber. I'm sorry you ended up in pain tonight. That certainly wasn't the plan when I asked you to dinner."

I plastered a smile on my face and tried to act cool. "That's me, a colossal klutz. I should be the one apologizing for ruining your dinner plans."

"I'm not worried about it, but I am worried about you. Are you going to be okay at home alone? Maybe you should call Haylee?"

I darted toward the side of the house as quickly as my leg allowed. "I'll be fine. Thanks for the first aid. I'll see you Saturday afternoon. I'm done at the bakery about two."

Before he could answer, I unlocked the door to my apartment and slipped inside, sliding it closed. "That was an even bigger disaster than anything I could have predicted," I said to the empty room as I stripped my dress off and tossed it in the laundry bin.

I stood in front of the mirror, the lights of the bathroom putting the reason for said disaster on display. With a sigh, I turned the water on in the shower and climbed in, letting the hot water soothe the sore muscles that still quivered from pain and fatigue.

The tears swirling down the drain had nothing to do with pain and everything to do with fatigue. My heart was tired, and after almost seventeen years, I should be used to it, but something told me I never would be.

Three

Haylee breezed through the door from the back of the bakery, grasped my hand, and helped me to her office. "Um, it's lunchtime. Who's going to watch the store?" I asked as she pointed at the chair across from hers in the tiny room. It was once a broom closet, literally.

"Brady. He said he's ready to schmooze the old ladies into buying some bread and buns."

I laughed and leaned back in the chair, sipping the lemonade she had waiting for me. I smacked my lips when I swallowed. "Thanks, I needed that. The question is, can I trust Brady with the cupcakes left in the case? He's always stealing them."

"You know you can't trust him with the cupcakes, but we'll overlook the ones he eats since he's helping us out. You need a break, and I need to talk to you."

I leaned forward and motioned for her to speak. "Whatever you need," I said instantly. "Is something wrong?"

"Not with me, no," she answered, a brow up in the air.

"You're implying there's something wrong with me." It wasn't a question since that would have been unnecessary. It was obvious she was talking about my leg.

"You're the one who mentioned needing to talk to me before your date the other night. Here it is Saturday, and you still haven't talked to me."

I tapped the desk twice with my finger. "As a matter of fact, I have another date with Bishop tonight."

"You do?" she asked, and I could tell she was trying not to sound too excited, but she was totally failing at it.

"Well, it's like a working date, but it involves food, so..."

"A working date?"

I grimaced and held up my hands where the red dots from the splinters were still visible. "He's going to take our fence out today. Since I knocked down half of it the other night, now the rest of it has to go. I promised to help as much as I could, but mostly I'll be grilling steaks while he does the grunt work."

"Your dad finally agreed to pull that old thing down?" she asked with surprise. "I swear he thought it was an antique or something."

I laughed and shook my head, letting my eyes drift to the ceiling. "I think he was hoping it would come down with a heavy snow or wind storm, so he didn't have to work too hard at it. It gave way the second I leaned on it, so I don't think Bishop will struggle to get it out. That eyesore has got to go."

"What are we really talking about here, Amber?" she asked, her head tipped to the side.

I glanced around and then back to her face. "Uh, the fence? It needs to go now that I smashed the front half of it."

"I'll send a cake for dinner tonight with my thanks to Bishop," she said dryly.

"I detect sarcasm."

She held her fingers close together. "Just a tiny amount. I want to know what happened the other night. You haven't been forthcoming."

"I told you, I fell on the fence and had to cancel the date."

"What you aren't telling me is why you fell on the fence. Though, I'm pretty sure I only need one guess."

I sighed and leaned back in the chair again. "I was tired after a long day on my feet—"

"And you didn't bring your crutches with you."

"They wouldn't have saved me," I said quickly. "I knew I should have canceled the date, but I didn't have his number."

"Then, you discovered he's your neighbor."

"Imagine my surprise," I added, playing her sarcasm card. "Good chat," I said, standing.

She pointed at the chair like I was a child. "It's not over."

I sat again and rolled my eyes, remembering in the nick of time not to cross my legs. "I don't have much else to say."

She leaned over and folded her hands on the desk. "I think you do, but you don't want to say it. You think you'll just add to my already full plate."

I pointed at her. "I will, which is why I haven't said anything. It's the same boring story."

"Hasn't seemed like the same story to me since at least February. What happened in February that made your leg so much worse?"

I rubbed my temple and bit my lip to keep from speaking while I thought my answer through.

"I'm not going to give you time to think of a workable lie, Amber."

I huffed and crossed my arms over my chest. "Fine, okay. I hurt it in February. It's not healing the way it should."

"How did you hurt it in February? I don't remember it being here at work. Did you fall at home?"

How was I going to tell her the truth now without making her mad? I wasn't. She was going to be angry, but I didn't have much choice. She'd see through every lie I came up with and make me sit here until I was left with nothing but the truth.

"I got into an altercation one night. I thought the leg was okay, but I'm starting to think I probably did more damage to it than I originally thought." That was such a lie. I already knew how much damage I did to it. I simply didn't want to tell her the truth.

Tart

"You think? You can barely walk by the end of the day. What kind of altercation are we talking about here? You aren't the argumentative type."

"This was more of a self-defense type situation. See, I was dating this guy," I started, and she stood, walking around the desk to squat next to me.

"And you needed to defend yourself against him? Who is he, and where do I find him?"

"I love you for always trying to protect me, Hay-Hay, but I didn't tell you about this for a reason. You don't need anything else to worry about."

Her hard eye roll right in front of my face spoke volumes. "Listen, the Darla thing is over."

"No, it's not," I said, shaking my head. "Not by a long shot. You have plenty to deal with when it comes to her nonsense. You don't need to add mine to the mix."

She growled at me in the way only she can. "Out with it. Now."

I tossed up my hand. "Fine. I started dating this guy after the new year. I didn't mention it because it wasn't serious. He was from St. Paul, and we'd been on a few dates in January. I invited him to my apartment for dinner, right before Valentine's Day." Her mouth opened, but I held up my hand to quiet her. "My parents were at home. I wasn't reckless or stupid about it, but it felt like the next step. He was a great guy when we first started dating."

"Until he wasn't."

I pointed at her and grimaced. "Until he wasn't. That night after dinner, he decided he wanted a few stolen kisses in the dark. When he was kissing me, and I couldn't stop thinking about what I had to do the next day, the answer was obvious. We weren't a match. I politely told him it was time for the evening to end since I had an early morning, but he refused to get off me. I couldn't get away from him, so I hit him in the balls with my knee, which was still in the brace."

She sucked in air while she held my eyes. "Bet he didn't like that."

35

"Not even a little bit. I got away from him and demanded that he leave. That's when he attacked me."

"He attacked you," she repeated, and I nodded. "He hurt your leg?"

"He knew my weakness and used it against me. He kicked me in the knee, and since I was wearing the brace, my knee just snapped—," I stopped to swallow around the surge of pain and anxiety the memory gave me. "I fell to the ground screaming and writhing in pain. My dad heard me in the main house, but by the time he got to the apartment, Rex was gone."

"Where is this asshole now? Brady and I are going to go have a chat with him."

I snorted with laughter but grabbed her hand tightly. "I love you for always coming to my defense, but it was months ago. I haven't seen Rex since."

"You should have pressed charges," she said, disapproval in her voice.

"He said, she said," I insisted, holding out my palms.

"Except you have an injured leg that says otherwise."

I rubbed my knee and swallowed back the bile that always rose in my throat when I thought about that night. "Honestly, I sent the cops to look for him, but he was gone. Good riddance."

"But the leg keeps getting worse instead of better," she said, her eyes taking in the mangled limb.

I shrugged casually as though what she said was wrong. "It's been slow to heal, but the x-rays didn't show any fracture of the bone. You know they can't do an MRI with all the metal in there, so there's little they can do with it anymore. The problem now seems to be more about sensation and pain. The doctors think I need a different kind of brace."

"Why haven't you gotten it yet?" she asked, one brow going down. "Show me the leg."

I sighed heavily and shook my head. I love her, but she worries too much. "I can't whip my pants down in the middle of the bakery, Hay-Hay. It just needs more time to heal."

She stood up and closed the door to the office, then gave me a pointed stare. I sighed again and stood up, pulling my pants down and unstrapping the top half of the brace. Her eyes roved over it, and she inhaled, her hand to her lips.

"Honestly, Amber. How are you even walking on that?" she asked, falling to her knees to inspect the hip and knee. She ran her finger over the hot, red, mottled skin of my leg and glanced up at me. "I've seen this leg at its best and its worst, and this is worse than I've ever seen it. It looks like it might be infected."

"It's not," I assured her. I yanked my pants up before she could freak out about it even more. "It just needs more time to heal. You know how that leg is."

She nodded and leaned her butt against the desk. "I do know, and that's why I'm worried. Does Phyllis know how bad it is?"

I made the so-so hand. "Mom can see I've been limping around, but let's face it, that isn't new. Also, you know—" I shrugged rather than finishing the thought.

"You know what?"

I folded my hands on my lap on a sigh. "I don't bother them with my leg issues. I'm an adult now. They took care of me long enough. They deserve to enjoy their retirement without always worrying about the adult child they're still forced to house."

It was painful how accurate that statement was. I was injured when I was thirteen, and I'd been dealing with this ever since. When it came to my leg, nothing was unexpected because the damage to it was so unexpected. All the doctors could do was keep treating the problems as they arose. Granted, the setback in February didn't help things, but regardless, I knew it was only going to get worse with age.

The face of Bishop Halla loomed in my vision for the thousandth time since last night. I held in a sigh as I thought about the way his strong arms wrapped around me and carried me to safety. The way he so lovingly cared for my hands when he didn't have to. He was genuinely concerned for me, and on the surface, he was one of those genuinely nice guys. That didn't mean he was a genuinely nice guy, but it was a shame I'd never find out. He'd be a friend and nothing more. Considering he's a physical education teacher, dating someone like me was out of the question for someone like him.

Her hand was on my right leg, and her sigh brought me back to the conversation we were having. "I know things have been difficult for the last few years with your parents."

"Difficult?" I asked, and she nodded. "That's true, but it's unfair to put any of the blame on them at this point."

"I wouldn't go that far, Amber. They want to pretend as if none of it happened, but it did, and you're the one dealing with the consequences. They let you live at the house, but they'd rather you moved out. They mention it in one way or another practically every time we're together."

I shrugged my shoulder, still staring at my hands. "I'm looking for a place, but there are very few places to rent that have a basement, and the ones that do, I can't afford. I will find one. Hopefully, by fall. I just might have to move to a different community and commute to work."

She squeezed my hand tightly. "No, that's not going to happen. Brady and I will help any way we can, okay?"

I smiled at the woman I loved more than my biological sisters. They were both so much older than I was, but Hay-Hay and I had been joined at the hip since we were four.

She was speaking again, and I forced myself to listen and not cry on her shoulder. "You were status quo and completely functional with the leg up until February, and now you're not. You have to do something. What kind of brace do the docs want for it?"

"Something expensive," I said immediately and then grimaced when she glanced up sharply. "I'm giving it time."

"You've given it since February. This is June. Get the brace."

"That's easier said than done, Haylee. It's a microprocessor brace and well over seventy thousand dollars. I don't have that kind of money."

Her eyes nearly bugged out of her head at my statement. "What on earth? They're going from low tech straps and dials to microprocessors?"

"It's the wave of the future," I said on an eye roll. "I understand why they want me to wear it, but I have to figure out how to pay for it first."

"We'll figure it out," she said immediately, hugging me tightly. "You shouldn't be in pain all the time. I know our insurance isn't good about paying for this stuff, so we'll come up with another plan."

I nodded over her shoulder and let out a sigh. I'd been so afraid to tell her the truth, and now that she knew, I was relieved. "They won't cover any of it, I already checked. That's why I'm giving it time. Anyway, thanks for picking up my slack lately. I know I haven't been as helpful to you and Brady as I usually am. I should have told you sooner, but admitting what happened makes me look weak. You know how I hate that."

She shook her head and held my shoulders lovingly. "An asshole who thinks he can take advantage of a woman, any woman, doesn't make you look weak. I watch you walk around here on that leg and wonder how the hell you stay so damn strong all the time. You deserve better than you've gotten, and through all of it, you're still here doing your job every day."

"I'm always here, but I'm hardly out front at all now. I've had to delegate a lot of the customer service work to the other girls."

She shrugged and motioned at her desk. "You have, but that has less to do with your leg and more to do with the fact that we're nearly drowning in orders. I'm so busy baking that I can't keep up with everything else. If Taylor weren't doing the kitchen manager job, it would be even worse. You haven't had a choice but to delegate the customer service work, or nothing would get done in the office."

I nodded with my lips in a grim line. "You're right, and I meant to talk to you about that. Do you want to make some brownies and have a meeting just you, me, and Brady?"

She shook her head and winked at me. "Not later today, no. You have a fence removal date with one hella sexy teacher. We'll do it tomorrow afternoon."

"It's not a date!" I exclaimed, frustration with her matchmaking filling me to the max. Ever since she'd gotten together with Brady, she insisted I needed to find someone to do the same. I had already sworn off men! The last one didn't work out so well, and I wasn't in the mood for a repeat performance. "Bishop's my neighbor, that's all. He's helping me out by getting rid of the fence. And actually, removing that eyesore benefits his property, too. That's all it is."

She nodded and tried to hide her grin by pursing her lips. "Okay, sure. Well, whatever it is, you've already committed to it. Let's have the meeting tomorrow afternoon after the bakery closes. For now, go home. We've got this covered. Put that leg up with some ice on it for a few hours before you have to help Halla Hottie with the fence."

"Halla Hottie?" I asked on a snort of laughter.

"Like what I did there?" she asked, grinning like a fool.

"Not even a little bit," I said, standing up and hugging her again. "Thanks for understanding. You've always been my best sister."

She chuckled and wrapped her arms around me. "You better not say that too loudly. One of your real sisters might hear you."

I leaned back and patted her face, a smile on mine. "They already know, and they don't have a problem with it."

I limped to the door and grasped the handle. "I'll let you know how dinner with Halla Hottie goes."

She pointed at me and winked as I swung out the door to the sound of her laughter.

Four

I pounded a post marker into the ground at the front of the driveway. I had done the same at the back of the property before I started pulling the wooden planks out of the packed soil. I was shocked when most of them came out with little effort from me. Only two or three planks were anchoring it in the ground, and the rest were rotted beyond help. I was honestly surprised it hadn't fallen over in a strong breeze.

I rolled the fence up and dropped it in my backyard, before heading back to Amber's yard to fill in the holes. I wanted to have most of the work done before dinner, so I could focus on her. If I were lucky, I'd have time for a shower before she started dinner. I knew she was home since her car was in the driveway, and I noticed her moving around inside her apartment, but I decided not to be pushy. She'd come out when she was ready to face me after what happened the other night. I could see how embarrassed she was, and she was going to struggle to keep her promise to cook dinner tonight. She had nothing to be ashamed of, but for some reason, she was.

I love a woman with spark, sass, and pizazz. Amber has all three in spades. Okay, so maybe the sass was on the high end of the spectrum, but something told me she used it as a defense mechanism. There was no doubt it had everything to do with that left leg of hers. I didn't need her to tell me that she had a problem bigger than she was letting on. Holding her in my arms made that obvious. She

41

wore a brace on her left leg, but the limb itself was nothing but skin and bones. She was a slight woman to begin with, but that leg was something else entirely. Hopefully, she'll tell me what happened at some point, but until she does, I'll continue to treat her with respect. I would always be here to listen when and if she decided to talk.

"You're hard at work," her sweet voice said as if I had conjured her from just my thoughts. "You were supposed to wait for me."

I leaned on the shovel I was using to fill the small holes left by the fence. "I figured after the other night that your hands would appreciate not having to deal with the old wood again."

She held up her palms, and the red marks were still apparent. It wasn't the splinters that left them red and abraded, but the gravel she landed in when she fell.

"They thank you, and so do I," she said with a smile. She lowered her hands to her hips and pointed at the small holes along the length of the yard. "Did it come out okay?"

I stomped down on a dirt-filled hole as I answered. "I don't know how the fence was still standing. I barely had to pull on it before it went down like dominos. I'm going to fill all these holes, and then tomorrow I'll plant some grass seed."

"I appreciate all your help," she said, biting her lip as she stared at the ground instead of making eye contact.

"It's no problem. Taking down the fence improves my property, too."

She searched around the area where I was working. "Where did you put the fence? Did you haul it away already?"

I leaned on the shovel again and pointed at the fence in my yard. "I was going to pull the boards out of the wire and burn them. Then all I have to do is take the wire to the metal recycler on Monday."

Her head nodded as I spoke. "I'll get a pair of gloves and help you cut the wires apart. I'd offer to help you fill the holes, but you look like you've got it covered."

She was putting all her weight on her right leg, and I could tell it took effort for her to keep from falling over.

"I only have a few holes left to fill. Why don't you grab a chair and talk to me while I finish?"

"I don't need a chair," she said defensively.

That was a kneejerk reaction. I sensed it was something she often repeated whenever someone even suggested she might need to sit down.

I held up my hand. "Whatever you'd like," I said, going back to packing dirt in the holes. "How was work today?"

Air blew from her lips in exasperation. "Exhausting. We're so busy this time of year we can barely keep up."

"That doesn't sound fun."

I noticed her shrug out of the corner of my eye as I stomped on another pile of dirt. "We've grown so much over the last couple of years that we need to reevaluate our plan. We're going to have a meeting tomorrow to figure out how to make the workday easier on everyone."

"You and Haylee are partners in the business, right?" I asked, starting on the last hole.

"Yup, we started The Fluffy Cupcake nine years ago. It was just the two of us running this little bakery that no one even knew existed. Word of mouth spread about Haylee's cupcakes, and soon, we had customers lined up out the door. Eventually, we hired Brady so we could offer bread and buns besides our cakes and pastries. He's such an amazing bread artist that now we have so many standing orders with restaurants around the area it's hard to keep up. We even do the buns and bread for the school. Though, at least during our busiest season, we don't have that order to worry about."

"Wow, I've had the buns and bread at the school and wondered how the cook had time to make such crusty, yeasty perfection. Now I know where I can get more of those buns. They were seriously New York quality."

She chuckled and pointed at me. "Now you see why we're busier than we've ever been. We have to start planning for our tenth-anniversary extravaganza in August, but we don't even have time to do that."

43

I finished filling the last hole and leaned the shovel I'd borrowed from her dad against the shed at the back of the property. "It sounds to me like a meeting tomorrow is necessary. I hope you guys can find a way to make it work. The town has a fondness for your fluffy cupcakes."

So did I, but I wasn't going to say that.

"Her cupcakes are all she cares about, other than Brady, of course," she said as I helped her by the elbow across the driveway.

"And you," I said, kneeling by her chair after she sat. "I bet she cares about you a lot, too."

Her heavy sigh stole the laughter from her lips, and I regretted uttering that sentence immediately. "Sometimes she cares too much about me," she whispered with her eyes on her lap.

Today, she wore a gorgeous red sundress with colorful daisies all over it in a willy-nilly pattern. I won't lie. It made my dick twitch every time it swished around her to reveal tiny glimpses of her figure. It swayed with the natural motion of her body in a way that told me I'd be taking a cold shower at the first opportunity tonight. It wouldn't matter, though. Every time I saw her, my lower half stood at attention. She was that damn beautiful. There was just something about the way she moved that told me she was a firestorm in bed. I wanted to know just how much, but I was smart enough to see that was likely never going to happen. This woman had too much on her plate and not enough forks or spoons to empty it.

"I don't think that's possible, sweetart."

"Sweetart?" she asked, a brow in the air.

I smiled to let her know I was teasing. "Like the candy. They're my favorite."

"I know what they are, but it's not a good term of endearment. Zero out of ten, do not recommend."

I frowned but never broke eye contact with her. "I thought it was perfect. That tart I got the other day was as sweet as the woman who made it."

"You should call Haylee that then," she said dryly. "She's the one who made it."

I tried to hold in my laughter but failed when it came out on a snort. I held up my hand. "I stand corrected. The tart was as sweet as the woman who handed it to me." I pointed at the house. "I'm going to go wash up and grab some cold drinks. When I come back, I'll help you with the fence. Then we can start dinner when the work is done?"

"Sure," she agreed, nodding her head along with me. "I'll wait here."

I stood and patted her shoulder on my way to the house. I hoped my face didn't show my surprise when she grasped my hand with hers for a moment. I squeezed her shoulder once and then made my way up the stairs into the house. I stripped my shirt off on the way to the bedroom for a quick shower before I joined her again. It was going to be a cold shower for the simple reason I needed to cool my overheated libido for a few moments. I was smart enough to know the only way to quench it for the rest of my life was to be the one who laid down next to her every night, though.

The idea should have startled me more than the cold water, but it didn't. I fell hard for Amber Larson the first time I met her. If only I knew where to go from here.

The lake was gorgeous in the late afternoon sunshine. I had purposely waited until later to come out and see how Bishop was doing. As much as I wanted to enjoy his company, my brain knew it was smart not to enjoy it too much. That could result in catching feelings for someone I couldn't afford to have. Down deep, I knew he was one of those good guys people talk about in this world. I'd met a few like him. Guys like my father, who willingly took in another mouth to feed because his daughter cried that her friend was hurting. Brady, who protects my best friend like she was a fragile porcelain doll who would break if you handled her too roughly. She wouldn't. She had survived a knife attack at the hands of a deluded woman, but that wasn't the point. The point was, Brady knew how strong Haylee was, and that was why he loved her the way he did. He had already experienced what it would feel like to lose her, and he was going to do everything in his power to keep her safe. With no family of her own other than me, Brady also knew she needed someone to prop her up in life. He was that kind of guy. Something told me Bishop was cut from the same cloth. That was the reason I had to be so desperately careful about how close I got to him.

I shook my head at the blue sky. Right now, I could use some propping up, but that was never going to happen, not after what happened with Rex.

"There you are," a voice said behind me.

I spun quickly, having been lost in thought, and lost my balance. My arms pinwheeled in the air, but Bishop was too far away to catch me. I fell backward, directly into the cold water of Lake Pendle. I came up sputtering, water running down my face in rivulets and my lips sputtering to clear it from my mouth.

"Amber!" he called, running onto the dock in shock. "Let me help you!"

I stood up on the lake bottom and laughed, pushing my hair out of my face. "It's not exactly deep here," I said, shaking the water from my hands. "I'm in no danger of drowning. I think you should come in. The water feels great." I leaned back in the water and let the gentle waves carry me across the surface toward deeper water. "I'm serious, Halla. Get your bones in here."

"I just took a shower. Besides, I'm rather enjoying myself right here," he answered.

I snuck a peek at him sitting at the end of the dock, his feet in the water, and his eyes on my wet chest. I didn't care. I'd prefer they were on my chest rather than my leg.

"Where are you from, Bishop?" I asked, lowering my leg a little bit more into the water so he couldn't see the brace. It was stupid since I was going to have to get out of the water eventually, but no one ever said self-preservation made sense.

46

"A little town smack dab in the middle of Illinois. It was loud, hot, and stunk like big industry most of the time."

"I bet you never thought you'd be sitting on a dock overlooking a small lake in an even smaller town."

His eyes drifted to the sky for a moment before he answered. "It wasn't on my radar, that's for sure. I just knew I needed a change. It was weird when the Lake Pendle position opened up. I can tell you how many times I've applied for a job that had one opening for physical education and one for English."

"One?" I asked, and he pointed at me with a strange look on his face.

"This was a first and I've been teaching for eleven years. I've worked for three different school districts, but never once saw an opening like this one."

"Serendipity?" I asked, and the air was filled with his laughter as his head nodded.

"I hope it's serendipity, for sure," he agreed. "I'm tired of being unhappy with where I am in life. Moving here in the middle of a school year and living in an old run-down cabin for months was the first time I found myself truly happy in years. My commute was short and stress-free, I had time to get to know my students and create a fun curriculum to keep them active in the winter, and I had something to look forward to with the new house," he explained, pointing to the place behind him.

"Do you miss the people you left behind?"

"I wasn't close to anyone but my daughter, and she's an adult now."

I sat up in the water. "Your daughter? You're divorced?"

He shook his head as I swam over and hoisted myself up to sit on the edge of the dock. I would dry in the sunshine while he explained that bombshell. "I was never married to her mother. My daughter is eighteen now and moved to Southern California for college. She plans to come to visit in July."

"Wait, she's eighteen? How can you have an adult daughter if you've only been teaching eleven years?"

"She was born just before I turned seventeen, that's how," he said, shaking his head slightly.

"Oh, wow, I guess that was a shock."

"Shockingly dumb on my part," he said on a chuckle. "Her mother and I were counselors at a summer camp and had a fling. We were responsible, but accidents happen when you're only using condoms and trying not to get caught by the other camp counselors."

"Not an infrequently told story," I agreed. "It must have been difficult."

He leaned back on the palms of his hands and bumped me in the shoulder. "Not as much for me as for her mother. She didn't live with me, so I didn't shoulder that responsibility for her, you know?"

I nodded while I squeezed the lake water out of my dress. "That's usually the case in those situations. Not your fault, just what it was."

"That's a refreshing statement."

"Why?" I asked, confused.

"Usually, when I mention my daughter, women make an instant judgment about the situation. That I was a deadbeat dad or didn't take responsibility for my actions."

"I would never assume that, Bishop."

"I did what I could while I went to college and worked to support her. I took care of her on weekends and took her as many weeknights as I could to give her mom a break. I made bottles, changed diapers, and cleaned up vomit. I was lucky that her grandparents on her mother's side were godsends and took care of her while her mom and I went to school. My parents weren't in the picture, and my grandparents raised me. I wasn't going to ask them to raise their great-grandchild, too."

"Some kids would have."

"The difference was, from the moment I knew Athena existed, I wanted her. I wanted to be part of her life. I wasn't going to be a no-show kind of dad. I might have been a kid myself, but if I was old enough to create her, I was old enough to take care of her."

"That's," I paused and made the mind-blown motion with my hands. "Not too many guys would do that, Bishop. You know that, right?"

He shrugged and stared off over the lake. "Maybe not, but I've never been like other guys. I loved pushing a baby in a stroller while I ran around the track. She didn't ask to be created, so she wasn't going to suffer because the timing of her birth was inconvenient for us. Her mother and I both agreed on that point."

"I'm absolutely certain now that not too many guys are like you, Bishop," I said, trying not to sound as shocked as I felt. "Athena. That's a beautiful name."

"The goddess of wisdom. Athena has always been wise. An old soul, my grandmother used to say. The first time I held her in my arms, it just didn't matter that I was sixteen, still in high school, and didn't have a clue what I was doing. She was mine, and I would take care of her forever."

"I would say that makes you a stand-up guy, Bishop Halla."

"No, it just makes me a dad, which most women don't want to hear. They don't want to be weighed down with the idea that I have a teenager and responsibilities."

"Which is strange because, at our age, we should have responsibilities. We should have a wide enough base of knowledge and understanding to see other people's pasts as not the end of the world, but as life experiences."

"And in my case, that life experience will be part of my life in a tangible form forever."

"I suppose some women might see that as a problem, but I don't. Those women probably think you aren't interested in having more kids when you've already raised one, or if you do have kids, your allegiance will always be to Athena."

He nodded while he stared out over the water. His head just kept nodding like he was searching for the right thing to say, but couldn't come up with anything. Finally, he turned his head to drink me in from top to bottom. "You are something else, Amber Larson. Refreshing. Wise. Understanding. Compassionate. Intuitive."

"I'll take those adjectives as a good thing," I teased.

"You should. I meant them all. I usually don't bring Athena up on a first date, or second or third for that matter, because it muddies the water."

"But this isn't a date, so that rule doesn't apply."

He froze and swung his head to stare at me. "Ri—right," he stuttered. "I just meant that's why I don't talk about her with women, even if it's just while getting to know my neighbor."

Did he want this to be a date? Was I reading his friendly dinner to make friends outside of school the wrong way? It was starting to feel like I was.

"I suppose we should get back to that fence," I said, unsure what else to say. "I need to fire up the grill for the steaks, too."

He stood and wiped off the butt of his shorts, while I took a good long drink of his tight buns in that denim. He was definitely as yummy as Haylee's tarts, but I wasn't going there. Not now, not ever.

"Sure," he agreed, his eye to the sky. "I suppose it's almost dinnertime, and we still have to finish taking the fence apart."

I suddenly realized there was no way for me to get up from where I sat. I couldn't roll over to my knees when I wore the brace, I couldn't push myself up from the dock without something to grab, and I wasn't going to ask him to help me. All that left was jumping back into the water and wading to shore. I hated to do it since I was almost dry from the first swim, but I didn't see much choice. If I was going to save face and keep my secret a secret, I was going to have to. I'd change when I went to grab the steaks from my fridge.

Before I could make my escape into the water, his strong hands were under my armpits, and he pulled me up into a standing position in one motion.

"I figured you might need a hand after being down there for so long," he said, slipping his hand into mine and helping me up the uneven dock to the grass. He didn't drop my hand then either.

"Tha—thanks," I muttered, my limp pronounced after sitting on the dock for so long. "Do you have a grill, or do you want to use ours?"

"I have one big enough for a couple of steaks. Why don't you get them while I fire it up? We can work on the fence and then, after dinner, have a little bonfire."

"Sounds like an excellent way to spend a summer Saturday evening," I agreed with a smile. "I'll be over in a few minutes."

We parted ways at the property line, where he dropped my hand and watched me walk toward my apartment, the leg dragging behind me in a bit of a swishing motion rather than any kind of proper gait. I hated that my issues were displayed in a way that he could see, but it didn't matter, because we weren't dating. I told myself that the whole time I fixed my hair, put on dry clothes, and dug the steaks out of the fridge.

Bishop Halla might have a kid, but that would be the least of his worries if he got involved with me. The smartest thing to do was to beg off from dinner and stay holed up in my apartment for the night. I couldn't do that, though. I grabbed my cane on the way out the door and made my way across the yard. I had to admit to myself that I didn't want to stay holed up in my apartment anymore. The admittance scared me more than thunderstorms, and that was truly saying something.

Five

The sun began to set just as clouds moved in across the lake. The oranges, reds, and yellows of the sunset made it stunning, but it also gave an ambiance to the space around us that made me entirely uncomfortable. Suddenly, the summer campfire felt close and intimate as we sat around it, drinking beer and talking about absolutely everything. We'd covered music, literature, and politics. I was pleased to see we liked the same music and tended to stand on the same side of politics, but our literature tastes differed significantly. Bishop assured me that was okay. He said there's a book out there for everyone, so we don't all have to like the same ones. I had to take that as the gospel truth, considering he taught literature for a living.

"I bet your dad will be surprised to learn the fence is down. I hope he doesn't get upset," he said, tipping his beer bottle up to his lips. He was relaxing more and more with every sip he took. It was nice to see him enjoying himself in his new home. I wasn't so arrogant that I believed it had anything to do with me, other than companionship at a time in his life when he needed a friend.

"I sent him a picture while you were in the house. He sent me back a picture of him doing a fist pump. He said he owes you a beer when he gets back. I promised I'd pass the message along."

"I would be honored to share a beer with him," he said, tipping his at me. "He raised a brilliant woman. I know that doesn't happen if you're a slouch."

"Is that what people say about you?" I asked, sipping my lager. It was hoppy, thick, and glorious on a warm, sticky night like tonight. The humidity had increased considerably, so I kept my eye to the sky to make sure a storm didn't take us by surprise.

"That I'm a brilliant woman or a slouch?" he asked, confused.

"As a father. That you raised a brilliant daughter, so you aren't a slouch."

He shrugged, but his eyes remained on the fire, which was unusual for him. He rarely broke eye contact during discussions. "Her mother does, but not too many other people know that I'm a father—those who do haven't even met Athena. As much as I hate to say it, she's in the periphery of my life now. She doesn't need me as much as she used to. Now that she's in college, I rarely see her."

"Sort of out of sight, out of mind." I waved my hand in the air while I swallowed the sip of beer I'd taken after uttering the words. "I didn't mean that in the literal sense."

He chuckled and leaned forward, setting his empty bottle under his chair. "I know what you meant. Athena is never out of my mind, but she is out of sight. There is nothing I can do for her when she's across the country. I'm geographically closer to her than her mother is at this point. It's new. It's foreign. I still struggle with it, but I know she needs her space and independence. She's a smart girl, and I have confidence she can take care of herself. She only lived with me during the summer, so I guess we have always had that independence from each other."

"Versus me who can't take care of myself, isn't independent, and still lives with my parents."

He swung his body toward me and lifted a brow. "Is that what you got from that whole statement? I wasn't implying that. Not even a little bit."

I finished my beer, setting the bottle down next to my cane, which I glared at with hatred. "Doesn't mean it's not true. I can't take care of myself. That's how I got here."

He tipped his head at me. "I'm confused."

I waved my hand at my throat to indicate he should forget it. "And I've had too much to drink."

We stared at the fire for several minutes, the uncomfortable silence stretching out before us. A flash of light caught my eye, and I glanced up at the sky sharply.

"Just heat lightning," he assured me almost like he knew my secret, which I was sure he didn't. I couldn't say for sure, since everyone else in town knew, but what were the chances that someone had told him? It's not likely that came up in general conversation.

I settled back against the chair and watched the last of the wooden posts burn down to ash. "Wow, there goes a piece of my childhood right there," I whispered, the red coals bright as they burned down to nothing. "I don't remember a time that fence wasn't a constant marker for every season of my life. If the grass grew past the first wire, it was time to cut it. The snow piling up along it marked how many feet fell throughout the winter. In the fall, the leaves would get caught in the wires, and we'd have to rake them out without damaging the fence. The crocus always sprouted in the spring to make it festive at Easter. The burning of the fence feels like an end of an era. Maybe it's time I accept it."

"What does that mean?" he asked, poking at the fire until it sparked to life again to throw more light on the yard.

"The end of my childhood. It's time to move out and get my own place. I know I should, but I also have my reasons for staying. I'm warring with it right now."

He leaned back against his chair and nodded. "And I don't think you need to explain those reasons to anyone, Amber. You can live wherever you want to live without justifying it. I haven't lived here long, but I can tell that your parents rely on you to take care of the place when they're gone, too."

"That's true," I agreed. "The question is, what do I do when I'm starting to justify it to myself? I'll tell you what the therapist told me as a kid."

He rubbed his hands on his thighs until he grasped his knees. Almost as if he was trying to keep his hands to himself. "The therapist doesn't have to live your life or war with your emotions. They can say what they want, but that doesn't mean you can implement it into your life just because they say it should be so."

I nodded and kept my eyes focused on the fire rather than him. "You make a good point. It's a lot to think about for me right now. I'm sorry for being a Debbie Downer. Alcohol does that to me, I guess. I'm questioning a lot of things in my life, probably spurred by almost losing Haylee last summer and now with her being married."

He swung his head back and forth. "You aren't a Debbie Downer. I don't think talking something out with a friend is a problem. You did promise to tell me the story behind the Berry Sinful cupcake, though. Does it have something to do with the woman who attacked Haylee?"

Oh, thank God. He was throwing me a bone, and I was going to grab it and hold on for dear life.

I turned my chair a bit so I could look at him without straining my neck. "Oh, that's right! Let me explain."

He held up a finger, grabbed a piece of firewood off a pile by the deck, and added it to the fire before sitting back down. "Okay, ready."

"Every year we have the Lake Pendle Strawberry Fest. It started small but grew into this big event every year. It's kind of like a county fair now."

"I'm familiar," he said, nodding along.

"Okay, so there's an event every year called the cupcake bake-off. No rule says professionals can't enter, so every year, Haylee and Brady team up to bake the best cupcake. The only caveat is, you have to incorporate strawberries into your recipe."

"I have to say that the berry sinful was berry good."

I chuckled and winked, wishing I wasn't flirting with him as much as I was, but also not able to make myself stop. "I think it's the best one they've ever come up with, to be honest. That filled strawberry on the top…" I rubbed my belly and licked my lips with vigor. "Anyway, as you know, Berry Sinful won, but she beat out a woman named Darla McFinkle. Haylee and Darla have had a hate-hate relationship for their entire lives. Darla was extremely vocal about her hatred for Haylee, but my bestie was smart enough to just stay out of her way as much as possible."

"Which, from what I'm hearing, wasn't easy. What was her beef with Haylee?"

"No one knows. It was just hate at first sight for Darla. As for trying to avoid Darla, that was like trying to nail down Jell-O. She hated that Haylee was successful, and she was angry that The Fluffy Cupcake won the competition every year. Darla argued that professionals shouldn't be allowed to compete."

He made the so-so hand. "I guess I kind of agree. It feels like an unfair advantage to me."

"And Haylee agrees, too. The problem was, everyone kind of expected her to participate, you know?" He nodded, and I sighed, wishing this story had a better ending than it did. "Hay-Hay decided it was going to be our last year to compete, but she had committed to the competition already, so she showed up and baked. When Darla got second place, to say she wasn't happy was an understatement. She said some nasty things to Haylee and Brady at the competition about Haylee's body and how she didn't deserve to be dating Brady."

Bishop grimaced and shook his head. "Darla sounds like a prime example of a bully."

"Oh, yeah," I said, nodding with exaggeration. "Darla has been a thorn in our side for our entire lives. You could never prove that she was a bully, though. She had all of the adults snowed. They believed she was wonderful, and everyone else was the problem."

"As is typical with bullies."

"I suppose you have plenty of experience with them as a teacher."

He laughed, but it was mirthless. "And as a father. More than I care to admit. Anyway, continue."

"Every time you mention being a father, I do a doubletake. I have to remind myself that you're not old, and you're extremely hot to boot." This time his laughter was filled with humor. I buried my head in my hand out of embarrassment. "Cripes, you can't trust me with alcohol."

"No, I think the exact opposite is true. You hold too much back when you're sober. A little bit of alcohol helps you loosen up and stop being so afraid of saying something you think the other person doesn't want to hear."

"That's not untrue. I've always been that way. I tend only to speak when I know what I'm going to say. I'm sure the reasons are obvious to you now."

He shrugged with a grin on his face. "I don't mind that you think I'm hot and not the least bit old. You're way ahead of the curve with most women."

"But you aren't old. You're only a few years older than I am. You just had kids when you were young. We can look at it that way."

"It was more like a once and done kind of thing."

"Wait, you don't want more kids?"

He waved his hand in the air. "I do. What I meant was, I made a mistake once, and I wasn't going to make it again. The next time I have a baby, if I ever do, it will be planned and what we both want. I will never put another woman in the position of having to decide between their future or a child's future ever again."

I sat there, nodding as I thought about what he said. "You're right. I'm sure Athena's mom felt that way to a degree."

"Her name is Sam. She's one of the strongest women I know. She grew up to be a social worker and is married to a super nice guy named Ken. He had as much to do with Athena being the kind of woman she is as I did."

"Sam got her happily ever after, but you're still waiting."

"I guess you could say that. What happened with Darla and Haylee?"

I threw my hands up excitedly. "Oh, right, sorry! Anyway, no one knew that Haylee had left the recording app open on her phone after the judge got done announcing the winner, so every cruel and disgusting thing Darla said to Haylee was recorded. When Haylee found the recording the next day, she took it to the festival committee to let them listen. She wasn't doing it to be vindictive, though."

"What did it matter? If Darla didn't win the cupcake bake-off?"

"She didn't win that, but she did win Strawberry Fest Princess and was going to represent the city for a year."

"Oh, crap," he said, his laughter evident. "I bet she wasn't happy that Haylee had audio of their interaction."

My head shook back and forth with all seriousness. "Not even a little bit. Especially after they removed Darla as the princess and took her crown before she could even get on the float. She went on an all-day bender and then waited for Haylee outside her apartment. She pushed my best friend down the stairs and then stabbed her."

He reared back with his eyes wide. "I hadn't heard that part of the story."

I nodded and tipped my head to the side. "Darla will be going to trial for attempted murder sometime next month."

"You have had a lot to deal with the last year. Not only is Haylee your best friend, but she's your business partner. That must have been hard running the business with her injured."

"It was harder knowing that she was in pain for no fault of her own. Worse, knowing that she could have died before anyone found her. Thankfully, Brady had figured out that Haylee was upset with him and went into work early to talk to her that night. If he hadn't, Haylee might not be with us. The police think Brady pulled up and scared Darla away before she could stab Haylee more than once. It was also good she was completely wasted and had a bad aim. Darla isn't talking, of course, but they have the knife with Haylee's blood on it, so it will be tough for her attorney to prove she's innocent."

"That's heavy, Amber. I'm sorry," he said, leaning forward and taking my hand. He held it in his warm one, and I liked it way too much for where I was in my life. He was a professional. He was in charge of educating young minds. Hell, he'd already raised one. Here I was, still afraid of my own shadow.

"I'm just glad that she's okay and healed quickly. Brady has been a rock for both her and the business. Now that they're married, it puts how we work together at the bakery in a weird place. We're supposed to have dinner and talk about everything tomorrow night, and I'm nervous about it. I have to remind myself that we've navigated the changes thus far, so I know we can do it again."

"I know you can, too," he said, squeezing my hand before he let it go. "Everything in life is about change. Every day brings about some kind of change. We either have to bend to it or break to it. I learned that very early on in life. My parents were killed by a drunk driver when I was six, which is why my grandparents raised me."

My hand went to my mouth as I gasped. "How awful, Bishop! I had no idea it was that type of situation. That's tragic."

He nodded and pursed his lips. "I can't say that I even remember much about them anymore, which is to be expected, but it is still hard for me to accept. My grandparents have both passed now, too, so there isn't much left to the Halla name. It's just Athena and me."

"Athena sounds like a badass warrior, though, so I know she'll carry the name proudly for many years to come."

He laughed and winked, his long lashes coming down to brush his cheek. "Maybe forever unless she takes her wife's last name in the future."

"Her wife's?" My mind caught up to my mouth, and my lips made an O. "Her wife's."

"She's been out for years, and I know that all parents say that they always knew their child was gay, but her mother and I did. I swear we knew since the day she was born."

I chuckled and shook my head. "I don't question any parent who says they know their child that well. I don't have kids, but when I have one, I figure I'll understand right quick what they're talking about."

He pointed at me and smiled. "You can become a parent without even thinking about it, but you can't raise a child without thinking about every single thing you do with and for them. It's the hardest job in the world. That's saying a lot when I take care of other people's children for a living."

"I've heard that before—from my mother," I said with laughter. "I suppose I better go to bed. I have to be at the bakery early tomorrow."

He stood and walked around my chair, picking up my cane for me and then steadying me by my elbow. "I'll walk you home. It's dark, and I don't want you to trip."

"It's okay. I left the light on," I said, taking a step and almost falling into the fire.

He grasped my arm and held it tightly until I righted myself. "You sure about that?"

I sighed with resignation and hung my head. "I'm not sure about much anymore, Bishop, other than I had a nice evening. I'm glad we got the fence down with no one suffering any further splinters."

He smiled, and in the low light of the fire, my heart flared to life a little bit. I made sure to pour a bucket of cold water on that feeling instantly. I couldn't fall for this guy. He was too hot, too educated, and way too out of my league to find me interesting for very long. Considering that he was helping me walk across the grass to my apartment, he would lose interest faster than most guys.

We arrived at my apartment, and I was glad I'd left the light on over the door. It's easy to pretend you don't want to kiss someone when a harsh light is making you squint.

"Thanks for the steaks and the company. We should do this again. I enjoy being able to sit outside and listen to the lake with a friend. There's something to be said for nature and a nice campfire."

I nodded and slid the door open, ready to step into safety. "I agree. Thanks for helping with the fence. I can't wait to show Haylee what it looks like tomorrow. She'll be jazzed that the eyesore is gone."

He smiled and stuck his hands in his pockets, bouncing up on his toes. "Jazzed, huh. Well, I'm glad I could make her happy."

"You made me happy, too."

He laughed and shook his head, staring at his shoes. "Well, you could have fooled me, but if I brought even a little bit of a bright spot to your day, then it made my day worth living. Sleep well, Amber."

"Thanks, Bishop. Have a good night," I said, stealing into the house before I kissed him like the fool I wanted to be. Thank God enough of the alcohol had left my system to keep me from making a bad decision.

He waited until the door closed, and then he turned and walked back to his yard. While he busied himself putting out the fire, I stood in the darkness and watched him work. Bishop Halla was less of a mystery than he was eight hours ago. Unfortunately, what I knew about him now made me want to turn the next page even more.

The truth was obvious. I was crushing on Bishop Halla. I shook my head as I limped to my bedroom. I was in so much trouble.

Six

I slid out the door of my apartment, and Haylee followed, carrying a salad and drinks for me, her, and Brady, who was manning the grill. We were cooking brats and having potato salad and cake for dinner. At this rate, all of Mom's meat would be gone from the freezer by the time they got home. I felt terrible not inviting Bishop over for dinner, but we were talking business and nothing else. I'd save him a piece of Haylee's famous orange creamsicle cake and wander across the driveway with it later.

Sure, you'll just wander over there, Amber. I rolled my eyes at myself. I would probably dart over there the second Haylee and Brady left tonight. I was dying to see him again, which honestly scared the crap out of me. After what happened back in February, I should want nothing to do with another man. Why did the guys you were interested in dating always come along after a bad experience? It's like the universe is testing you or something. Will she know a good guy when she sees one? Stay tuned to find out!

I huffed, and Haylee snickered behind me. "Maybe you should just invite him over for dinner. We can send him home when we're ready to talk shop."

I sat down at the table and took the drinks from her. "Invite who?" I asked innocently.

My best friend rolled her eyes at me with massive precision. "The guy you've been obsessing about all day."

"You know, your neighbor," Brady said from the grill.

"Wow, you two have so many assumptions," I said, biting my cheek, so I didn't smile. "Is that meat almost done? I'm starving."

Brady swung over with the platter of brats, and we sat down to fill our buns and shovel in the food. "That was some kind of crazy today," I said after I swallowed a bite of potato salad. "I can't believe we didn't lock the door until nearly five. That's unheard of."

Haylee pointed at me while she chewed and swallowed. "It is, but I know if we stayed open until six during the summer, we'd always have customers."

I lowered my fork slowly and swallowed. "I'm sure we would, but I'd be dead in two weeks."

"Which brings us to another point," Brady said immediately, setting his brat down. "You can't keep up this pace any longer."

I chewed thoughtfully and forced the food down over the lump in my throat. "I'm thirty, not ninety," I said, washing the meat down with a swallow of beer. "But if we're thinking about having the storefront open twelve hours, even six days a week, we're going to need more help. I can't work four a.m. to six p.m. that many days in a row."

"We already need more help," Haylee agreed, stabbing a potato. "We're barely keeping our heads above water, which is great for the business, but not so great for us. Now that Brady and I are married, we'd rather not be there twenty-four seven if possible."

We all shoveled in more food, our thoughts on the business, and how much things were changing. At least that's what I was thinking about, but probably not in the same way they were. They wanted more time to be together outside of work, and I got that, but I didn't know how to make it happen without sacrificing my own free time, not to mention my leg.

Brady finished his food first and sat back with his beer, tapping it on the edge of his chair. "We could use Taylor full-time in the kitchen."

I shrugged with frustration. "I'm sure you could, since Taylor's great at what she does for you guys. I know she's expressed an interest in baking, too. The problem is, I need her for the front, or I'm sunk."

Haylee smiled and winked. "We know, which is why we haven't said anything yet. We wanted to talk to you first. From what we can see, you need at least another full-time and half-time person in the front."

"But we think it should be two full-time people so you can go down to half-time in the front," Brady finished.

"Or two full-time and a half-time. Then you don't have to be in the front at all," Haylee said, a brow up.

"My leg isn't that bad," I said on an eye roll.

"Yes, it is," they said in unison, and I grunted.

"I need to work more than part-time guys. The last time I checked, I am the co-owner of that business, not you two," I said, standing angrily. Haylee grabbed my arm before I could leave, and Brady grabbed the potato salad from the table. "I'm going to put this in the fridge and grab the cake." Before I could say anything, he was gone.

Haylee pointed at my chair and waited for me to sit down again. The sun was sinking in the sky, and I just wanted to finish this business meeting so I could go home and cry myself to sleep.

"We aren't trying to take over the business, Amber."

I sighed and let my chin drop to my chest. "I know, but it does feel like that sometimes. I'm just out of sorts if I'm honest. It used to be the two of us against the world. Now I feel like a third wheel to the dream team. I wish I hadn't come up with that stupid saying last year."

She snickered and shook her head at me. "I don't exactly think you came up with it, but we have noticed you stopped using it. You aren't a third wheel. There are still only two of us powering the bike. Brady knows and respects that. He didn't even want to be here tonight."

"But he is."

She nodded and tipped her head to the side. "I asked him to be, only because I knew I'd need back up with you. You have stubborn in spades, and you don't always listen

64

the first time I say something. Sometimes, you need it said in both ears. That doesn't mean he's making any decisions in regards to what we do going forward at The Fluffy Cupcake."

"But he'd like to," I said smartly. "I can tell when he's biting his tongue."

"No, he doesn't want any part in managing the bakery beyond what I task him with in the kitchen. When he's biting his tongue, it's to keep from saying that you need to take care of yourself and stop pushing before you do damage that you can't walk back."

"I'm lucky to walk at all," I muttered.

She pointed at me again. "That's our point! Gah, you're so stubborn!"

I tossed my arms up in frustration. "I'm not stubborn, but what the hell am I supposed to do? I can't just decide to stop working!"

She held her hands out to quiet me. "I know, that's not what I'm saying. What I'm saying is, sometimes you have to slow down when things get tough, so you don't have to stop working."

"Easy to say, hard to do when people are counting on you, Hay-Hay. I didn't think I had to explain this to you of all people. We take care of each other, and I'm not walking away during the busiest season at The Fluffy Cupcake."

"We don't want you to walk away. We want you to work smarter, not harder."

"If I'm not working in the front, then I'm not working."

"That's not true," she said, taking out a notebook from her purse as Brady arrived back at the table with the cake. He handed out plates and sat quietly, eating his cake and watching the lake beyond the trees. "You'd be working."

"Hey, there's Bishop," Brady said, pointing into the yard across from us.

I swung my head automatically, my cheeks heating when our eyes locked. I waved awkwardly, and he waved back equally as awkward.

"Mind if I go chat with him?" Brady asked.

Haylee and I shook our heads at the same time.

He bussed her on the cheek on the way by and jogged across the driveway to talk to the guy I wished I was talking to, just to be anywhere but here, I realized. Faced with the truth of how my life had already changed was uncomfortable and challenging to grasp fully.

"As I was saying," she said, pointing to the notebook, so I leaned in to read it better. Out of the corner of my eye, I noticed Brady and Bishop walking down to the lake, laughing like women at a coffee klatsch. I huffed and tried to focus back on Haylee. Unfortunately, my mind wanted to focus on a sexy teacher and single dad who had the most expressive, understanding eyes of anyone I'd ever met.

"And then we're going to sell fish from a tank against the far wall to go with the bread."

I tipped my head to the side and studied her for a moment. "What now?"

She snorted and shook her head. "You're a million miles away tonight. Or rather, across the yard, it seems."

I rubbed my face and sighed. "Sorry, I'm just—"

"Spread too thin?"

"Maybe a little bit in the current climate," I agreed.

"More like you're stretched so thin that you're close to snapping. You're carrying more than your share of the burden. You can't do it all, but you're trying to, and it's wearing you out."

"Truer words," I muttered while I shook my head. "I have a lot of ideas I'd like to do with the bakery, but I don't have time to implement the marketing strategies or work with you and Brady to brainstorm new product ideas. The business has exploded over the last three years—there's no doubt about that. The last year, though." I made the mind-blown motion with my hands and shook my head. "We rake in cash hand over fist, but it feels like we're just treading water."

"We are," she agreed. "I feel the same way in the kitchen. I want to try new things, but we just don't have the time with all the special orders."

"And having a third baker would help with that?"

She nodded immediately. "Having a third baker would let us spread the baking out throughout the day. Another baker could get all the basic cakes made and ready for me to decorate. They could help Brady by starting some of his doughs or panning and pulling from the oven to prepare for pickup in the morning. I know those orders are bringing in a shit ton of cash, so we need to keep them, but we need help. Desperately."

"You think Taylor is right for the job?"

"Absolutely. Taylor already knows the ingredients and what orders go to what companies since she's doing all the ordering and prep for them every day. She's quick to pick up new things, and the other day when I was called away, she pulled all the cakes and organized them in the cooler for me to finish."

"I've noticed she seems happier now that she's not up front all the time. Not that I can blame her. The customers can sometimes be overwhelming. That said, if I give you Taylor, then I'm down another part-time front person."

"If I have my way, you'd be down one full-time and one part-time person."

I leaned in and twisted her notebook around to read it better. What I saw there had my heart sinking and my heart soaring at the same time. I always thought that was something people just said, but when faced with a situation like this, there was no other way to feel.

"Howdy, neighbor," a voice said from the driveway. "Are you okay?"

My head snapped to the left, and I sat up in the chair, surprised to see the sun was down and the crickets were chirping. Brady and Haylee had left an hour ago, and I had stayed outside to think about what she had to say. I must have fallen asleep.

"Hi," I said, wondering if I could stand up without falling after sitting for so long. "I'm fine. I was just sitting out here thinking." I registered a crackling and then noticed the campfire in his yard. "I guess you've been watching me sleep."

He chuckled and motioned at the missing fence. "I suppose the fence did keep the nosy neighbors away, but I didn't mind the view one bit. Want to come and sit by the fire?"

"Sure," I agreed, pushing myself up. "I have some orange creamsicle cake. Are you interested?"

"Do fourth graders love dodgeball?"

"My assumed answer is no, but something tells me it's yes."

He chuckled and bounced on his toes. "Secret aggressions and all that."

"Boy, do I know about those," I muttered, taking a moment to make sure my leg was under me before I moved. "I'll grab the cake and meet you over there."

He jogged over and grabbed my elbow, helping me to the door. "I'll wait here and carry the cake for you. It's dark, and I don't want you to fall."

I nodded vaguely and slid the door open, thankful the lights were off. There was enough ambient light from outside that I could make it to the bathroom where I quickly checked my hair, washed my face, and used the facilities. I grabbed a couple of Tylenol from the bottle in the kitchen and swallowed them down before I pulled the cake from the fridge along with two forks, and made my way back to the door.

He took the cake in one hand and my elbow in the other and helped me across the uneven ground to a chair by the fire. He pulled his chair closer to mine and held the cake out. "This looks delicious."

"Well, Haylee Davis made it, so yeah, it's delicious."

He chuckled and took a fork, stabbing into a piece and savoring the flavor on his tongue. "Man, you aren't kidding. Everything she makes is amazing."

"Orange creamsicle is her favorite, so she's especially good at this one. I swear she can bake it in her sleep."

He laughed and leaned back in the chair while he finished his piece. "She probably has. I can't imagine being a baker and working that early every day."

I nodded without speaking, staring into the fire and then up into the sky. It was cloudy like it had been all day but also humid and hot. I was worried about storms, and I was searching the horizon for any sign of a problem.

"I had a nice talk with Brady," he said, and I nodded, my eyes still on the blackened sky. I didn't want to miss any early signs of a storm. "We talked about grilled cheese on his famous sourdough bread, which he promised me a loaf of, and how Lake Pendle is filled with sharks. I'm told they like to nibble at your toes."

"Mmm-hmm," I said, nodding along as he spoke. His laughter filled the air, and I whipped my head in his direction. "What's so funny?"

He was shaking his head at me as he finished his slice of cake. "I just told you Lake Pendle was full of sharks. You said mmm-hmmm." `

I rubbed my temple with fatigue. "Sorry, I'm a little bit distracted tonight."

"I can tell. Want to talk about it?"

"No, but only because I haven't worked it out in my head yet."

"Which is kind of the point of talking it out," he said on a chuckle. "At least that's what they told me in college."

A rumble of thunder filled the air, and I jumped, my gaze back on the sky to search out the lightning.

"It's a long way away," he said immediately. "There wasn't even any lightning."

His words didn't comfort me the way he expected them to. I understood that the way I felt about storms wasn't normal. I understood that other people thought I was looney tunes, but that didn't make being me any easier.

"How was your day?" I asked to change the subject. "I suppose the summer is full of to-do lists you don't get to finish during the school year."

"You aren't kidding. There's always something to do around here, and that's not even taking the curriculum work, classroom orders, and reading recommendations to finish into account. People think teachers have the summer off," he said in quotation marks, "but that's so far from the truth."

"At least you get paid, right?" I said on a laugh.

He shook his head. "Actually, I don't get paid. I mean, I get a paycheck, yes, but only because they take my pay for nine months and spread it across twelve. I have the choice to take it all from September to June and just get bigger checks, but then you have to be dedicated to saving money to get you through the summer, or you have to work a summer job. By taking smaller checks across the twelve months, you always have income."

I tipped my head to the side. "So wait. If you're getting paid in the summer, but it's money you earned during the nine months you were teaching, that means you aren't getting paid for the extra work you do in the summer."

He touched his nose. "Ding-ding, you win the prize," he said, laughter filling his voice. "That's being a teacher. Sure, if we're doing heavy curriculum writing, we will get a stipend to do that, but for the most part, all of the other stuff we do during the summer to prepare for the next year isn't paid."

"I had no idea," I said with a shake of my head. "Like none. I always thought teachers got paid to do nothing in the summer."

He laughed, but it wasn't his usual laughter. He wasn't amused, which was easy to hear. "You aren't alone. The majority of people think the same. The truth is, we don't have the summer off," which he put in quotation marks again. "We aren't on family vacations and frolicking in the water all summer. The thing is, I love it enough not to care. It is super annoying when people yell loudly about teachers making all this money to sit on their butts all summer and do nothing. If only they knew what we do, the programs we plan, the classrooms we organize and stock from our own funds, and the planning and collaborating we do during those twelve short weeks. Teaching always has been and always will be a thankless profession, which is okay by me. My job satisfaction comes from knowing my students will go on to do great things."

"That's true," I agreed, holding the cake on my lap, but not eating it. "I'm sure that's a perk every teacher appreciates as the years go on."

Another clap of thunder hit, and I jumped up, nearly tossing the cake into the fire before he caught it, bringing it into his chest. A raindrop landed on my nose as a jagged bolt of lightning streaked across the lake.

"I want to go inside," I said, my voice shaky.

"It's just a little summer storm, Amber. It will pass."

"I want to go inside," I said, louder this time and with less stability in my voice when more thunder and lightning filled the air. "I want to go inside! I want to go inside!"

The rain came down heavier now, and he grasped my elbow and helped me up the rickety steps of his deck. "I'll go home!" I said over the sound of the thunder rumbling overhead.

"Get inside," he ordered, sliding the patio door open and pushing me through, then coming in behind me to close it just as the wind picked up. He set the cake plate on his small dining room table that was circa the 1980s and eyed the yard. "I want to make sure the fire goes out," he explained as the rain came down in a sheet.

The wind started to howl, and I backed up toward the front of the house, fear filling me. "I want to go home. I have to go home. I have to go home now."

He turned away from the door and shook his head. "Not wise. Better to stay here until the storm blows over. It shouldn't be too long. The good news is, the fire is out."

He was teasing, but my heart was pounding as the rain drenched the front of the patio doors. I kept backing up into the room and fell over the arm of the couch rather ungracefully. I was on my feet again instantly when another clap of thunder shook the house.

I had my hands over my ears now, my whole body consumed by fear. "I want to go home!"

He held his hands out while he walked toward me. "I finished my man cave in the basement the other day. Would you like to see it?" he asked, opening a door and flipping on a light.

I nodded, afraid no words would come out if I tried to speak. I walked toward him, and he grasped my elbow. "Be careful going down. The stairs have carpet so they can be slippery."

All I wanted to do was run down them, but my hands and legs were shaking, so I took them as slowly and carefully as I could until I made it to the bottom. I was grateful when Bishop followed me down the stairs after shutting the door. I was also thankful that the small windows in the basement didn't let in much evidence of the storm raging outside.

My legs were shaking so hard I had to sit, or I'd fall. I sank onto the L-shaped couch that lined one side of the room, glad for the coolness that grounded me. It was leather and enveloped you into the soft, buttery cushions. I put my hands to my ears and leaned over my knees, my body rocking slightly. The cushion depressed next to me when he sat, his hand rubbing my back up and down. After a few minutes, his hand chased away the shaking and calmed me down enough that I could breathe again. The thunder was lessening, which meant the storm was moving out and away from us. My hands slowly slid from my ears, embarrassment likely tinging my face a bright red.

He kept his hand on my back but motioned at the room in front of us. "Do you like it? It's kind of a movie room, man cave, and guest room in one. I have the projector set up for movies, and back there," he said, pointing at a wall, "is an extra bed for guests. I have a second bedroom upstairs, too. I have that set up as the main guest room for when Athena comes to visit. There's also a large loft room on the top floor. I'm just using that for storage right now."

"It's unexpectedly roomy. The house looks smaller than it is," I said, my voice trembling when another clap of thunder rumbled over us.

He nodded his agreement. "Exactly what I thought when I saw the place. It's nice to have a finished space like this, even though I live by myself. I hope eventually to have a family to share it with." He held my gaze for a beat before he spoke again. "Feeling better?"

"I'm—I'm fine," I stuttered, clearing my throat. I stood up off the couch and inspected all the pictures he had hung on the wall. "Is this Athena?" I asked as another crack of thunder made me jump. I grimaced and bit my lip to keep from whimpering, but instinctively covered my ears at the same time. I was glad I had my back to him.

"It is," he said, standing behind me now with his hand to my back. I couldn't tell if it was a protective gesture or a steadying gesture, but either way, I liked it way too much for it to be smart. "She was an adorable little girl who grew up to be a beautiful young lady."

"You're not kidding," I said as I stared at the girl in a senior photo. "I see all of you in her." I jumped again when thunder rumbled through the room, and his hands grasped my upper arms tightly, as though he knew I needed that comfort.

"All of me in her?" he asked. "I don't know if her mother would like to hear that."

"She would," I said on a nod. "Athena is beautiful, and she is her daughter. Regardless of what's happened since she was conceived, a mother's love accepts every feature of their child. At least it should," I added. "Besides, you were a standup guy when you were nothing more than a kid yourself. She could have had to raise Athena alone with no help from her birth father. I'm sure she's grateful you're here to help, even though she has a husband now."

He was silent for several moments while his fingers rubbed up and down my back like they had a right to do that. I suppose as long as I didn't tell him to stop, then they did. "You have an interesting way of looking at life, Amber Larson."

"You make that sound like a bad thing," I said, a tremble rumbling through me.

Katie Mettner

"Not at all. It's more like something tells me that you have experience with it in a painful way."

I didn't—couldn't—answer him. I didn't know how to answer him. I did have real-life experience with it, and it was painful, but not in the way he was thinking. My hand trailed across a frame sitting on the stand next to the couch. I picked it up to look at it closer. "This is you and Athena. What a wonderful picture."

"It is. That was when Athena liked having her picture taken with her old dad. I think she was about ten there and we were going to a school event. She was so happy that I took the morning off to go to the Donuts and Dads event. Usually, her step-dad went because I was teaching. She was in fourth grade that year, and I just wanted her to know that she was always more important to me than work or anything else I was doing. It became a tradition after that. I invited Ken, and all three of us sat together, ate donuts, and got to know her and her friends. I thought that was important, even if I didn't live in the same town. I wanted to know who she was hanging out with, and I wanted to know their dads. It was also important that Ken was there, too. He was raising her for the most part, and he saw her friends more than I did. We found ways to make it work."

"Sounds like you more than made it work, Bishop. You are the very definition of co-parenting. I can promise you that Athena now understands how rare that is after spending a year at college. I'm glad she had both of you in her life. Strong male role models for a girl always help them make good decisions."

I lowered myself to the couch again on a sigh and kept hold of the picture, just to have something to do with my hands. "It sounds like the storm is easing."

He nodded and walked to a mini-fridge next to the small table. "It is. I wouldn't be surprised if there aren't a few more here and there tonight. It was hot and muggy all day." He walked back and handed me a cold can of Sprite, which I accepted with a smile. I cracked it open and took a gulp, lowering the can to my leg. "Thanks. I don't like storms."

"Some people don't. Nothing to worry about."

"No, I mean, I really don't like storms. I don't—I have," I stuttered about, looking for words that wouldn't come. Finally, I just shook my head. "I can't."

"Storms are the reason you live in the downstairs apartment, right?" he asked, motioning at the side of the house that faced mine.

"It's hard to find a rental with a basement," I agreed.

"Especially in a resort town like this one."

"How did you know that's why I live in my parent's basement?" I asked, my head tilted. "I bet Brady told you, didn't he?"

He shrugged and leaned back, sipping on his can of Diet Coke. "He said you'd never tell me the truth, so he did."

"What an asshole," I moaned, dropping my head back to the couch. "Way to make a girl look like a head case, Brady!"

"I don't think being afraid of storms after what you went through makes you a head case, Amber. On the contrary, I think you've earned the right to feel that way about the power of Mother Nature."

"You might be the only one that thinks that besides Hay-Hay then. Even my parents want me to get over it and be normal," I said, using air quotes.

"If only it were that easy, eh?" he asked, shoulder bumping me lightly.

"Trust me. It's not. I've tried everything, but I still work my plans around the weather all these years later. That bothers them. No, it's more like it drives them batshit crazy."

"Brady didn't tell me everything. He just said you were injured in a storm as a kid, and that's why you walk with a limp."

"Ha!" I said, sarcastic laughter filling my voice. "That's an understatement." I was getting angry and defensive now. "Brady had no right to tell you that and then to underplay the truth!"

"What's the truth then, Amber?" he asked, leaning forward to rest his forearms on his thighs.

I pulled up my dress to show him the scars on my calf. "Intramedullary rod and nails in my tibia and," I said, turning my arm outward so he could see the underside. "My left humerus. We aren't even going to talk about my knee and thigh. A tornado hit the campground where we were camping when I was thirteen. They found me in a tree yards away from where the RV had been. It took everyone by surprise that night. Every bone on the left side of my body was broken, but I was lucky and survived, some people didn't. The tornado split our RV right in half. I was unlucky enough to be sleeping on the bed in the middle of it."

His hand came up to rest on my back, and his eyes closed. "I'm so sorry, Amber. I can't even imagine. The idea of how scary that had to have been just made my stomach tremble. I understand why you don't want to mess with Mother Nature now."

"You mean, why I freak out about storms?" I asked sarcastically. "For your information, I have diagnosed PTSD." My shoulders deflated, and I sighed. "Sorry, my heart is still pounding wildly. I need to run and hide, but I can't."

He rubbed my leg soothingly through the brace and all. "Don't apologize. I didn't know that," he said with understanding. "I wish I had. I wouldn't have played tonight's weather off as no big deal. I would have respected your request to go inside the first time you asked. It won't happen again. I stick by my earlier statement, though. I understand why you don't want to mess with Mother Nature now. Why don't you want to talk about your knee and thigh?" He had his head turned to gaze into my eyes, and I hated that it felt like he could see all my secrets so easily.

Tart

I shook my head and gazed up at the ceiling to keep the tears at bay. "I'm sure you noticed I wear a brace on that leg."

"I felt it the other day when I picked you up," he answered. "I didn't know why at the time."

"I'm just going to show you. Normally, I hide it, but whatever you think is happening here between us will eventually end. This is the quickest way to the finish line." I grasped my dress, but he grabbed my hand to stop me.

"I don't know what's happening between us, Amber. I had hoped we'd be friends, but it feels like something more. Something on a deeper level than I've ever experienced with any other woman before, my daughter's mother included. Regardless, the fact that you wear a brace isn't going to make it end. I think you've earned the right to hold your head high after what you've been through, brace or no brace."

My eyes closed, and I swallowed around the lump in my throat. "Why is it that the one guy who could make you entertain the idea of dating always comes along at the wrong time? It's like the universe is conspiring against me."

"It's only the wrong time if you continue to let it be the wrong time," he said, one brow going down to his nose.

"It is the wrong time, and you'll understand once I show you this," I answered, tears filling my voice as much as they filled my eyes. One tipped over my lashes and ran down my cheek when I glanced down at my dress. His hand left mine to wipe away the tear while I pulled the material out of the way. I removed the Velcro off the top of the brace and let it fall open, leaving it wide open for his inspection. When his gaze swept across my skin, and I swear to God, if I believed such a thing was possible, it healed me just a little bit more. His face was stoic. He didn't grimace or look away from it the way most people do. He remained engaged even as he asked his first question.

"Is it painful?" he asked, his hand hovering over the red, mottled skin.

77

"This part is," I said, making a circle over the top of my knee. "I don't know why it's so red other than it might be infected."

"The skin?"

My eyes closed and the tears I'd been holding back dripped down my face. "I, um, I was injured back in February. The doctors think the nerves in the knee were damaged," I said, clearing my voice to rid it of the tears. "They asked me to come back for more tests, but I haven't."

"This is June," he said, not disapprovingly, just clarifying. "Could the nerve issue be causing your pain?"

"Some of it," I agreed, nodding. "I haven't had time to deal with it. The bigger issue is—"

"The muscle atrophy," he said instantly. "More like there is no muscle." His finger went to trace a divot in the leg, but he pulled it back. "I don't want to hurt you. It looks like it hurts. The muscle is why you wear the brace?"

"It hurts a lot," I said, my head nodding. I captured his hand in mine instead of letting him touch it. "The brace is even hard to wear some days, but it's the only way I can stay upright."

"Amber, I'm not trying to sound pushy, but I think you need to see the doctor. At least address the skin issue if nothing else."

I rubbed my temple and leaned back on the couch, my frustrations spilling over onto my cheeks. "Haylee told me tonight I can't go back to work until I do," I said, swiping at a tear angrily. "She doesn't have that right—"

"No, but she's concerned about you. Brady is beside himself. He says he hasn't known you as long as Haylee has, but even he can see the drastic change in how you walk. From what he tells me, Haylee is out of her mind with worry."

"Tonight has been," I paused, looking for a word that encompassed everything, but there wasn't one. "Hard. I'm sure that's a lame word to use in front of an English teacher, but I can't come up with anything else. I'm sorry."

Tart

"Don't ever think you need to apologize about something just because I'm a teacher. You can't walk around using words like arduous and toilsome all the time. It just doesn't work."

Laughter spilled from my lips, and I shook my head on the back of the couch. "You always know how to make me laugh. Thank you."

"Anytime," he said, laughter filling his voice, too. "Besides, I think hard was the perfect choice to use. I felt it here." He pointed to his stomach. "Because I understand hard."

"I wish my mom were here for a hug, but at the same time, I'm glad she's not. She's been bugging me for months about this, and she'll just say I told you so."

"Moms can be like that. I am happy to offer a hug without the I told you so."

He shifted just enough to pull me over onto his shoulder, where he wrapped his arms around me. "All the little kids at school say I give pretty good hugs."

I rested my hand on his chest. I liked the way I fit into him perfectly, almost like he was made for hugging me. "They're right. You give pretty great hugs." We sat in silence for a few minutes, and then I sat up, his arms dropping from around me instantly. "I suppose I should go home and wallow in my self-pity over there so you can get some sleep. It sounds like the storm is over."

"I'm not in a rush to go to bed. I'd rather help you sort out what to do about the bakery. What does Haylee want you to do?"

I shrugged and rolled my eyes to the ceiling. "So much more than I expected. To begin with, she wants me to get the leg treated. She says I can't continue with it the way it is."

"I would argue that she's correct there," he added, just to rub it in.

"I know, but it costs money, Bishop. Lots of it."

"You don't have insurance?"

I made the so-so hand in the air. "We do, but it's a high deductible. You pay everything up to the first ten thousand.

Since we're young, that's a pretty safe bet, but as we learned with Haylee last year, when you get hurt, it gets expensive. We carry special insurance, so if we get hurt on bakery property, they cover it. I didn't get hurt on bakery property this time."

"This time?" he asked with a brow in the air.

My head barely nodded in response to his question. "I was in a situation in February."

His hands rubbed up in down on his thighs with frustration. "Let me translate that. Some asshole tried to take things too far in February."

I tipped my head in acknowledgment. "I got away from him and asked him to leave, but he kicked me in the leg before he did. I suppose it was payback for me kneeing him in the nads."

"Good for you," he said vehemently, "I just wish he hadn't decided to pay you back. Did you have him arrested?"

"I tried, but they can't find him."

"They can't find him?" he repeated, and I nodded.

"I guess he moved on immediately upon leaving my place since I sent the cops the next day. It doesn't matter. There's nothing I can do about it now. I tried to give it time to heal, but it doesn't appear to be happening."

"Well, it can't heal by magic," he said, shoulder bumping me again.

"I know, but the cost of fixing the entire situation is out of my league, Bishop." He opened his mouth to speak, and I held up my hand. "Let me explain. This kind of brace isn't working anymore. I used to be able to walk almost normally when I wore it. Now, I just drag the leg around behind me. If I don't wear the brace, I can't stand on the leg at all. It won't hold me up."

"Do the doctors have a solution?"

"Oh, they do," I said on a chuckle. "A seventy-thousand-dollar solution."

"Come again? I didn't pay much more than that for this house."

80

"You just made my point," I said, shaking my head in frustration. "My insurance won't pay for the kind of brace I'm wearing, much less one that expensive."

"Why is it so expensive if I may ask?"

"The brace is computerized, from what I understand. The doctor likened it to one of those prosthetic knees that runs on a computer. The microprocessor adjusts your gait for what kind of terrain you're walking on and that kind of thing. I have a very rudimentary understanding of it because I will never have one, so it doesn't matter."

"Okay, that explains the expense. Why do the doctors think you'll benefit from it?"

"Honestly, I tuned out after he told me how much it cost. It wasn't going to happen, so I didn't worry about the explanation. I do remember him saying if I got the new brace, the leg would be functional again."

"And if you don't?"

I gave him the palms out. "Probably end up on crutches, then eventually a wheelchair. I won't be able to work at the bakery anymore, and my life will be over."

"A lot of people live very productive lives from a wheelchair, Amber," he said logically.

"Well, it looks like I'm going to be one of them, but that doesn't mean I'll be doing it in the bakery. Haylee already doesn't want me there. Imagine if I'm rolling around in a wheelchair. The office isn't even big enough for a desk chair."

"Then you do the office work at home."

I tossed my arms up and huffed. "That's exactly what she wants me to do!"

"Something tells me a lot is going on below the surface with the bakery that has nothing to do with your leg."

"Let me guess, Brady told you," I said sarcastically.

"Not in so many words. He just said that you were having a business meeting. I'm a relatively smart guy and figured out the rest all by myself."

"I'm really tired," I said, "tired of talking. Tired of being in pain. Tired of thinking. Just tired."

81

He nodded and motioned at my leg. "Why don't you put the brace back on and I'll walk you home. Tomorrow is a new day. When the sun comes up, it might be easier to sort out what you're going to do."

I strapped the Velcro down and let my dress fall again before I stood. "I hope that's true, but I sincerely doubt it. Thanks for listening, Bishop, and for the hug."

"Anytime," he promised, putting his arm around my waist and walking me to the stairs. "I'm always here to listen, even if I don't have the answers."

I eyed the stairs, and frustration mounted. "I don't suppose you have an outside entrance to this basement."

He shook his head. "Sorry, I didn't even think about it when I suggested we come down here."

"You didn't know how bad my leg was. I can go down, but going up is impossible now. The leg won't hold me up long enough to step up with the other leg. Mind if I go up on my butt?"

"I don't mind at all," he said with a smile, waiting while I worked my way up the stairs one at a time. He followed me up so I didn't slip and, at the top, helped me stand again. "See, no problem, but we'll stay on the first floor from here out."

I nodded and hung my head. "I'll stay at my place when there are storms."

He helped me to the door and then out into the night, the sky already clearing off to reveal a smattering of stars here and there after the earlier downpour. There were puddles of rainwater on the sidewalk, but it was cooler, and a soft breeze blew across the lake. "It's going to be nice sleeping weather tonight. I'm glad it cooled off. I love sleeping with the window open and the night air pouring in."

"That sounds like heaven. Living in a basement, I don't get much of the night air unless it's from the patio doors." I paused at the doors to my apartment and grasped the handle. "Thanks for walking me home, and for listening, again. I feel like that's all you do for me. I'll bring you that loaf of sourdough bread and a cake to make up for listening to me whine."

He waved his hand at his neck and then grasped my shoulder. "Stop apologizing, Amber. I love talking with you, and I don't mind listening. It's not a huge burden to spend the evening with a beautiful woman like yourself. I'd do it all over again tomorrow night if you'd have me."

I nodded and offered a genuine smile. "More like if you'd have me because I love sitting in your yard around a cozy fire. I guess I'm not going to work tomorrow, so I might be over after all."

He returned the smile and squeezed my shoulder gently. "I'll be there. Shout if you need anything before then, and I'll come over. Until then, goodnight."

"Goodnight, Bishop," I whispered, sliding the door open without turning. I was lost in the green eyes of the guy who, during any other time in my life, would have been real relationship potential. Unfortunately, that time in my life had passed.

His head lowered until our lips were nearly touching, but it was me who closed the distance to make sure they finished the journey.

Seven

Was this happening? My lips were on hers, and I was instantly lost in the sensation of softness, warmth, and passion I didn't expect to course through me the way it did. Lord, she was delicious. The kiss was closed-lipped, but she vibrated with a need for more. She vibrated with a need to be kissed hard by someone who would still respect her when the kiss was over. Hell, someone who would come back for more again and again. I was that someone.

A moan rumbled deep in my throat, and she returned it with a soft mewling that made me instantly hard. Pressed up against her the way I was, there was no way to hide the evidence of what she did to me. I was a goner with this woman. She owned me already, and I had only spent a few hours with her. She was wounded but strong. She just needed to see that someone—anyone—understood her pain, her desire to stay independent, and her need to be held and comforted when life got to be too much.

I poured that idea into the kiss, my lips gentle and undemanding of anything she wasn't ready to give. When it was her who traced my lips with her tongue, my dick pulsed against her belly, an uncontrollable reaction to the way she took what she wanted without care. She was beautiful, talented, smart, and sexy as hell, and I wanted all of her. I had to bide my time, or I'd scare her away. Our discussion tonight made that obvious.

She moaned low and needy when I opened my lips, tipped her head, and took a tour of her warm, silky tongue.

Tart

I returned the moan, the sounds rocketing around under the portico of her apartment like an echo. She pushed my tongue out of the way, using hers to delve into my mouth. I wrapped my hands in her hair while hers were wrapped around my neck to stay upright. I made sure to lean back so she could rest against me and feel secure.

The kiss was burning hot, both of us wanting more than we were going to get tonight, but knowing the promise was there for more the next time we saw each other. And there would be a next time. Amber Larson was more than I ever dreamed of dreaming about when I thought about my perfect partner. I had steered clear of relationships for years, too afraid to repeat the same mistakes I made with Sam. I swore that I would never let my libido lead me again, but this soft, unbelievably beautiful woman under my lips was making that resolve extremely hard to keep. It was making other things extremely hard, too.

My thumb caressed her cheek while I slowed the kiss, and finally, with deep regret, let my lips fall away. I lowered my forehead to hers and gazed into her soulful grey eyes. "You're incredible, Amber Larson, and I mean that exactly the way it sounds."

Her eyes danced with the smokey hue of a turned-on woman, but I also saw fear and uncertainty in those eyes. I couldn't make that disappear with just one kiss, but maybe, after one thousand more, the fear and apprehension would float away and leave her eyes clear and bright again.

"I think you're rather incredible yourself, Bishop Halla. I admit that it scares me, but I can't deny the truth. Now I have to try not to think about you and your lips for the rest of the night."

"I will have to do the same, but the memory of your soft lips on mine will make that as hard as other parts of me are right now. Good night, Amber. Sleep well," I said, dropping her hand and walking up the pathway. I turned to make sure she made it into the house safely. She slid the door closed and offered a wave through the glass that I returned before I walked back to my house.

She made my body throb with desire and want in ways no woman ever had before. That wasn't an exaggeration or dramatization of what just happened. That was the truth in ways that cut to my core and forced me to rethink my life. I had spent the last eighteen years alone, save for a few relationships that I knew would go nowhere, which made them safe. I was focused on my work and raising my daughter to be a decent human being. Now, my job was established, and my daughter was a wonderful woman who made me proud every day.

It hit me that I was just given a new assignment to teach. That realization dawned when I walked back into my house, and the scent of Amber's perfume still lingered there. It would be the most demanding assignment I'd ever taught, but if I did it right, the rewards would last a lifetime. I hadn't known Amber long, but I knew she was worth the effort it would take to heal her. She would always suffer the consequences of that night, but she didn't have to suffer them alone anymore.

I grabbed a fork and my computer then sat down at the table and opened the laptop. The cake still sat on the table, so I stabbed a piece, bringing it to my lips before I typed information into the computer. It wasn't hard to find the brace that she was talking about earlier. I chewed and read, clicking through on videos and spec pages until I was well-educated about the product. She was right. It was ridiculously expensive, but what it could do for her pain and her mobility was startling and obvious. She needed that brace.

I surfed through some articles about the rods and nails they had put in her bones, so I had a little bit of background information about those procedures, too. Looking at some of those pictures, I couldn't imagine the pain she must have been in after those surgeries. Needing one rod looked painful enough. I couldn't imagine needing three. I had to force myself not to think about the asshole who decided to kick her just to hurt her more. His abuse was the reason Amber's leg had gone downhill so quickly over the last few months. I could see why Brady and

Haylee were scared shitless for her. When you love someone, you don't want to see them in pain.

Yes, loved someone. It didn't matter that I'd only known Amber a few weeks and only spent a handful of hours with her. Those few hours had been some of the best hours of my life. She made me think. She made me smile. She made me want more out of this life. That was the most surprising part of all. I had found in that little tart all the things I'd been searching for over the years but just couldn't find. There is love there, and where there is love, there has to be action.

I rubbed my temple as I chewed absently on the sweet cake. I wanted to help Amber, but there wasn't much I could do. She wasn't going to accept money from me to help pay for the brace. I couldn't bully her into going to the doctor to get the leg checked when her best friend couldn't even convince her to make an appointment. All I could do was support her and try to understand the position she was facing. Her position was precarious, and that was the problem. It wouldn't take much to push her over the edge, and she'd be lost forever.

I suppose I could try to find her parents. I had their phone number, given to me by Mrs. Larson in case I ever needed anything. Contacting them felt wrong, though. She was an adult, and from what I could gather tonight, they weren't great at accepting her issues since the tornado had ripped through their lives. I didn't want to make that worse for her.

I tapped my chin with my finger while I stared at the Google search bar on the screen. It waited for me to tell it what to do next while I waited for some grand vision to tell me what that was. A thought struck me, and I hit a bookmark at the top of the page, waiting for it to load.

The frequently asked questions page came up, and I searched for the information I was seeking. A plan was forming in my head as I read the information, clicking through other pages to find the exact information I would need to convince Amber even to consider the crazy plan I'd just hatched.

Katie Mettner

Sleep hadn't come easily. Between thinking about Haylee and the bakery, and lusting after my kind, sexy neighbor, I spent most of the night staring at the ceiling. I had come to a few conclusions about the bakery, but conclusions about Bishop were more elusive. The pros and cons were easy to delineate when it came to the man. He was sweet, gentle, a good listener, understanding, supportive, sexy as hell, and after that kiss we shared last night, obviously interested in me.

The cons were more complicated because they had nothing to do with him and everything to do with me. My life was a dumpster fire, and I didn't see that changing anytime soon. Not to mention, he was a gym teacher. He's not going to date someone like me for very long. Not when the only physical activity I can manage is sitting at a campfire. The cons of Bishop Halla don't outweigh the pros. The cons of how Amber Larson would destroy Bishop Halla's life do.

My previous dating experience was a nightmare. I wasn't in the mood for round two. Did I think Bishop was going to hurt me? No. Not even a little bit. That didn't change the fact that I was experiencing too much upheaval to trust myself right now. It wasn't fair to draw someone else into my nightmare, either.

My fingers left the steering wheel and traveled to my lips. *Why were you kissing him last night, then?* I asked myself for the nine hundredth time since the kiss. *It wasn't like anyone was forcing you to stand there and let him stick his tongue down your throat.*

I growled and banged my head on the headrest. This morning was starting the same way last night ended—too many questions, too few answers, and not enough patience. I pulled the key from the ignition and unbuckled my seatbelt, deciding the only thing I could do was start trying to solve my problems instead of making more for myself. The only way to do that was not to be run roughshod over. I know my best friend and her beau had nothing but good intentions, but that didn't mean I had to agree with them completely.

The one thing I did agree with them on was we needed to change how we were doing business at The Fluffy Cupcake. We were all run down, short with each other, and running on fumes. If we didn't make some changes immediately, we weren't going to survive another year at this pace. That was the reason I was at my business this morning. I had worked out a plan last night that would mostly satisfy everyone. We'd all have to give a little on our demands to be successful, though. Having spent the last twenty-six years with my bestie, I already knew she'd agree to the changes I'd come up with during the night. Her forte is baking. Mine is business.

I pulled the door open to the bakery and stepped in, immediately enveloped by the loving scents of fresh bread and sweet pastries. The sun was shining, the coffee was brewing, and Taylor was loading the bakery case with the last of the fresh Danish.

"Hey, Taylor," I said, crutching behind the case to greet her. "How are things this morning?"

"Hi, Amber," she said, standing upright from the case. "Busy as always, but that's good, right?"

"Busy is good, but overworked isn't," I said, deciding that honesty was the only thing that would start to sort out where we were going with our business. "I think we're all feeling the overworked part."

Taylor shifted nervously, uncomfortable with the situation, her answer, or both. "It's always this way in the summer."

"Tactful," I said on a chuckle. "I know you've only worked here for three summers, so you'll have to take my word for it that it hasn't always been like this."

I shifted the crutches under my arms better to take some weight off my leg. "We're in a bit of a crisis here, Taylor."

She motioned at the crutches with a slight grimace to her brows. "I'm scared to death about your leg. It's not getting any better, is it?"

"It needs some work," I said, deciding that going into how bad things were would only muddy her decision. "Nothing I'm not used to. I'll be seeing a doctor about it this week. I do have a question for you."

She leaned her hip on the edge of the cashier's counter and nodded. "Sure, hopefully, I can answer it."

"If you had the opportunity to work in the back of the bakery full-time, is that something you'd be interested in doing?"

Her eyes widened double in size, and she swallowed nervously. The answer was evident on her face while she searched for a way to say it without losing her job or making me angry.

I held up my hand to calm her fears. "You don't have to worry about upsetting me. I want to solve the problem we're having here. I can't do that if people aren't honest with me."

Her shoulders deflated, and she nodded, but I noticed her neck bob with emotion all the same. "I would love to work in the kitchen full-time, but at the same time, I know that you need me in the front. I'm not going to make things harder for you than they already are."

I waved my hand in the air. "No, you wouldn't be making things harder on me. You'd be making things easier on my business partner and sister, so either way, it's a win for me. I already know I need to hire help for the front of the bakery. In that process, I want to move people around to do jobs that interest them the most. I want you to stay at The Fluffy Cupcake, Taylor. You're a wonderful person and employee. You are talented in so many aspects of the business that it's hard for me not to spread that around, but I know that spreads you too thin. If I can count on you to help me train a few new counter people, then I'm more than happy to let you find some happiness again working here."

"Seriously?" she asked, her excitement obvious now that she knew I wasn't going to be upset. "I would love that so much!" she said on a squeal. "I would never leave you in a bind here, so whatever you need, Amber. I'm here to help. I know a couple of people looking for part-time hours if that helps."

"It would," I said quickly. "Have them come in and fill out an application, please? We need at least two more part-timers and a full-timer. If I don't have to advertise, that saves time. Besides, I know you don't hang out with people I can't trust."

She grinned and bounced up on her toes. "I would never let anyone work here I didn't trust, Amber. Never. I'll text them and have them come by today." She cleared her throat and looked over my shoulder for a minute. "My good friend, Sara, she just got laid off from her server job in St. Paul. She's looking for full-time work right now. She's organized, a quick learner, and knows customer service like the back of her hand. Should I start with her?"

I folded my hands and shook them. "Please. That would be heaven if we could get someone in here this week. The other boss has told me I'm not allowed in this place until I get my leg fixed."

"Which makes me wonder why you are here," said a familiar voice from the doorway.

I rolled my eyes at Taylor, where only she could see. "I'm here because even though my bestie thinks she runs the place, she doesn't. Blindsided or not, I have decisions to make."

Hay-Hay made the snorting sound she always made whenever I decided to pull the drama queen card. "Blindsided. Please. You'd have to be blind not to see what was going on here the last year. I'll be in the office. Join me with a pastry or two when you're done here."

My eyes rolled again, and Taylor was biting her cheek to keep from laughing. "She's so bossy. Geez, you'd think she owned the place or something."

Taylor couldn't hold in her laughter any longer and let it out, filling the bakery with a light that even the sun couldn't

Katie Mettner

offer. "She loves you, so we'll forgive her. We all love you, and we don't want to see you in pain the way you have been the last few months. You can't keep going like this."

"I know," I said on a sigh. "It sucks to get smacked in the face with the truth sometimes, but at least it was by someone who cares and wants what's best for me. We'll figure this out together, I promise," I said, taking her hand in mine. "Just be patient with us as we shift things around. Hopefully, by August, you should be in the back full-time, especially if your friend works out. I need to find someone I trust to take over the majority of my hours up here for the foreseeable future."

She held up her finger and grabbed a bakery paper and a container, setting two Danish in it. "I'll call her as soon as I carry these, and two hot, black coffees into the office for you. Even if you weren't offering to let me work in the back full-time, I'd be doing anything I could to get you out of pain. I know Sara will be here before your meeting with Haylee is done."

"It's seven a.m.," I said, laughing. "You can give the girl a chance to wake up."

"She's up. She's an early bird like me."

I waited while she poured two cups of coffee and then followed her back through the bakery to the office. Brady was at the bench, and I growled at him as I went by.

"Geez, who spilled your coffee this morning?" he asked lovingly.

"More like who spilled my secrets to my next-door neighbor," I responded in kind.

"I didn't know it was a secret, Amber. Everyone in this town knows what happened to you. Besides, he might be a man, but he's not obtuse. He was the one to bring it up. I apologize if trying to put his mind at ease upset you."

"I'm messing with you, Brady. I know he could ask anyone on the street, and they could answer him without even thinking about it. I appreciate that at least you were discreet."

He smiled in a way that softened his eyes and smoothed out the lines of his face as he leaned on the bench, his hands still full of flour from his dough kneading. "I'm always discreet, but he was so worried after you fell the other night that I felt like I should at least try to put his mind at ease a little bit. I'm glad you're not upset."

I winked and returned his smile. "I could never be upset with you, Able Baker Brady, but I would appreciate if you'd let a bitch have a little bit of mystery about her, eh?"

He snorted and saluted me, flour floating through the air from his fingers. "You got it, sarge."

I laughed aloud and realized how long it had been since the bakery was filled with our laughter. That used to be the only sound you heard other than the drumming beat of the mixer or the timer going off on the oven. Now, there was a pervading silence to the place I worried we couldn't fill. Taylor passed me on her way back to the front and patted my shoulder.

When I got to the office, I was surprised to see the disarray. "What's going on here?" I asked Hay-Hay as I sat in the chair across from the desk, piled with papers.

"I thought about what you said last night, and you were right. I can't just kick you out of here and expect you to be okay with that. What I can do is make this office functional, so you have a place to manage the business better. My crap is always strewn around here, which makes it hard for you to find anything. I have to do better."

I motioned at the paperwork while I sipped at the coffee Taylor had brought for us. "Seeing this, I know you're right. We do have some work to do if we want to get this place running smoothly again. It's been neglected for too long. The majority of that is my fault."

"No, you were just stretched too thin, and that's on both of us. Should we have seen this sooner and done something about it? Yes. The problem is, we were both so damn busy doing our jobs that we didn't have time to stop and think about how to make life easier."

"You must have found the time somewhere."

She shook her head and looked to the ceiling. "No, I was forced to see the light, too. I, um, had a scare," she said, looking around me to check the doorway.

I leaned forward and stared at her under my eyebrows. "A scare?"

Her eyes rolled to break contact with mine. "A pregnancy scare," she clarified.

I hopped once in my seat and squealed. "What? And you didn't tell me?"

She held her finger to her lips. "Shh, geez. I said it was a scare, not that I was. I'm not, for the record."

My shoulders slumped back into the seat. "I don't know how to feel now. I can't wait for you and Brady to have a little one!"

"And we will, when the time is right, and things here are in a better place."

"But, the scare forced you to see the light?"

Her head nodded up and down in such an exaggerated manner it would have been funny if it weren't for the fact it wasn't. "I lost it, Amber," she said, lowering her voice. "I was a week late, hadn't even taken a test yet, and he found me sobbing in the bathroom. It all crashed down on me, I guess. After the test came back negative, and I could breathe again, he forced me to talk to him about my reaction. He knew it didn't have anything to do with the idea of being pregnant, but rather the idea of being pregnant right now. It was at that moment I knew the business was running us instead of the other way around."

I rubbed my forehead and agreed with a nod. "I came to the same conclusion last night at about three a.m. while staring at the ceiling. That's why I'm here now. I decided you were right, to a degree, last night. I can't keep going like this. So, I made some decisions."

She leaned forward on the desk with her hands folded. "Okay, one of them better include having your leg looked at again, or we're done here."

I forced my eyes not to roll and tipped my shoulder up. "I'll call later and see when I can get in. In the meantime, I'm going to start sorting out this," I said, motioning around at the mess around me. "I can't—" My voice broke, and I rubbed my temple, trying to swallow back the tears. I cleared my throat and tried again. "I can't work out front for a few days. I hurt too much." A tear ran down my cheek until I wiped it away.

She was around the desk and hugging me before my hand fell to my side. "I'm sorry, honey. I didn't mean to make it worse, but I'm desperately worried."

I nodded over her shoulder. "Me, too. That's why I've avoided the doctor. I can't any longer, though. I'm in bad shape. I don't want to make things harder for you, but I'm scared, Hay-Hay. My knee looks atrocious today. Last night, I could still walk with only a cane, but this morning, I can't do anything without the crutches."

She leaned back and motioned for me to show her. "I had to wear a dress because I couldn't even get pants on." I pulled the dress up, and her eyes widened.

"Brady!" she yelled in a voice that told me how scared she was.

"Don't bother him," I hissed. "There is absolutely nothing he can do."

He skidded to a stop at the door and didn't get to ask what she needed before his eyes landed on my knee. "God almighty, Amber." He took a step in the door. "You have to see a doctor."

"I will," I promised, my head nodding. "It wasn't like this last night, so something has changed."

Haylee looked up at Brady. "Would you get some ice for it? She can ice it while she's sitting here. It won't help the underlying problem, but it might make it feel better."

He promised he would and left the office, while she hugged me again, rubbing my back and rocking me gently. "You took care of me last summer, so let us take care of you now. I wish I had understood what was going on, but now that I do, I'm not going to let this go on. I'm mad at Phyllis for not putting her foot down sooner."

I laughed, but the sound was more sad than amused. "Don't be mad at her. She tried. So did Dad. They can only do so much when I'm a grown-ass adult."

She leaned back and smiled, but it was forced. "Don't try to pretend that I don't know the dynamics that go on there, Amber. They didn't push you to do anything because their guilt doesn't allow it. I wish they would see, even all these years later, that it wasn't their fault. You can't predict Mother Nature."

I gave her the palms out. "You're preaching to the choir. All I know is, I still have to find a way forward with my physical health and the business. I took the first step before I came in here."

She tipped her head to the side. "How?"

Brady came back with a bag of ice wrapped in a bar towel. I accepted it from him with a smile and held it to my knee. I prayed it would numb the explosive ache that was overwhelming me quickly. I wasn't sure how I'd even finish this conversation without throwing up. I needed to go home, but first, I had to finish addressing my business situation.

"I asked Taylor about working in the back full-time," I said, picking up the conversation. "I promised her if she helped me get the new employees trained, that she could move to the back with no guilt."

"Did she agree?"

"Faster than you agreed to marry Able Baker Brady."

She snorted and rolled her eyes. "I guess we better get an ad in the window then."

I held up my hand to stop her. "Taylor is calling a friend of hers who was just laid off. The woman is looking for full-time work. If we could get her full-time, up Monique's hours, and hire one more part-timer, we'd be in good shape. Taylor said she knows a couple of people looking for part-time work, too. With any luck, I can do interviews later this week and get them started. In the meantime, I'll ask Monique about picking up more hours. I can't take Taylor from you guys right now to cover my front hours. You need her worse than I do."

She nodded and sighed. "Especially with all the summer orders."

I rubbed my hand on my thigh and eyed her, unsure how to say the only solution I could find last night. "I thought about our discussion, and I know you're right. It's time for me to take control of this place. The only way I can figure to do that is to become the manager over everything but you and Brady."

"Meaning?" she asked, confused.

"I don't work in the front anymore except for emergencies or to cover vacations. I'll do all the scheduling, marketing, ordering, paperwork, payroll, and be the face of the business for the community. I'll make deliveries and meet with brides and those looking for special occasion cakes and buns. That gives you breathing room to bake without spending hours every week doing everything else."

She clapped once and grinned. "Thank you! You don't know what a relief that will be. Both for my schedule and my worry about your leg. I know you don't want to admit that you have to slow down, but you do."

I nodded and gave her a lip tilt. "Bishop reinforced that opinion last night. I know you're both right. That doesn't make it any easier to do."

She held my hand and patted it. "I understand. I remember what it was like last year when I couldn't bake. I knew it was temporary, and it was still frustrating. Yours isn't temporary. That's what makes it that much harder. You saw Bishop last night?"

I shook my head at her. "Yes, but we aren't talking about Bishop right now. We're talking about business. That's why I'm here. I've decided I'm going to load all of this nonsense up," I said, motioning at the paperwork on the desk. "Then I'm going to take it home and spend the next week sorting, shredding, storing what we need in bank boxes, and bringing the rest back here for the file cabinet. When I finish that, I'll get all those digital accounts set up that we keep saying we need to do, but never find the time to get done. That will keep this paper explosion from happening again. I'll also set up a new way to keep track of everything on the computer, so we all know where to find anything at a moment's notice. Once all of that is finished, I'll start planning new campaigns and marketing ideas. We'll have a meeting once a week to keep everyone on task and up-to-date. How does that sound?"

"Like you're a lifesaver," she said, her chin trembling. "I'm already overwhelmed, and I knew I was going to have to get this all done somehow, too. If you take all the paperwork, Brady and I will redo the office. It will be your office when you come back. I'll allow you to work from home as long as you keep that leg up while you're doing it, and you make an appointment to see the doctor."

I crossed my heart and winked. "That's my plan. I'm hoping by taking time off my leg that it will improve drastically." She opened her mouth, and I stuck my finger against it to keep her from speaking. "I'm still going to see the doctor. I have to find some relief from the pain. It's wearing me down to the point I can't control my emotions. I nearly lost it last night with Bishop when the storm took us by surprise."

"Oh, no," she sighed. "I wondered if you were okay."

"We were outside by the fire, so I had to go into his house since mine was too far away. As the storm got worse, he figured it out pretty quickly. I guess Brady said something to him about the accident. Anyway, he took me downstairs where we stayed until the storm passed, then he walked me home."

She rubbed my shoulder compassionately, the same way she has done since the accident happened. "You weren't too embarrassed?"

"I most certainly was," I said on a laugh. "It was too late to do anything about it, though. He asked appropriate questions, and was more than understanding about it. Then we talked about his daughter and—"

"His daughter?" she asked, leaning back in surprise. "He's got a daughter?"

"Yes, Athena. She's eighteen and away at college in California. He was a teenage father."

"Holy man," Haylee said on an exhale. "Proof positive that you never know what's going on in someone's life."

"He told me a few nights ago. He never married Athena's mother or even lived with them, but he has taken an active role in Athena's life. Considering he was sixteen

98

when she was born, he stepped up and did the right thing by her."

"For sure," Haylee agreed, her head nodding. "As a foster kid married to a foster kid, I know where that girl might have ended up if he had walked away."

"It sounds like her mom had very supportive parents who helped. Sam is a social worker now, and married to Athena's step-dad, who helped raise her. They co-parent well together."

"How does that make you feel?"

"How does what make me feel?"

"Bishop being a father."

I gave her the palms out. "Uh, fine? It's not like she lives with him. She's an adult and goes to school across the country. Besides, I have no right to have any feelings about it. I'm his neighbor, not his mother."

"I see," she said as if she didn't. "Did you explain to Bishop about your leg."

"Yup, and my arm, and the situation as it stands. I also told him my best friend ripped the rug out from under me, and I needed to sort out what to do."

"What did he say about that?"

"He said you were right to call me out. If I didn't do something about my leg, I was going to require more than a short, forced time-out."

Her brow went up. "Smart man."

"I promised him I was going home to think it over. He walked me there, kissed me, and I went to bed. End of story."

"What!" she squealed instantly. "Next time, lead with that!" Her laughter, dancing in the chair, and foot-stomping on the floor told me she was excited.

Brady came racing around the corner, nearly running into the wall when he tried to stop short. "What's the matter?" he asked out of breath.

"Nothing," Haylee said, finger-waving at him. "Sorry, I was just excited to find out I don't have to do all this paperwork because Amber's going to do it."

Brady did a fist pump. "Excellent. Give me ten minutes to get my buns out of the oven, and I'll help you load it all."

"Buns in the oven, you say. I hear that was almost a thing between you two," I said, snickering when Haylee groaned.

"One day, it will be a certain thing," he said as he walked away.

Haylee leaned in and took my hand. "I can't believe you kissed him already."

I swallowed and looked anywhere but at her. "It just kind of happened. It wasn't planned. The moment was there, so I took it. I mean, he was going to kiss me, all I did was encourage it."

She made the *out with it* motion with her hand. "Was it completely panty-melting as expected?"

"Panty melting?" I asked with laughter in my voice. Her brow lowered, and she growled until I answered. "My panties didn't melt off, but it was close."

She clapped her hands like a little girl, excitement radiating from her. "I knew it! I'm thrilled that you guys are moving forward with this!"

"Moving forward with what?" I asked, confused.

"A relationship!" she exclaimed, throwing her hands up in the air.

I stood instantly and shook my head hard. "No. No, no, no. No relationship," I insisted, stepping toward the door. "It was just an innocent kiss, Haylee." I took another step backward and never found my footing before I was falling to the floor.

"Amber!" Haylee yelled, grabbing me before I fell onto the hard concrete. "Stop before you hurt yourself."

She swung me back into the chair carefully and knelt, taking stock of me. Her hand went to my forehead and held it there. "You're warm."

"It's warm in here," I said, shaken by the near fall. I had to remember to keep my crutches with me at all times now.

"No, you have a fever."

I looked to the ceiling because making eye contact with her would only make me cry. "I think the leg is infected or something. I don't feel right."

She yelled for Brady again while putting the ice pack back on my knee. He came running and stopped at the doorway. "We need to get her home," Haylee said, standing up. "I don't want her driving. She's got a fever."

I swatted at her, and my dress fell to cover my leg again. "I'm fine. I drove myself here. I can drive myself home. I'm not a child."

Brady knelt in front of the chair and gazed up at me with his bright blue eyes. "We know you aren't a child, but you can't let this go any longer. You have a serious problem and one that's going to cause serious consequences if you don't have it looked at by a doctor. If you have a fever, then you have an infection. You can't pretend anymore, Amber."

I nodded once. "I know. I was already planning to call Dr. Newton today."

Brady glanced at his watch and then to his wife. "I'll cover the bakery. The clinic is open. Take her there. She needs a doctor, whether it's the one she always sees or not. No more waiting or she'll be in the ER. I'll have Taylor drive over to pick you up, so Amber has her car once she's done at the clinic."

Haylee stood and untied her apron on a nod, then held her hand out for my car keys. I sighed. I had officially pushed my luck.

Eight

I lowered my head to the seat of my car and rolled it back and forth a couple of times. I was exhausted, and it was only two o'clock. Somehow, I had to find the strength to get into my house. It had been a long day already. Maybe I could just go to bed and hope things looked better in the morning. I glanced over at the seat where a bag from the pharmacy was sitting. Chances weren't great for that.

There was a knock on my window, and I jumped, letting out a little yelp until I recognized the face in the window. Bishop. I wanted to let out a deep sigh, but he would see me do it. The last thing I wanted to do was hurt his feelings. It was nothing against him, anyway. The fact that I was overwhelmed wasn't his problem. It was mine.

I waved and opened the door, thinking hard about how I was going to swing my left leg out the door of my Subaru. "Hey, Bishop," I said without moving.

"Hi, Amber. Sorry if I scared you. I was concerned when I realized you'd been sitting in your car for ten minutes. It's going to get warm in there."

"I've been sitting here for ten minutes?" I asked, glancing at the clock on the dashboard.

"I think you fell asleep," he said, his gaze sweeping across me. It drew heat and fire to my gut and made me swallow hard when I recognized the desire in his eyes. After what I had just gone through, I had a way to make sure that disappeared and never returned.

"I may have. I didn't get much sleep last night. I was at the bakery bright and early and then the clinic. How are you?" I asked, just to stop the diarrhea of my mouth. "Why were you watching me sleep?"

He laughed and pointed at his yard. "I was finishing up the deck demo. I'm having it replaced, and my handyman was here helping me get the old one gone. He just hauled all the old wood away, so now I'm looking for wayward nails. He'll start building the new one in a few days." He held up his hand before I could say anything. "Don't worry, though. There won't be any pounding. I bought a modular deck, so all he does is snap it together after he levels the ground."

I tipped my head in confusion. "They make prefab decks now?"

"Yes! I didn't know it either. I was doing a little research online and found them. I can't wait to show you. You'll love it." He held the door all the way open and stepped back. "I should let you get out."

I nodded, but my head just kept bobbing because I wasn't sure how to accomplish that simple task.

He knelt next to me and turned my chin until I made eye contact. "Can I help you get out?"

"I wish I could tell you how," I said on a sigh. "The clinic brought me out to the car in a wheelchair and now," I paused to take a breath when he interrupted.

"Can you swing your legs out or not?"

"Only if I lift the left one out. It's in bad shape," I said, biting my lip.

He bent over, gently lifting the left leg out and lowering it to the ground, giving me the freedom to swing my right leg out and sit on the edge of the seat. I grabbed my purse, but before I could get my crutches, he scooped me out of the car and strode toward my apartment.

"You're going to hurt yourself, Bishop," I scolded, hanging on tightly to his t-shirt.

"You weigh nothing, my little tart," he teased, his voice full of laughter.

His little tart? Were we back to that?

"Shows what you know," I said, shaking my head. He waited while I unlocked the door to my apartment before he strode in and lowered me to the couch. "Thanks for the ride, but now I'm in the apartment, and I don't have my crutches." It was my turn to laugh when he held up his finger then jogged back out the door. When he returned, he had my crutches and the pharmacy bag. He set the bag down on the table by me and the crutches on the floor. "Let me get a pillow for that leg."

I pointed down the hallway. "On the bed," I said, ready to say more when he disappeared to get it.

"Holy hell!" His words were distant, but I snickered at the tone. When he reappeared, he was holding the pillow and shaking his head. "It looks like an office store exploded in there. What the hell?"

"I was going to explain," I said, still laughing. Bishop handed me the pillow and sat opposite me in the chair by the doors. "You didn't give me time."

"I wasn't expecting," he motioned his hands around, "that."

"Stop being dramatic. There aren't that many boxes."

"I counted like ten or twelve," he said, a brow raised. "I missed something over the last eighteen hours. What's going on?"

I sighed and let my shoulders drop back after I fixed the pillow. "I am officially out of the bakery except for interviews and paperwork."

He leaned forward and clasped his hands together. "What do you mean out of the bakery?"

I held up my hand to clarify. "Sorry, not out of the bakery. I'm no longer working at the front counter. I'll be doing all the management and marketing work from here on out. All of the customer service work will be employees only. Those boxes hold the paperwork and filing that we haven't had time to deal with for over a year. My job is to spend the next week here at home, sorting it all out. Then I have to devise a new computer filing system for us, set up some accounts to go digital, and hire several new workers."

His eyes widened, and he shook his head slightly. "That sounds like it's going to take a lot more than a week."

I laughed, glad it was relaxed for the first time all day. "Oh, it will. I'm just saying that I'm not allowed back in the bakery for at least a week while my leg heals a little bit, so I'll work here with my leg up. It's not in good shape."

"I would never have guessed that," he said, winking. "Actually, the need for two crutches was a dead giveaway."

I nodded, biting my lip while I did it, so I didn't cry. "I've been at the clinic since eight o'clock this morning. Um, things didn't go well."

"How not well did they go?"

"I should just show you," I said, "unless you're squeamish."

"I'm a physical education teacher for elementary kids. I'm not even a little bit squeamish."

I laughed and nodded, letting my chest relax a little bit more. "Good point." I hiked my dress up to show him the knee that now sported a bandage. The rest of the leg was fire engine red.

He stood up and walked over, dropping to his knees to get a closer look. "God, Amber," he hissed, his words barely audible, "this looks worse than it did last night."

"It is," I said, letting my head fall back. He held the back of his hand to the skin and then grabbed my gaze with his. His hand went to my forehead, and he shook his head, his lips in a thin line.

"You have an infection. That fever is something else. You must be miserable."

"I've had much better days," I admitted. "The doctor said I have septic arthritis in my knee. I guess the leg is more susceptible to it because of the hardware. He did a needle aspiration, which surprisingly made it feel better. The skin is also infected. I had to stay at the clinic for I.V. antibiotics before they'd let me leave."

"Do you need to go back for more?"

I pointed at the bag on the table. "No, I picked up oral ones to start today. I'll have to take them for at least two weeks and possibly up to six weeks."

"Did he do x-rays?"

I sighed and rubbed my forehead. The heat of the day mixed with the fever made me want to take a cold shower and curl up in a ball. "He did after draining all the fluid out of the knee. There was a new fracture that wasn't there after the original accident. He thinks Rex fractured the femur again when he kicked me."

"And you walked around on a broken leg?" he asked in shock.

I made the so-so hand. "Remember, there's a rod in there already holding that bone together, and it was just a small crack in the bone, so not a fracture the way you're thinking. I should have said it was relatively new, but healed. It was painful because he cracked the bone, but it was always stable."

He fell to his butt and grasped his knees. "I'm so sorry. You must be miserable. I guess you do need to spend some time off it. Does he think once the infection is gone that you'll be able to walk better again?"

I laughed, and the sound took him by surprise until he glanced up and noticed my face. He stood and lifted my legs carefully, sitting on the couch and setting my legs over his lap. He pulled me into his arms and held me in a hug, not speaking or doing anything other than comforting me for a few moments. When he did finally speak, his cheek was resting on the top of my head, and my face was buried in his shirt.

"Maybe you should call your parents and have them come home? I'm sure they'd want to be here for you."

I shook my head slightly. "Not unless I have to. My issues have ruined a lot of plans they've made over the years. I can handle this."

He lowered me back to the pillows on the couch and held my hand in his. "Tell me what else happened. I can tell he gave you other news you don't know how to process."

I shrugged and leaned my head back on the pillow. "He was surprised to see how I just drag the leg around rather than have any kind of natural gait. When he took the

Tart

brace off, and I couldn't hold myself up at all, he was extremely unhappy that I'd waited so long to see him. I used to be able to walk on the leg without the brace. It wasn't correctly, but it did hold me up. Since February, it hasn't."

"Don't you think maybe that was a good reason to see the doctor before now?" he asked gently. He was concerned, which I understood, but he didn't understand the life I've led up until now. I couldn't get mad at him for that, but I also didn't want to defend myself all the time.

"In the beginning, I thought it was from the injury and would improve. When it didn't, I adjusted to it just like I always do when something changes. See, you've known me for less than two weeks, Bishop. You haven't been part of the last seventeen years of constant changes with this leg. I know it's easy for you to sit there and judge my decisions, but those decisions are never easy, cut, or dried."

His fingers tightened on mine, and he shook his head. "I'm sorry if that came off as judging you. I should have worded it differently. I should have asked if that concerned you, but you answered the question in a roundabout way. You didn't think anything of it because the leg is always changing."

"At the beginning, that's true," I agreed. "It was when it didn't start to improve again that I got worried. Then work got busy, and I kept pushing it day after day. As long as I wore the brace, I could walk, but I didn't see the way I was walking. Haylee and Brady did. When I almost faceplanted on the bakery floor this morning, Haylee drove me to the clinic and deposited me there. Now it's too late to fix it."

"The doctor must have some kind of treatment, Amber," he said gently. "What did he suggest?"

"In two weeks, he wants to do nerve conduction studies. He said the nerves aren't firing correctly anymore. He suspects the damage is too great to reverse it. According to him, all that's left for treatment is the current brace and both crutches all the time, a wheelchair, or the microprocessor brace he told me about before."

"The nerve conduction study will give them more information, though, so that sounds like a good place to start, right?"

"It would be if it weren't for," I rubbed my fingers together to indicate money. "I don't have it. I also don't have seventy thousand dollars, so that brace is out. I can afford a wheelchair. Would you get me a drink of water? I'm not feeling so great."

"Anything you need," he said, lowering my legs back to the couch and disappearing into the kitchen.

What I needed was a few minutes to myself. I just told Bishop more than I'd told my best friend. It was hard to admit defeat, but I think I just did. When you're up against a rock, all you can do is bend or break. I couldn't bend because I was already broken.

I inhaled a breath of cold air from the freezer while I dug around inside it. I needed a moment to steady my nerves. Now was the time to bring up my idea, but I was terrified Amber would laugh at me. Then again, maybe she'd cry. Either way, I knew she was going to say no. I just wasn't sure how I was going to convince her that this was the only way.

I grabbed the water, a washcloth wet with cold water, the bottle of Tylenol, and an ice pack, then carried it back to the living room. I handed her the glass of water and held up the ice pack. "Would this help at all?"

She reached for it and settled it across her knee. "Can't hurt, right? My skin is burning as if someone lit it on fire. I was thinking about a cold shower, but that's more effort than I can expend right now." She swallowed two Tylenol with the cold water and smiled. "Thanks, I appreciate your help. You don't have to stick around. I'm sure you have better things to do than sit around and nurse my sorry ass back to health."

"It's summer. I have nothing else to do," I promised, rubbing the cloth around her face to cool her.

Her finger roved around my face in a circle. "That's a lie. You're the one who spent five minutes explaining all the things teachers do in the summer."

I laughed, and it made the tension flow out of my chest in a way I was grateful for at the moment. It was hard to speak when my sternum was crushing my lungs. "I'll give you that, but I enjoy your company, and I'm not in a hurry to get home. I wanted to talk to you about something."

"Sure," she said carefully, as though she was afraid that I was going to ask her out again. Little did she know.

"First, I have a question." She motioned for me to ask, so I cleared my throat. "If you could afford the nerve test and the brace, would you do it?"

Her head tipped to the side, and she blinked twice. "That's a ridiculous question. If I could afford it, then I would have done it already."

"If that's the case, then I might know how to help you get those things accomplished."

"Did I win the lottery on a ticket I didn't know I bought? If not, I don't see how that's going to work."

"We get married," I said in one breath.

The room remained deathly silent. I had to check to see if her chest was even rising and falling, or if she had just stopped breathing to avoid answering.

"This is like one of those fever-induced delirium dreams, right? Am I awake?" she finally asked, the words barely audible.

I swallowed and rubbed my hand on the couch to keep from making eye contact with her. "You are most definitely awake. Let me explain. I was thinking about all of this last night. I realized that if we get married, then I can add you to my insurance. My insurance will cover it all without deductibles or copays."

"Um," she said, the word hummed more than spoken. "I don't think that's legal, Bishop. Thanks for the offer, though."

"It's not illegal," I said quickly.

109

She held up her hand. "Okay, maybe more like sketchy and not exactly ethical."

"I'll give you that," I agreed, "but then again, there have been sketchier things done in the world. Listen, I already carry insurance on Athena, so I have the family plan regardless. Adding a spouse," which I put in quotation marks, "isn't going to change the premiums or raise any red flags."

"Except we've only known each other for two weeks!" she exclaimed.

"They don't know that. I've been employed in the district for six months. For all they know, I moved here for you."

"And then after I have expensive tests and they pay for a ridiculously expensive brace, we what, just get divorced?"

"We cross that bridge when we get there," I said hesitantly. I couldn't say that I was already in love with her. I couldn't say that I'd fight like hell to stay married to her if I ever convinced her to agree to this crazy scheme. What she didn't know wouldn't hurt her. If, in the end, it didn't work out between us, her quality of life improved in the process. There was no downside to the plan other than my broken heart, which I would keep to myself for right now.

She waved her hand in the air. "Wait, it's a preexisting condition. That's not going to work."

"They can't deny treatment because of preexisting conditions anymore, Amber. Is that why your insurance is refusing to pay for anything? If it is, you have a lawsuit on your hands."

Her head shook instantly. "No, they would pay for the nerve conduction tests, but not until I meet the first ten grand. That said, I don't have any coverage for durable medical equipment, so they aren't going to pay for the braces no matter what."

"My insurance doesn't have that condition," I explained. "We pay the first thousand dollars, and then everything else is paid after that. I've already spent that between Athena and me this year. Durable medical equipment is paid one hundred percent after the deductible, too."

"Seriously? I thought it was always twenty percent."

"Teachers don't make a lot of money, but we do have decent benefits in most districts."

She was quiet while she pondered the things I said. Her eyes remained focused across the room rather than meet mine.

Her cheeks were rosy from the fever she was still fighting, so I took the cold washcloth and held it to those cheeks for a moment. "Listen, Amber. I don't have all the answers, okay? I just know that I have one answer. I can do one thing to help you over this hump right now. I can't tell you what will happen in the future because I don't have a crystal ball. All I can say is, if you marry me, we can get you the treatment you so desperately need to stay part of the bakery and living life the way you want to live. If you want to think of it as a business arrangement, that's okay with me. Take some time to think about it, okay? I'll let you rest and try to kick this fever, but if you need anything, you have my number, right?"

"Right," she whispered, her voice soft and unsure. "I think I'll go take that cold shower after all."

"Do you need help getting to the bathroom?" I asked, brushing a piece of hair off her forehead.

"No, I'll be okay. Thanks, though."

"You bet. Maybe after that shower, you should take a nap. You look worn out."

"Yeah, I'm kind of tired," she said on a yawn, still avoiding eye contact.

"I'll let myself out. We'll talk soon," I said, sliding the door open and letting myself out before she could say anything that would only make my heart hurt more. I had probably just blown my chance at ever marrying Amber Larson, for love or any other reason.

Nine

The scent I followed as I walked across the driveway to my neighbor's yard was heavenly. I don't know what he was grilling, but I wanted a taste. It was nearly nine p.m., and the sun was setting lower in the sky. After my cold shower, I decided that a nap was necessary before I could even think about the bombshell that he'd dropped on me.

Truth be told, I still couldn't wrap my mind around it. Most of my heart melted when I thought about his offer to marry me and his reasons behind it. He'd thought it out, but there was a lot he didn't take into consideration. I was going to have to let him down easy and hope it didn't ruin our friendship. I gave an internal snort. Sure, you're worried about the friendship. You're more concerned that you'll never get a kiss like last night ever again.

I told myself to shut up and crutched carefully over the old fence line to save distance to his yard. "That smells amazing whatever it is," I called, so I didn't scare him with his back turned to me.

He spun around and set the tongs down, hurrying over to me. "Hey," he said, moving to take my elbow but thinking better of it. "How are you feeling? I don't think you should be up and about."

I kept crutching until I could lower myself to a chair in front of the fire. "I'm fine," I insisted. "I had a shower and a nap. My leg is already feeling better after the fluid was drained off it. I think the antibiotics this morning already helped because my fever is gone."

Tart

"That's good news," he said, dropping a hand to my shoulder for a moment before he went back to the grill. "Have you eaten?"

"No, I was getting up to make something when I smelled your dinner. I hoped to mooch some of yours."

"You're always welcome to mooch some of mine. Do you like wild rice brats?"

"From Johnson Meat Company?" I asked, rubbing my hands together. It was a tiny butcher and processing shop in town that did huge business.

"That's the one," he agreed, pulling the links off the grill. "Let me get them ready in the house, and I'll bring one out. Unless you want to come inside."

"I'll wait out here," I said, already settled in the chair. "I take my sausage wrapped in nothing but a soft bun."

I swear he moaned as he climbed the stairs to the house. I swear he also said *me too*, but I couldn't be sure. My phone beeped, and I pulled it out of my pocket, checking the message. It was from Hay-Hay. I opened it and read it twice with my head cocked to the side. She had big news to tell me tomorrow, and she'd be over when she finished baking. I wondered what that was about since she hadn't mentioned any *big news* when we talked today.

"A wild rice brat wrapped in nothing but a soft bun," he said, breaking into my thoughts when he handed me a plate. I dropped my phone to my lap and took the plate, offering a smile.

"Thank you. My mouth is watering. I appreciate your willingness to share."

He sat down in the chair next to me and set a soda in the cupholder on the chair. "I don't mind sharing my sausage with you."

The double entendre was less than subtle, and I smirked. Okay, so I was a child, but now I couldn't stop picturing him sharing his sausage with me. "This bun looks familiar," I said, picking up the hot meat. "I think I might know the baker."

He was grinning when I looked up at him. "You might. Everyone in town swears by his dill pickle buns."

113

"You won't be sorry," I promised, taking a bite. I know Bishop moaned, but he quickly covered it with a bite of his brat.

Neither of us spoke again until the food was gone and we sat sipping our sodas in the night air. The fire crackled to keep the bugs and the chill away as the sun finished its journey into the good night.

"I talked to Athena this evening," he said, tapping his can on his leg.

"How is she? Missing home?"

His head shook, and he laughed heartily. "Not that girl. She loves her independence. She got a job working at Disney and is going to spend the summer selling Mickey Mouse ear balloons."

"Wow, that sounds like fun for someone her age. Not to mention, a long way away from my experiences growing up in Minnesota."

He nodded again, his head bobbing rhythmically. "It's certainly not your typical summer job. She has always loved everything Disney, though. She felt bad that she had to push her visit here back to the end of August and will only be able to stay a few days. I assured her that I love her and that I want her to take these opportunities when they come up, not let them pass her by because she was trying to please someone else or do what someone else thinks she should do."

Oh boy, it didn't sound to me like he was talking about Athena anymore. Was he sending me a message in dad language? I chuckled at the thought inside my head and rolled my eyes. If he was, he was the hottest damn dad I'd ever met. There was no dad bod on this guy. He was one hundred percent ripped. I couldn't stop thinking about him inside me, his breath hot on my ear when he asked, *who's your daddy, my little tart?*

I rubbed my forehead and took a steadying breath. It must be the fever. It was the only thing to explain the nonsense floating around in my head right now. Maybe I hadn't had sex in so long I'd forgotten how, and the hot man next to me already proposed. Okay, so he didn't *propose* propose, but he did suggest we get married—kind of the same thing.

"I hope I get to meet her when she comes to visit. She sounds like an awesome young lady," I said, clearing my throat. I was thankful that the sun was gone, so he couldn't see how those thoughts of heated sex brightened my cheeks with blush.

"You will, and she is. I'm pleased she's confident enough to go out and do the things she wants to do without one of us holding her hand."

My phone beeped again, and I held up my finger, glancing at the screen. "It's from Hay-Hay. She should be in bed, but she's texting me about some news she has to tell me tomorrow."

"Don't you love that?" he asked, laughter in his voice while he took a drink.

"No, I don't," I said, shaking my head. "If you have news to share, either tell me what it is or don't say anything until you show up at my door." I held up my finger and texted her that we'd talk in the morning after she finished with the baking. I added that I was super stoked to hear about the big news, just to settle her down a little bit.

"Do you think she's pregnant?"

I snapped my head up, sliding my phone back into my pocket. "No," I said, shaking my head. "That was already a scare that occurred and prompted all of this messiness."

"Messiness?"

I nodded and stared into the fire, my mind racing. I had so much to think about, and now he'd thrown the whole marriage thing into the mix. I didn't know where to start to sort any of it out.

"Hay-Hay thought she was pregnant and had a meltdown thinking about the business, all the work that already wasn't getting done, how many hours she spends there, and how she was going to do it with a baby on her hip."

"I see," he said. "That would be a lot if you hadn't planned for it."

"Yeah," I agreed, finishing my soda. "The test was negative, but Brady used her reaction to the situation to force her to see things had to change. He told her she had to think hard about how to stop letting the business run us."

"I feel like he's good at that. He kind of has this quiet way of needling you about something you already know has to happen, but you haven't accepted yet."

"God, you're so right," I said on a sigh, but my lips wore a smile. "He's the only guy in the bakery. We need his cool head on a daily basis, to be honest. He's the break in the dynamic between Hay-Hay and me. When we get going on something that could spiral out of control, he's always the one to bring us back down to earth and remind us that there's more to consider. Come to think of it—I could use his wisdom now, too bad I don't have that luxury."

"His wisdom about what?" he asked, his head tipped to the side.

I held my hand out and sighed. "Well, see, someone asked me to marry him today, and I don't know what the right answer is."

He chuckled and stared into the fire. "I thought that question was asked and answered. I can rescind the offer if that makes it easier for you."

I shrugged, my curiosity winning out over my logic. "I can't get past the idea that it's deceptive, Bishop. It's probably insurance fraud."

"Surprisingly, according to the definition by the FBI, it's not," he said. "Do you know who commits the most insurance fraud in this country?" I shook my head as an answer. "Doctors. The little bit of money the insurance would payout for your tests is a penny in a full bucket of what they pay out to doctors filing fraudulent claims."

"That still doesn't make it right, Bishop," I insisted.

He held up both hands in surrender and went back to staring into the fire.

"I mean, how would it even work?" I asked, not sure I needed him to answer as much as I needed not to have it

116

in my head anymore. I needed to work it out in the air by the fire.

"It's not hard. We apply for a license, get married by a judge, and file it. My district allows me to put you on the insurance immediately."

"I mean the marriage. How would that work? It's not like I can live over there and you over here," I said, pointing at his house.

"True, that wouldn't look like we were newlyweds. I suppose we'd have to live together for a while."

"In your house?"

"I do have more bedrooms," he said. "You can have a guest room."

"Or the basement," I said casually, but my voice wavered at the end.

He reached out and squeezed my hand. "You can't stay in the basement here with your leg the way it is. If storms are predicted, and you can't get down my stairs, we can always hang out at your apartment for the night."

I squeezed his hand back in acknowledgment of his understanding, which was something I didn't get a lot in my life. "I mean, marriage would put a huge crimp in your social life, Bishop. You wouldn't be able to date or anything."

"Damn," he said, shaking his head with serious vigor. "I'll have to clear my social calendar. Think of all those calls I'm going to have to make and all those disappointed women who will have their hearts broken. It's going to take days."

I snorted and crossed my arms over my chest. "Smartass."

"I understand that this is a small town, and if we get married, we'll have to live as such."

"A fast marriage in this town only means one thing to everyone. Can you handle that?" I asked, angling my head toward him.

"I know the truth. You aren't pregnant. It won't take anyone else long to figure that out, too. I'm not worried about it. People do fall in love and get married quickly for other reasons."

"They do?" I asked, surprised. "I don't have a lot of experience with falling in love. Haylee and Brady took nearly seven years to kiss the first time."

He laughed, and I was glad it didn't sound so tight this time. "That's the exact opposite of instantly falling in love. I used to work with a guy in my last district who took the elementary school secretary out on a first date, and they were never apart again. He took her home, she stayed, and they married the next week. They're still married twenty years later."

"Those cases are rare, though."

"They are, but not unheard of when it comes to love. Besides, why are you worried about what everyone else is going to think?"

I laughed and rolled my eyes to the sky. "You didn't grow up here, Bishop. You don't understand the nuances of having been born, raised, injured, and running a business in the same town. Certain expectations are had for the hometown girls."

"Courtship and marriage to a hometown boy?" I tipped my head in agreement. "Screw that antiquated idea, Amber. You're a modern woman who can do whatever the hell she wants without worrying about what the knitting club or ladies' aid groups are tutting about."

"Tutting about?" I asked, laughing. He lowered his brow at me, and I sighed. "I know what you mean. You're right, but it's hard when you grew up in that environment. Even my mother still believes I'll marry a nice boy from my class," I said, using finger quotes.

"Maybe she'd be happy with a nice boy who lives next door," he said with a wink. "Then again, I'm not a boy. I'm a nice man, so I suppose that's going to be harder for her to accept. Your dad will probably be an even harder sell."

I shook my head, the motion jilted and twitchy. "Understand that when I do get married, whenever that may be to whoever that may be, my parents will rejoice and be glad. I'll no longer be their problem. They won't be faced with the constant guilt of this," I said, motioning at my leg stretched out toward the fire. "They'll be happy to pass me off to the first guy who is remotely interested in taking care of me, so they no longer have to do the job."

He stood and knelt next to my chair, hugging me. "I'm sorry you have to live like that, tart. You don't deserve that kind of treatment. Nothing that happened was your fault." His arms squeezed me tighter, and I put mine around him unconsciously, needing the closeness of someone to comfort me. I was worn out. Being strong all the time was hard work. I just laid there on his shoulder and let him comfort me in a way that I usually found hard to accept. Maybe that was because the comfort came from someone with pure intentions.

I sighed, my eyes heavy as they stared into the fire. "I know it's not their fault either. People deal with trauma in different ways."

He tucked a piece of hair behind my ear then sat back down in his chair. "That's true, sweetart, but it's still not right."

I cleared my throat and motioned at his house, ready to change the subject. "What about like, you know," I said, gesturing around with my hand until he grabbed it and held it down. "Wifely duties."

"That's not a thing, Amber. I'm capable of cleaning and doing laundry just the same as you are. I don't expect you to clean up after me or wash my boxers."

I stared into the fire to avoid eye contact, uncomfortable with him still holding my hand. "I didn't mean those kinds of duties," I whispered. "I meant like wifely duties," I said, emphasizing wifely this time.

His hand squeezed mine, and he sighed. "Okay, first of all, if sex feels like a duty, you're doing it wrong. That said, marrying me in no way enters you into a contract that requires time spent in my bed." I nodded without saying anything because part of me wanted to spend time in his bed. A big part of me. "Unless you want to, of course."

My head snapped to the left, and I eyed him in shock. "Do you want to?"

He rubbed the front of his shorts absently. "You have no idea how much," he said on a moan. "But I can control myself, so you don't have to worry about that. I'm not a teenage boy fumbling around in a cabin in the dark, desperate to get laid. I have better ways to deal with those urges now."

I don't know what possessed me to do it, but I stood and braced a hand on each arm of his chair, leaning down. "What if I want to worry about it?"

My lips crushed his then, and the swoop of my stomach told me I wanted to do a lot of things with this man. My heart pounded when he pulled me over onto his lap and held me tenderly, his tongue exploring mine. When it caressed the roof of my mouth, his moan filled the night sky louder than thunder.

He buried his hands in my hair and ripped his lips from mine to hold my gaze. All I saw in those eyes was desire. The firelight reflected in his green garnet globes was indicative of the fire inside him. I could feel it as I sat on his lap. I could feel every hard ridge of him.

His nose touched mine, and he stared into my eyes like they were wells without a bottom. His thumbs rubbed my temples while he took a shuddering breath after the kiss. "I swear to God, Amber Larson, all I need is thirty days to convince you that love is easy, and taking a chance on marrying me will be the best decision you've ever made."

"Thirty days, eh?" I asked, my lips seeking his for another sexed-up moment of lusty desire. "You're pretty confident, Mr. Halla."

"That's because we're not that different, Miss Larson. We've both spent years alone yearning for the one person that we had an instant and easy connection to in this world. I found that person in the back of a cupcake van on a rainy morning a few weeks ago. She peddles bread and tarts by day, but by night, she's the only thing I see in my dreams. This," he whispered, pressing his hard rod into my thigh, "has never reacted this way to a woman so immediately or viscerally. You turn me on in the blink of an eye and make me harder than I've ever been. All I need is thirty days to teach you how to accept that as the truth."

"A lesson from the teacher?" I asked before his lips were back on mine. He pried my mouth open with his tongue and dodged in, stroking, caressing, and thrusting in a way that said he had every intention of one day showing me his tongue wasn't the only thing capable of those motions.

I dragged my lips away from his to suck in air and calm my pounding heart. "If you keep kissing me like that, it won't take thirty days."

His deep, sexy, and soulful laughter filled the night. "My secret weapon is working," he moaned, his gaze holding mine. "You're such a beautiful tart. My mouth waters every time you walk into the room."

"Thank you…I think," I said, my lips dangerously close to his again.

"That was definitely a compliment. My mouth waters just thinking about how you'd taste under my tongue. Would you melt like butter the moment my tongue touches you? Do you taste sweet? Those are all things I want to know. Those are the things I have to know," he hissed, pressing his hardness into my hip again.

"I'll give you your thirty days, Bishop Halla," I whispered into the night, my heart pounding from desire and the words I was about to say. "But first, you'll have to marry me."

I heard his fake proposal and a real one solidify into my reality, when another moan erupted from his lips right before they slammed into mine again.

My bedroom at the apartment was emptying out. It was weird and exciting at the same time. I was moving out of my parents' house for the first time in my life. I'm aware of how stupid that sounds, considering the circumstances, but

I couldn't help it. Watching Bishop carry my things from here to his house all day made my belly quiver with excitement. Yes, I was only moving next door. Yes, I was going to have my own bedroom and not be sleeping with that sexy hunk of a man, but none of that kept the excitement about a new adventure at bay.

I glanced around the bedroom and shuddered in a way that told me this was real. My life was changing. I was going to be a wife before I was even a girlfriend. I was also a burden to the man who was trucking around heavy boxes like they weighed nothing more than a pillow. I had to remember that. Last night, he said he'd prove to me in thirty days that I was what he wanted, not just as a fake wife, but as a real one. I gave it fifteen days before he regretted those words. I wasn't going to hold him to this marriage. If either of us showed signs of unhappiness, I would end it immediately. It would break my heart to do it, but I would do it. Bishop was a good guy who deserved happiness with someone who didn't jump at every loud noise and wasn't broken in mind and body.

I folded the bedspread up on the bed and finished tucking it under the pillows. I was finally satisfied with how neat and orderly the room looked and felt. When Bishop came back, I'd have him lift the boxes onto the bed, so they were within easy reach. Since I wouldn't be sleeping here, I planned to use the apartment as an office to get all of the bakery paperwork sorted out. I didn't want to move it all to Bishop's house only to move it back to the bakery. Besides, it would be nice to have time away from each other every day. He had work he needed to get done for school, too. Not being in his atmosphere all the time would guarantee me time away from this constant thrumming inside me to lay down in our marriage bed for real.

"Did we get everything?" he asked when he strode back through the door of the bedroom.

"I think so," I said, looking around me. "Once we put the boxes up on the bed, I can use this room as an office. I have the desk set up so I can prop my leg up on the bed while I work."

He hefted the boxes up on the bed and rested his hand on one of them. "I like this set-up. It gives you a good space to work while protecting your leg."

I waved my hand at the bed, which was now filled with boxes. "I agree, but it just dawned on me that with the bed covered, I can't sleep here if it's storming. Maybe we should just put one up at a time."

He dropped his hand from the box and walked over, taking my shoulders. "You won't need to worry about it. I have a guy coming tomorrow to install a chair lift for the basement. You'll be able to go up and down without worrying about falling. We'll get a second pair of crutches to leave in the basement, too. That way, you don't have to worry about taking them down with you."

I tipped my head to the left in wonderment. "Bishop, you can't put an expensive chair lift in your house just for me. That's too much!" I hated how my heart pounded in a pitter-patter pattern at the thought of it.

He grasped my hand and held it to his chest. "Listen, my little tart. There is nothing too expensive if it means you're safe. A friend of mine had one he was taking out of his parents' basement, and he just wanted it gone. I bought it, and tomorrow it will be installed. You still won't be able to go upstairs to the loft, but I decided as far as you were concerned, the basement was a better bet."

I threw my arms around his neck and hugged him, my words a whisper against his ear. "Thank you so much, Bishop. I'm so relieved to know I'll be safe at your house."

He held me tightly and swayed with me, the warmth of him soaking into my chest like a soothing balm. "I'll do anything and pay anything to keep you safe, sweetart. That's why we're doing this, so you can get back to living your life. I hope I'll remain part of it, but if I don't, at least I'll know I had a little part in getting you back to the Amber you used to be."

I didn't know what to say to him. I didn't know how to tell him all the things inside me, so instead, I pressed my lips to his and let the kiss tell him what I couldn't find words to say. "You're the best, Bishop Halla," I said against his lips before I dove back in, my tongue caressing his. He had me pressed so tightly against him that I felt the second he went hard and rigid against my belly. Was I the reason he responded the way he did when we kissed? Logically I knew I was, but at the same time, it was hard to believe that a girl like me could turn someone like Bishop on that fast. He was the epitome of the perfect male specimen and by the feel of things, generously endowed in the steel rod department as well. I moaned, tipping my head to the left to give him better access to the roof of my mouth. I loved it when he stroked it with his velvety tongue. He made me want to come every time he did it. I rubbed my belly against him until a moan ripped from his throat that was absolutely panty mel—"

"Knock-knock," came a voice. Bishop and I jumped apart. I would have fallen to the floor if Bishop hadn't caught me.

I cleared my throat. "Hay-Hay, I wasn't expecting you."

She was snickering when she answered. "As I can see. I don't mean to interrupt."

Bishop held up his hand and smiled at my best friend. "Hey, Haylee. You aren't interrupting. I was just heading back home." He turned to me and winked. "See you later?" He mouthed *lunch,* and I nodded.

He strode past her, not bothering to hide the fact that I was the woman who turned him on. He was barely out the door before Haylee was squealing. "Amber!" I swear she was about to hyperventilate. "What the hell are you doing in your apartment, kissing Bishop Halla?"

I glanced around and shrugged. "Should I be standing on the sidewalk instead? His house? The dock?"

She stomped her foot with frustration. "You know what I mean!"

I held up my hand and motioned for her to go out and sit on the couch. "I told you Bishop kissed me before. This isn't new."

"A second kiss is new," she said, lowering her brow. "You sometimes let a guy kiss you once, but you never allow it a second time."

I shrugged, having no idea how to tell her that not only had he kissed me more than once, but I was marrying the guy. "That was more like the fifth or sixth kiss, but who's counting? Last night, while I was kissing him on his lap, his Johnsonville was pretty excited to see me."

She threw her hand to her chest and nearly hyperventilated. It took her a full minute before she could speak, and then it was more like high pitched moaning of *oh my God*. Cripes, if she was this excited over a kiss, imagine what would happen in a few minutes when I dropped my bombshell on her.

"You were on his lap?" she finally got out.

I patted her shoulder and winked. "I'm not a virgin, Hay-Hay. I have slept with men before. For Pete's sake, you make me sound like I'm sixteen and just been kissed."

Her head swung back and forth. "No, but it's been a long time since you trusted anyone to be in here when you were alone, especially without your parents or me on call."

"Huh, I guess that's true," I agreed. "I don't even think about it with Bishop. He's here all the time. Hey, didn't you have some big news to tell me?"

She jumped up and clapped her hands together. "God, witnessing the kiss knocked everything else out of my brain! Yes, I have huge news!"

"Well, I know you aren't pregnant. What's left?"

"Brady and I bought a house!"

I didn't jump up quite as quickly as she did, but when I was standing, I threw my arms around her. "I'm so happy for you both, Hay-Hay," I said, hugging her tightly. "You've worked so hard to get here!"

She leaned back and grasped my shoulders, so I didn't fall. "I know we already own the apartment, but with both of us there, it's just too small. We need something bigger."

I nodded and smiled, patting her face. "I agree. It was fine when it was just you, but not both of you. Besides, I know you want to start a family, and you're going to need a much bigger place. Where is the house?"

She pointed out the patio door. "You know the place on the corner?"

"Mrs. Daniels's old place?" I asked with my brow knotted. "I don't know who owns it now, though."

"We do!" she said, clapping again. "That's the house we bought."

"Wait," I said on a breath. "We're going to be neighbors?"

Her head nodded up and down, and I had to grasp her chin to stop it. "Why didn't you tell me before now?"

"I wanted to, but Brady said it would be better to wait just in case we didn't get the place. He didn't want me to get your hopes up and then be disappointed."

"I can't believe we're going to be neighbors!" I squealed, grabbing her again. "Mom and Dad are going to be freaking ecstatic!"

"I hope so," she said, holding me tightly. "We will own the first half of the block as one big happy family. At least until you move out and move on."

I lowered myself to the couch and nodded. "Can you imagine when Mom finds out she's going to be living next door to some of her grandkids. She's going to freak out!"

She tipped her head to the side and shook it slightly. "When I have kids, you mean?" I nodded. "They won't be her real grandkids, Amber," she said on a sigh.

"Okay, I'll let you tell the woman who considers you her daughter that she can't call your children her grandkids. Knock yourself out, just do it when I'm not around, please."

She gave me the har-har face. "You know what I mean."

"I know you're always hung up on the idea that family requires shared blood, and that couldn't be further from the truth. My parents would have adopted you if that had been a thing when we were kids. We both know it."

She frowned, duly chastised. "You're right. You know I consider them my parents. I guess I just don't want them to think they have to feel that way, too."

"Yeah, I don't think that's an actual thing when they've taken care of you since you were four, Hay-Hay. That's just something you made up in your mind to be true. If anything, they feel guilty that they didn't do more for you

126

during the early years of your life. If our old house hadn't already been bursting at the seams, I know they would have. Then this happened," I said, motioning at my leg, "and it was several years before they could even think about it again."

She brushed a piece of hair off my face and smiled. "You're saying I should stop being so resistant to the idea that they want me to be part of their family just like their three biological girls are."

I pointed at her and winked. "Yes, because you already are. You're here for every holiday, birthday, celebration, loss, and all those in-between days. Just stop fighting against the need to stay on the sidelines of the family and be part of it."

Her hand came up to her forehead, and she saluted me. "I will. I'll even call them tonight and tell them about the house, if you think I won't be interrupting."

"You won't be," I promised, grasping her hands tightly. "Make it a video call. They'll be thrilled to see your face and hear your news, I promise."

"Have you told them your news?" she asked. My eyes widened, and I swallowed hard. There was no way she could know my news. Unless someone reported to her that they saw us buying wedding bands in town this morning. I wanted to go to St. Paul to get them, but Bishop said if we bought them in town, it would make the sudden marriage more believable. We'd found the most beautiful set of turquoise and titanium wedding bands, and we swore the owner to secrecy, but I knew that would only last until the door closed behind us. The bands were simple, understated, and perfect for our situation.

"About your leg," she added when I stayed silent.

"I told them that I had an infection but nothing else. Please, don't say anything else to them, okay?"

She squeezed my hand again and nodded. "I wouldn't do that. Besides, I don't know much more than that, either."

"The knee infection was septic arthritis, but the antibiotics will clear it. It feels much better today already, and my fever has been gone for almost a full day. The doctor did x-rays that revealed Rex did more damage than I knew. He fractured the femur, but since there's already a rod in it, I didn't realize that it was broken."

"How did you walk on that?" she asked, her head tipped to the side. "God, you must have been in horrific pain."

I held my hands out in a shrug. "It was sore, but nothing earth-shattering."

"In comparison, I suppose," she muttered.

"Exactly," I agreed. "It healed just because the rod was already in there. The knee is a bigger problem."

"How big?" she asked, grasping both my hands in hers.

"The x-rays showed damage to the joint, but that's not surprising considering the amount of metal I have in that leg. Unfortunately, he thinks the nerves are damaged. Once the infection clears, he wants to do some nerve study tests. I assume after that, we'll know more."

"And you'll do the tests?" she asked.

I crossed my heart and let my hand fall to the couch. I would do the tests because when this infection was healed, I'd have insurance that would pay for them. I didn't like that I felt sketchy about how that insurance was going to be obtained every time I thought about it, but I also didn't like the idea of never being able to walk again. When you're stuck between a rock and a hard place, there is never a good answer.

I pointed at the kitchen. "Would you get me a drink?"

She jumped up and grabbed a couple of Cokes from the fridge. I nervously took a long gulp, working up the courage to tell her what was about to change in my life.

I set the can down on the table and folded my hands. "Um, I have some news of my own," I said slowly. I was going to wait to tell Haylee until after we were married, but Bishop made a good point earlier when we were shopping for the bands. He pointed out if I didn't tell her that I was getting married beforehand, she'd question why. She knows I'd never get married without telling her and inviting her to be my witness. I hated that he was right, but he was.

The time had come, and I had to clear my throat again while I waited for her to speak.

"More news? I hope it's better than the last news you had to share with me."

"Much better," I said excitedly, grabbing her hand and scooting to the edge of the couch. I was preparing myself for the performance of the century. If Haylee Davis didn't buy that I was marrying Bishop for love, then no one would. "Bishop and I are getting married!" I squealed, stomped my foot on the floor, and shook her hands in mine. She just sat there in silence. Her mouth opened once and then closed while her eyes blinked. "Hay-Hay?"

She opened her mouth again, and this time words came out. "Did you say you're marrying Bishop?"

I nodded quickly. "We want you and Brady to be our witnesses. Will you?"

"Let's back up. When did you decide to marry him? You've only known him a few weeks."

"I fell in love," I said, trying not to laugh at myself in the process. *Smooth, Amber.*

She tossed up her arms. "What is going on right now? When did he propose, and why didn't you call me?"

I hadn't considered that question, and I had to come up with an answer quickly. "He proposed late last night by the fire. It was so romantic, Hay-Hay," I said, my eyelashes batting. "You were already in bed, and I knew you had that big order to get out this morning, so I didn't want to bother you. You had already texted that you were coming over after work, so I waited. It killed me, but I waited. In the meantime, Bishop has been moving my stuff to his house, we bought wedding bands, applied for our license, and we're getting married tonight!"

"Tonight?"

I guess she was just going to repeat everything I said. "Yes, tonight. There's no waiting period in Minnesota anymore."

"Don't you want a big wedding with your parents and sisters there? What about Bishop's family?"

I swung my head back and forth. "No, we want to keep it small and easy. We just want to get married and be living together before he has to go back to school."

She rubbed the back of her neck with confusion. "Amber, don't you think this is a little sudden?" She leaned in close to me. "Have you slept with him yet?"

"No, we're waiting for our wedding night," I said, forcing myself not to smile.

She motioned around my face. "You know you can have sex before you get married, right? You can even have casual sex. You don't have to get married, just do it."

I gave her the har-har face this time. "I'm aware, smarty pants. I'm not marrying Bishop for the sex." She snorted, and I held up my hand. "Okay, so the sex will be absolutely amazing, but that's not why I'm marrying him. I love him the same way you love Brady. Like Brady, he'd do anything for me." If only she knew how much he'd do for me. "He has a lift chair being installed in the basement tomorrow to make sure I can go down safely if there's a storm."

Her brows went up. "Wow, that was some forethought on his part."

"You're not happy for me," I said, frowning like a spoiled child. I felt terrible playing her, horrible actually, but she had to be all in if I was going to convince the rest of the town I was marrying for love.

"No, because I'm not buying your story," she said. "Not for a second do I believe you're marrying Bishop because you fell in love and want to get married without your parents here."

"You agreed to marry Brady after only a month of dating," I said smartly. If she wanted to question my reality, I'd question hers.

"After knowing him for years. What is really going on here?"

I thought about the news from the doctor and swallowed around the lump in my throat. I was keeping a lot of secrets from her that I felt guilty about it, but she had enough to worry about with the trial and our business. Her hand came up to wipe away a tear I didn't realize had fallen. "My leg is way worse than I let on," I finally whispered, nearly choking on the tears I was trying to hold back. I was afraid if I didn't fight it, I'd never stop crying.

"We can see how bad it has gotten, honey. Tell me the truth about your appointment."

I sucked up a breath of air and let it back out shakily. "The doctor thinks after all these years, the nerves in my knee and lower leg aren't working anymore. I can't put any weight on it without the brace on, and even with the brace…"

She brushed a piece of hair off my face and behind my ear. "Are you saying your leg is paralyzed?"

"Mostly," I whispered. "I have some movement at the hip, but from the knee down, it's limp. I can't bend my knee or ankle without using my hands. That's why my leg just drags around behind me."

She pulled me over onto her shoulder and rubbed my back tenderly, giving me time to pull myself together. "Why didn't you tell me? You don't have to be strong all the time. Sometimes you can just admit that you need help."

"I know, but I don't want to pile more on you than I already have. You've dealt with this for as long as I have now."

She sat back and held my shoulders, her head shaking. "No. I've witnessed you deal with it. There's a difference. I get to go home at the end of the day while still having the use of both my legs. You don't have that luxury. You get to lean on us for support, Amber. What tests does he want? An MRI or something?"

I wiped away another tear. "No, there is too much metal in that leg for an MRI. He wants to do the nerve conduction studies. The results will tell him what nerves are damaged and how to program the brace that they want me to get."

"The one that costs more than a house?" she asked, her brow raised.

"That's the one," I agreed. "It's programmed with a microprocessor, so it does the work my knee no longer can do."

"How are you going to pay for it?"

"I wasn't going to," I said, swallowing back more tears and wiping my face on my shoulder. "I was going to buy a wheelchair and give up, but Bishop wouldn't let me."

"Bisho—" The word died on her lips, and she gazed at me, her head tipped to the right. "I'm trying to figure out how marrying Bishop comes into play here because something tells me it does."

I took a drink of Coke and let out a shaky breath, breaking eye contact with her so I could give it to her straight without seeing the disappointment in her eyes.

"Bishop has insurance for him and his daughter that pays for things like braces. If we get married, he can put me on his policy, and that will pay for the tests and the brace." I hung my head because I was so ashamed. "It was his idea," I stuttered, swallowing back more tears. "He asked me after the appointment yesterday, and it hit me that I couldn't keep pretending it wasn't necessary to get the brace. I can't ask my parents for money, and I don't have the money to do it, either."

"So last night, you agreed to marry him for insurance instead of love," she clarified.

"I know it's wrong," I said on a sob. "I know it's morally and ethically wrong, but I don't know what else to do. I'm so scared, Hay-Hay. I'm barely thirty, and I'm facing life in a wheelchair. How am I going to work?"

"Rock and a hard place, right?" she asked, wiping a tear off her face.

I nodded and rocked a little on the couch, my arms wrapped around my waist. "You know I can't use crutches for long periods because my arm has rods in it, too. I'm just screwed. It's so wrong to let Bishop's insurance pay for this. I know that, logically, but emotionally, I'm petrified. I have to do something."

She pulled me back into her chest and smoothed my hair, running her fingers through it like she has since she was a tiny girl. "I can see how scared you are, Amb. You never talk about your pain or challenges, so I know it must be bad. Here's what I think. Are you listening?" she asked as I rested on her shoulder. I nodded, so she would know I was. "I think you've made the right choice."

I sat up instantly to stare at her. "What?"

She nodded with her lips in a grim line. "I'm not going to judge you for this. I'm not going to judge Bishop for it, either. He saw a need and found a solution for my best friend, which was something I couldn't do. Do I agree that it's on the outskirts of morally not legit?" she asked, and I snorted at her choice of words. "Yes, but I also know that you're stuck without any kind of choice right now. If he can provide for you what you need to remain a productive member of society, working and paying taxes, then I say you should do it. If that pays back a little bit of the hell you've gone through in life, then I say the insurance company wouldn't bat an eye. If you can pay that forward someday, I know you will."

"That was what I finally decided," I said, nodding.

"Here's the thing, the cost of that brace is a drop in the bucket of what insurance companies pay out in fraudulent claims every year."

"That's what Bishop said, too. The problem is, I feel like I'm committing fraud. It technically is."

"Sure, okay, if you want to look at it that way. The thing is, Bishop is paying his premiums, and you know he's paid them for years and never used much on the plan, right?" I nodded. "This isn't like when a doctor's office bills out for expensive tests for imaginary patients from multiple different insurance companies to rake in millions. You are a woman trying to keep her head above water while faced with outrageous medical bills that were no fault of her own. You have insurance, and you've paid for years on those premiums with no claims. You paid for all your braces out of pocket, since they wouldn't pay a dime. You've paid your money into the pot. It's time you get something back from it."

I toyed with my hair and sighed. "I mean, you're right, but I still feel bad about it. I'm also worried about dropping the insurance I have now. I have to since I can't carry both plans, but what happens when we get divorced?" I asked, using finger quotes. "What if I can't get insurance again?"

She waved her hand in the air. "It's not a problem because the business employs you, so they have to allow you to pick it up again. If you get divorced, that is."

"You know I'll get divorced," I exclaimed. "This isn't forever, Hay-Hay."

She shrugged while she twirled her finger around my face. "I don't know, that kiss I just witnessed was too damn passionate to consider this nothing more than a business arrangement."

My shoulders slumped at her words. She wasn't wrong, but I didn't want her to think this was anything more than it was. At the same time, I couldn't stop thinking about his words last night.

"When we were at the campfire last night, he said if I gave him thirty days, he'd convince me that he wanted this to be more than a business arrangement. He said in thirty days that he'd convince me that I married him for one reason, but was staying married to him for a hundred others."

She winked, her grin growing wider with every passing second. "And that is what I saw when I walked in on that kiss. You may have just met, but that man is fierce when it comes to you."

"You're right," a voice said from the door. We both turned to see Bishop standing there. "I will protect her until my dying breath. Call it whatever you want, but I don't think it needs a label right now."

He strode to me and knelt, wiping another tear off my face. "You okay? Can I get you anything?"

I leaned my cheek into his hand. "I'm okay."

He offered me a tender smile but never broke eye contact. "She knows, right?"

"And she doesn't care," Haylee said, surprising him enough he turned to look at her. "She will convince everyone that you married for love because, in her opinion, love can be shown in a multitude of ways. You're doing for her sister what she can't. She will forever be grateful. She will also be rooting that maybe, in the end, this arrangement lasts much longer than anyone could predict sitting here this afternoon."

Bishop turned back to me and winked. "I know a guy who wouldn't mind if she was right."

Ten

I stood in the yard, holding Bishop's hands like a lifeline. He was as handsome as ever in his suit and tie, a small rosebud pinned to the lapel. I wore a white, sleeveless summer sundress that had eyelet lace in the perfect places to make it look like it was made for the occasion. I could tell he appreciated the way it hugged what little bit of figure I did have. His eyes had drifted from my face to my chest several times before grabbing my gaze again with those beautiful sapphire green eyes.

Hay-Hay and Brady had shown up dressed in their Sunday best, ready to be witnesses for the surprise matrimony. Brady didn't ask any questions, which meant his wife had filled him in on the reasons behind the nuptials. I was thankful. I didn't want to explain it to yet another person, but Brady would have to know the truth. I wouldn't ask my best friend to lie to the man she loved. As far as everyone else in this town was concerned, though, including my parents, we were marrying for love.

I eyed the man in front of me again and sighed outwardly. He was so dreamy, and I would so marry him for love. I couldn't say I was there yet, was I? Lust? Absolutely. Like? That's a solid yes. He's kind, considerate, compassionate, and helpful. All of those things are what makes him sexy as hell in my eyes. But people don't fall in love at first sight, right? I thought back to the first time we met and wondered why he was still hanging around my pathetic butt. He kept coming back, though, over and over to cheer me up and now, to help me stand on my own two feet, quite literally.

I was surprised to learn that the secretary from the elementary school, Lucy Novarty, was also an ordained minister à la the internet. Bishop had asked her to officiate the ceremony. Admittedly, I was uncomfortable with the school secretary, who used to make sure I had a barf bucket on my lap while I waited for my mom to pick me up, was now marrying me, but I understood why he asked her. This marriage would now be legit in the eyes of everyone in the school district. I made eyes at him, batting my lashes and smiling coyly while Lucy started her opening remarks. Since it was just the five of us in Bishop's backyard on a Tuesday evening, we told her the bare minimum to join us legally was all that was necessary. It didn't look like she was going to listen to us, though. She had already launched into a story about how she knew Hay-Hay and I would be something big in this community from the day we walked into kindergarten.

Bishop smiled and winked at me, clearly enjoying the story she was telling about the antics I used to participate in at the elementary school. He was unknown to everyone in this town still, but I was not. I was maybe a little too well-known, and it was showing.

My eyes drifted to the tripod, where Brady set up his iPad to record the ceremony for my parents and Athena. While we were *eloping*, he insisted we needed a video of the ceremony so our families could eventually see it. I wasn't going to argue with him. If nothing else, it would lend credence to the union upon the return of my parental unit.

"So now, I ask, Bishop Halla is there any legal reason why you cannot be married to this woman?" Lucy asked, motioning at me.

"Absolutely not," he said, his smile firmly in place.

She asked me the same question, and I shook my head, squeaking out a no at the last moment, too lost in the way his eyes were turning a dark forest green as the sun set lower in the sky. Tonight was the very definition of a romantic wedding in my book, real or not.

Once the legal questions were out of the way, Lucy launched into all the do you and I do's that you expect to say at a simple civil ceremony. We promised to have and to hold from this day forward, to love, cherish, and honor all the days of our lives as we slipped those wedding bands on each other's fingers. He held my gaze the entire ceremony, mine probably petrified in the face of what we were doing. He kept me calm and balanced by holding my forearms, so I didn't have to have my crutches with me the whole time.

"With the power vested in me by the state of Minnesota and the Church of the Flying Spaghetti Monster, I hereby pronounce you man and wife. Bishop, you may kiss your bride."

It was honestly the most surreal thing when I remembered that I was now the official wife *and* the bride about to be kissed.

"It would be my pleasure," he whispered, taking me in his arms and planting a kiss on my lips that was more rated R than PG-13. When he set me back on my feet, Haylee was clapping with her hands near her chin and tears in her eyes. I forced myself not to meet her eyes, or I'd be crying right along with her. I figured my cheeks had to be the color of tomatoes, which made me glad the sun had set, and the sky was filling with stars.

"Congratulations, you two," Lucy said, hugging us both. "Let's get that marriage license signed so you can enjoy your wedding night!"

I took my crutches from Brady, and Bishop helped me to the table where we had the official license ready to be signed by all. Once it was finished, we smiled for the camera, first with Lucy, then Brady and Haylee. Finally, Haylee insisted we have some pictures alone with the rising moon over the lake as our backdrop. Bishop snuck in a picture of him planting a kiss on my lips, taking me by surprise at the last minute. I swatted at him, laughter filling the yard and my heart.

Tart

Something told me marriage to Bishop Halla, whether real or fake, would be filled with more laughter than tears.

"That was a day, huh?" he asked, standing in the doorway of the second bedroom.

I was brushing out my hair and stopped with my brush midway through the locks. "It sure was," I agreed, offering him a smile. "If I didn't say thank you, I should have."

He stepped into the room and took the hairbrush from my hand, finishing the job for me. My moan was soft as he stroked the hair into long, straight lines. It felt so good to let someone else take care of me, even if it was something as simple as brushing my hair. "You don't have to thank me, but you did, multiple times. I care about you, Amber, for real. That's not the fake marriage talking."

I smiled, and my heart was suddenly lighter to hear his words. "I care about you too, Bishop. I just don't want you to get any backlash for this. I'm worried about that. Like really worried."

He set the hairbrush down and turned me to face him. "I won't. We're together now, just relax, okay?"

"Okay," I took a deep breath and let it out. "I guess I'm just trying to put everything straight in my mind. It's hard to do that when you feel like a terrible person."

He knelt and grasped my chin gently. "You aren't a terrible person. We aren't terrible people. I prefer to think of this as doing things backward."

"Doing things backward?" I asked, tipping my head to the side.

"First comes marriage, then comes love, then comes a baby in the baby carriage," he sang, laughter in his voice. "We got married first, but my little tart, I still want to date you. I have since that first day you ran over me with a cart full of cupcakes."

I swatted at him with laughter on my lips. "I didn't run over you. I bumped into you slightly because you were in the way."

He held up his hands. "Okay, since you bumped into me slightly with a cart full of cupcakes. When I turned around and locked eyes with you, I'll admit, I was a goner. When you cowered in that van, and I couldn't do anything to help you, I was instantly gutted. My soul kept telling me I had to get to know you. That's why I finally showed up at the bakery. I just had to see you again. If only I'd known that you lived next door."

I broke eye contact with him and stared at the floor rather than his face. "I was equally as taken, but the difference is, I know a guy like you doesn't end up with a girl like me."

"To begin with, never say that again. I don't play leagues. I never have, and I won't start now. Second, what do you mean by a girl like you?" he asked in confusion.

"No chest, no hips, a bum leg, and no hope of ever being able to keep up with you, at least recreationally speaking."

"Recreationally speaking."

I nodded with exaggeration, so he understood how important it was. "Hiking, biking, tennis, volleyball. Those are all out for me. Hell, even walking is out for me right now."

"There are plenty of other things you can do recreationally speaking while sitting down."

"Name them," I said, rolling my eyes.

"Canoeing, kayaking, biking with the right kind of bike, and sex."

My head snapped up, and there was laughter in his eyes when I punched him playfully. "Sorry, but you walked right into that one," he said.

"More like limped into it," I moaned, shaking my head. "It's late, but I think I could use a drink. I can't stop all these weird thoughts that keep running through my mind, which means I probably won't sleep."

"If they're anything like the ones running through mine, I think a drink is in order. I'll bring it in here. I bet you would like to relax without the brace on, right?"

"Like you don't know. My knee is improving, but overall, it still sucks in the pain department."

He stood and scooped me up out of the chair, carrying me to the bed while stealing a kiss from my lips.

"You shouldn't carry me, Bishop. You'll hurt yourself."

He lowered me to the bed with a laugh. "Yes, your whole one hundred pounds is going to give me a hernia."

"I'll have you know it's one hundred and nine."

"I stand corrected," he said, still laughing. "Let's take the brace off and prop the knee up."

Since I was wearing sleep shorts, it was easy for him to get to the Velcro, but I clasped my hand over his. "I'll do it. You don't have to do it."

"I don't mind," he said patiently, stripping the Velcro off while I let my head fall back to the pillow slowly. He took my shoe off, and the brace stayed inside it when he set it next to the bed. "Better?" he asked, moving my shorts aside to check the skin. "It's still red, baby," he sighed, running his finger over it gently. "I'll be right back."

While he was gone, I let my body sink into the soft, down mattress topper. The bed was easily a queen size, and much bigger than the one I had at my apartment. It was much easier to sink into, too. I was afraid I was going to like it too much by the time I moved back to my apartment. I decided tonight I'd enjoy a little bit of comfort for once in my life. Maybe I should enjoy Bishop, too. I wondered if what he said was true. That his soul had to see me again. It was a poignant thing to say, and my heart melted when he said it. I had to admit that I wanted to get to know him better, too. Even when I was in the middle of a terror episode during a storm, he calmed me. I hadn't met anyone before who could do that.

He came back in the door carrying a tray full of drinks and other various bottles. He set it on the nightstand and held up the Tylenol. I nodded eagerly, and he dumped two in my hand. I swallowed them with the glass of water he brought, and then he handed me a bottle of cold hard lemonade. "Not a lot of kick, but I figured with the meds you're taking, you didn't want anything too strong. It will take the edge off. So will this." He sat next to me and pushed my sleep shorts up higher, his fingers trailing the inside of my thigh and making me suck in air, a skitter of pleasure flowing through me at the sensation.

He unfurled something and rested it across my thigh and knee. It was cold and sent a shiver through me, but offered instant relief. I glanced down at it and then to his face. "What is it?"

He grabbed a bottle of lemonade and crawled over me, sitting on the other side of the bed. "It's an ice blanket. I found it online and ordered it. I thought it might help the pain more if you could ice the whole thing down at once. When you're not using it, you can roll it up and leave it in the freezer."

"You thought to order me an ice pack?"

He motioned at it. "Did I overstep?"

I waved my hand and lowered my bottle from my lips. "Not at all, I'm just not used to other people wanting to take care of me. I know I live with my parents, but they're pretty hands-off."

He cocked his head and let his hand rest on the ice pack. "I know you're a grown woman, but I want to offer you whatever comfort I can. I want to stay hands-off, but you make that hard. My hands want to be on you, taking care of you, holding you, comforting you."

"Is that the dad in you or the teacher in you?" I asked, setting the empty bottle on the tray again.

"Neither," he whispered, his bottle forgotten as he stroked my hip. "It's the man in me. The other two parts of me offer experience in how to treat an injury, but it's the man in me who wants to take your pain away and offer you comfort for a few moments each day, at least until we can make you more comfortable for longer stretches."

I turned on my side halfway and tucked my hand behind his neck. "You're so good at it that it scares me most of the time. I don't want to admit how good you make

142

me feel because then I have to explore what I've always believed about me, men, and my ability to make one happy."

The look he gave me was enough to make my panties wet if I had been wearing any. "You explore all you want, but I will say that you make me happy without even trying. Catching a glimpse of you while I'm in the yard, you oblivious to me, makes my heart race with happiness."

"Are you sure that's not lust?" I asked, not even jokingly. "Mine does the same thing. I'm not kidding about the exploring part. I'm not super good at this stuff."

His head shook slightly, and he slid his hand up the inside of my leg to cup my thigh carefully. "I know the difference between lust and happiness. Lust is when my dick hardens at nothing more than a look from you. That's all it takes, just a look that says you're thinking about the same thing I am, and I'm instantly hard. Happiness is the rest of the day."

"The rest of the day?" I asked, confused.

"The times you cross my mind and my lips tip up in a smile. When I think about dinner, and want it to be with you. When I'm setting up a fire, hoping you'll see it and come over so I can spend time with you again. When I lay down at night after we've been together and smile because I know when I wake up, I'll have another chance to see you again."

I nodded slowly, mostly because his hand on my leg was preventing me from thinking straight. "I see what you mean. I do the same thing, but I usually question and second guess every step of it until mostly the only thing I feel is scared."

He frowned and leaned down, his lips almost touching mine. "Then, my first goal in this marriage is to teach you the difference between happiness and fear. Are you going to be a good student and do your homework?" he asked, holding my gaze.

I swallowed because suddenly, all I could think about was being hot for teacher. "I will," I agreed, my lips aching for his.

"Excellent. The first assignment is to kiss me, but instead of worrying about what anyone else will think, concentrate on how it makes you feel."

"That feels closer to the lust side than the happiness side," I said, my lips almost touching his.

"Mmm," he hummed. "The extra credit is to tell me if a kiss can be both."

His lips crashed into mine then, and he held himself over me, his hands braced on the bed to keep from crushing me while his tongue swept inside my mouth. I grasped the back of his neck tightly and let him have his way with me until I needed air so desperately I was sure I would pass out. He sensed it and broke off the kiss, trailing his lips down my jaw to the crook of my neck, where he kissed and suckled the tender skin there. The sensation made me suck in a breath, and my hips thrust up off the bed into his leg that he'd braced between mine. He moaned, the sound ricocheting through my body to drag a moan from my own lips.

I buried my hands in his hair and pulled him back to my lips, his pliable and swollen against mine. "God, Bishop, what is happening to us?" I asked around his lips as I felt his hardness against my hip. "I feel like I'm drowning in you."

He tightened his hold on me and rolled me over on top of him, his lips barely leaving mine. "You're not," he promised, caressing my cheek. "I'm your flotation device in this crazy life," he whispered before his lips were back on mine.

Our moans of pleasure filled the room, making me want nothing more than to strip us bare and finish what we started. I couldn't do it, though. I couldn't risk being blinded by the lust of a guy like Bishop. Eventually, we'd have to go our separate ways, and if I had found a lover and had to give him up, I would never be the same. All I could do tonight was offer him a token of appreciation for marrying me when he didn't have to.

His hard dick was trapped between us, and he thrust against my belly with needy desire. His basketball shorts couldn't contain the length of him when he was hard, and he moaned when I pushed back against him. His hands tightened in my hair as I braced my right knee between his thighs and rubbed my belly up and down across his length. Every motion dragged a moan from him as he kissed me.

"If you keep that up, I'm going to come," he moaned, his lips in my neck now as I pushed upward again, his responding thrusts growing stronger with every passing second. "God, that feels so good," he sighed, his eyes closed. "You feel so good."

"I can make it feel better," I promised, and before he sensed my move, I slid down and captured the tip of him between my lips, t-shirt and all, where I suckled tenderly. I loved the disbelieving gasp that left his lips and I laughed naughtily, dragging another gasp from him. I flipped his t-shirt back to get to the meat of the matter, and the sound I made when I laid eyes on him for the first time was more than needy. It was damn near weeping. He was a god of a man like I'd never seen before, with a six-pack you could count, his manhood nestled perfectly in the ridge of his navel, and a bead of desire on the tip just waiting to be stolen.

My tongue darted out and licked it, his hiss of pleasure making me want to come in place, too.

"Fuck, my little tart. Who said you don't know what you're doing?" Bishop moaned, thrashing while I sucked him into my mouth almost to his hilt and held him there, the heat of my lips and tongue stroking him until he slid from my grasp again, all of him quivering with need. I didn't give him a chance to say more before I sucked him into my waiting lips and rubbed his tip against the back of my throat. He had grasped the sheet for dear life, but he wouldn't last long if his shaking thighs were any indication.

Letting him slide from my lips again, I sucked him back in, picking a rhythm I sensed was the right one to make him come apart in my arms. "Oh, God, don't stop," he moaned. Suddenly, he grasped my hair and pulled me away at the last second. "I'm going to come," he hissed, his eyes closed and his head thrown back.

I grasped him, my hand offering pressure at his base for a moment before he exploded with need across my chest, his moans low, hot, and filled with emotion my inexperience couldn't decipher. His chest rose and fell, but his eyes remained closed as I stroked him a few more times to draw out his pleasure.

"I think I sorted out the lust part," I said, my lips tilting up when he opened his eyes to glance at me.

"You are a naughty little tart, you know that?" he asked, using his shirt to clean me up. "That was." He fell to his side and made the mind-blown motion at his head. "I was not expecting that."

"Me either," I agreed, falling back to the bed and sighing. "I don't know what came over me."

"Probably the same thing about to come over me," he said, sliding his hand up my thigh and under my shorts. His fingers caressed the thatch of soft hair there while his lips sought mine again. His kiss brought me back to a heightened sense of desire while his fingers stroked their way closer to my center. When he encountered unexpected moisture, his breath caught again, and his lips tugged upward against mine. "It seems you weren't unaffected by your shenanigans, my student," he teased.

I thrust my hips into his hand and moaned. "I've never been this hot for anyone before, Bishop," I said, my voice wavering. "I don't know what's going on."

He gazed into my eyes, his holding mine while his thumb rubbed my cheek. "Do you trust me?"

"I shouldn't, but I do," I whispered, my breath catching when he stroked the engorged bud at my apex.

"Correction. You trust me because you know you can. You know I'm not going to hurt you, right?" My head nodded without even thinking about it, and then my shorts were gone.

"What are you doing?" I asked the words in barely a squeak.

"Repaying the favor." He was pushing my legs apart carefully, making room for his head.

I grasped his hair and stopped him instantly. "No. No, I don't let anyone do that."

His gaze lifted to mine, and he waited. "Why not?"

"I—I don't know. I just don't."

"Close your eyes," he said, his fingers straying back to my bud. "Close your eyes, and remember that you trust me."

My eyes closed against my will, and I held myself stiff, waiting for him to make a move I didn't like so I could jump up and run away. Well, not run away, but get away from him. Hide. Pretend I wasn't now his wife.

Instead, heat filled me slowly as he caressed me with a tenderness I had never experienced before. His tongue stroked the length of my lips, and then he rested his tongue on that bud, waiting and watching for any sign I wasn't okay with what he was doing. I moaned a little and shivered, pressing my hips toward his face, wanting more even when I didn't want any of it. His lips encompassed the bud, and he suckled on it, teasing the rest of my womanhood with his fingers. I was moaning. I couldn't help the sound as the sensations rocketed through me at such a lightning-fast pace that I couldn't hold them back. "Bishop," I called, my hips in the air until he held them down to the bed gently.

"Say my name again," he begged, his tongue stroking me while his finger slid inside. When I didn't object, he slid in a second one at the same time he pulled me back between his lips and sucked hard.

His name fell from my lips instantly. "Bishop," I moaned, my voice shaking. "God, Bishop, I can't stop."

His laughter and the exquisite pressure from his fingers sent me right over the edge. I called his name into the room like a dying woman using the last of her breath. When it was over, I found myself in his arms, the lights off, and his legs supporting my bad one. He had even managed to put my shorts back on while I came down from that earthshattering orgasm.

"I wasn't expecting that kind of wedding night," he said, kissing my temple.

"But we didn't, you know," I trailed off, and he tightened his arms around me.

"Consummate the marriage?" he asked, and I nodded. "Not by the true definition, I suppose, but as far as I'm concerned, you trusting me to bring you to orgasm that way was better than any wedding night I could ever imagine."

"You're just saying that," I insisted. "Men always want sex."

He snuggled deeper to get both legs of mine to rest over his. "Men want sex because it's easy, Amber. Sex doesn't require emotions. What we just did required emotion. Whether you want to face those emotions or not, that's up to you, but I was never happier to see that you didn't ask me for sex. You trusted me to make you feel good after you offered me the same release. That's the mutual respect you want in a relationship."

"Are you saying I got an A on that assignment?" I asked on a yawn, the heat of him relaxing me after a long day and longer night. Add in that rocking orgasm, and I was so relaxed I could barely keep my eyes open.

I registered that he had fixed the ice pack over my leg again before he kissed my temple. "Tart, not only did you get an A, but you got all the extra credit, too."

Eleven

The first seventy-two hours of marriage had been blissful. That's what you're supposed to say, right? The first few hours were at least, but then real life reared its ugly head again in the form of work, work, and more work. We did manage to get our marriage certificate the next day, and that allowed him to put me on his insurance immediately. He had taken the day off on Tuesday to deal with the wedding, but he still had to finish out the week working on the curriculum with his team at the high school. Per his report, our nuptials had shaken up the town more than we expected. That meant one thing, I had to video-call my parents and tell them we'd gotten married while they were in Florida. It wasn't ideal, to say the least. They were silent for so long I was afraid the connection had frozen. When I heard the kids playing in the background, I realized they were just struck dumb.

I had to hand it to Bishop, though. He had a real knack with the parental units. He had my mom eating out of the palm of his hand, telling her how he just fell instantly and deeply in love with me. My dad was a harder sell. I'm still not convinced it won't come to blows when they get back to town, but for now, at least they're still talking to me. I think my mother was secretly pleased to hear that I'd found a man, any man, to marry me. She was convinced I'd never get married or have kids because of my *fears*, as though having a diagnosed condition was something to be ashamed of or hide from people. Once she came around to the idea that I'd eloped, she couldn't stop talking about how we were all going to live on the same street and how close she would be to her grandbabies, both mine and Haylee's. I tossed my attention right then to Haylee's new house to avoid more discussion about my marriage, which wasn't nearly as real as Haylee's was.

It felt damn real the other night, though. That annoying voice in my head had been doing that since my wedding night. Like it enjoyed pointing out all the ways he'd made me feel in the span of fifteen minutes. I hated that voice. Okay, so I know the voice is me, but I wished I'd shut up more.

I shook my head and leaned back on the chair, my leg propped up on the bed while I finished sorting and organizing the final batch of bakery invoices. Monday, I would interview two more part-time people for the front of the store. I had hired Taylor's friend on Thursday, and she had started today. The report I got from Haylee was glowing. The girl was a natural at the job and schmoozed with all the gentlemen while their wives were busy shopping. I was thrilled to hear it. If I could find someone who wanted to work the hours I used to cover, that freed up my time for better managing, marketing, and new campaigns, we'll have time to implement.

"Amber!" A voice yelled from outside, and I tossed the papers, letting out a scream while my heart pounded. "Oh my God, Amber!"

I let out a breath when I realized it was Hay-Hay. When the blood stopped rushing through my head, I noticed her tone of voice was frantic. I pushed away from the pile of papers and grabbed my crutches. By the time I made it down the hallway, she was already coming through my unlocked patio doors.

"Hay-Hay, what's the matter?" I asked, crutching my way to where she stood by the door with her chest heaving.

"It's over."

"What's over? You and Brady?"

Her head swung wildly while she gathered herself. I pointed at the couch for her to sit, and got her a bottle of water that she swallowed in one gulp. I took it from her and sat. "Okay, start at the beginning."

"Right, the beginning," she said, taking a deep breath. "I was working over at the new house, and I got a phone call from the DA."

"Is this about the trial? Is it ever going to start?" I asked, my tone of voice overly irritated. "I'm so tired of Darla thinking she is going to get away with trying to kill you."

"She's not, that's what I'm trying to tell you!"

"They didn't find her guilty because the trial hasn't even started, Hay-Hay. Are you feeling okay?"

"I'm better than okay. I'm thrilled! She took a plea deal! There won't be a trial." Her hand went to her heart, and she flopped back against the couch, her face ruddy with exertion from her run over here.

"What? They offered her a plea deal? When did that happen?" I asked with suspicion.

"Just recently. The DA knew he could win in court since they had the knife with my blood and her fingerprints. It was going to be almost impossible for her lawyer to find a defense. When the courts refused to move her trial to a different county, that put another nail in the coffin. Her lawyers were going to struggle to find any sympathetic jurors no matter how hard they tried."

"Who went to them with a plea deal? Did you okay that?"

She held up both hands and waved them. "I don't get a say in that, Amber. The DA gets to decide those things. I just got a call saying she'd accepted, and I wouldn't have to go to court."

"She better not get just a slap on the wrist."

"She pleaded guilty to assault with a deadly weapon. She'll be in prison for five years with ten years of extended parole after that."

"But she tried to kill you! She should have gotten more than five years!"

"The DA was going to have a harder time proving the attempted murder part. They couldn't prove that she intended to kill me."

"She had a knife!"

"Which isn't illegal to carry by law. I guess what I'm saying is, I'll take it. It gets the whole looming trial off our backs this summer and puts her away for long enough that she just might wise up while in prison. Maybe she will be a nicer person once she gets out."

"I'm just afraid of what will happen when she gets out," I said, grabbing her hands.

"When she agreed to the plea deal, she agreed that she wouldn't live within fifty miles of Lake Pendle after her release. If she ever makes contact with me, Brady, or anyone affiliated with The Fluffy Cupcake, her probation will immediately revert to prison time."

I leaned back and eyed her. "And you're okay with trusting her?"

She gave me the palms up. "I don't have a lot of say in it. I'm just hoping that she finds some kind of passion or path while in prison. Even if she doesn't, I'll never have to see her again. Her father put their house up for sale, and rumor has it he's retired and moving to Florida. Without her family here, she won't have a reason to return. I wouldn't doubt that she won't try to get placed in a facility in Florida for her sentence. The DA said she was being taken into custody today."

"It's really over?"

She nodded once. "It's finally over. I hugged Brady for a solid twenty minutes and cried. I'm so relieved that I don't have to deal with the trial or the debacle she would turn this town into again. I want her to go away quietly, which, if you ask me, is what she deserves. She thrives on undue attention. She's about to find out what it's like to be no one special in a room full of people far more violent than she is. I wish her well."

I snorted while trying to hold back my laughter. I reached up and fixed her hair over her shoulder until I could speak. "You are so diplomatic. I hope she's somebody's little bitch every day she's in that prison."

Hay-Hay bent over laughing, the sound filling my happy meter another few notches. I was learning how to feel joy for the first time in years. I glanced down at the band on my finger and smiled. The guy who put it there wasn't doing a half-bad job of teaching me.

"Bishop, are you home?" her sweet voice called out.

I pulled the shirt over my head and jogged to the door, my feet still bare, and my hair wet. "I sure am," I said, holding the door so she could swing through on her crutches. I closed the door behind her, and she let her crutches fall, grabbing me around the shoulders in a death grip.

"It's over," she sighed, her arms wrapped around me and her face buried in my neck. "It's finally over."

I swung her up into my arms and stepped over her crutches, carrying her to the living room while she nestled into me. When I sat, I kept her on my lap, cradling her in my arms. "Tell me what's over. I don't understand."

"The trial and the nightmare of Darla McFinkle," she explained, resting on my chest.

"I thought the trial hadn't started yet?"

"It didn't, and it won't. Darla took a plea deal. We don't have to go to court. She's going away. She won't be able to bother Hay-Hay ever again." Her words were solid, but they were rough. They told of the unbelievable fear that sudden trauma often brought out. They told me how much she hated what Darla did to her sister and how glad she was that Haylee didn't have to go through a trial.

I rubbed her back to soothe her and planted a kiss on the top of her head. "How long is she going away for?"

She glanced up at me, almost as though she just realized she was in my arms. "Hay-Hay said five years and

153

then she'll have ten years of probation. Darla won't be allowed to live within fifty miles of Lake Pendle, and she can't contact any of us, or she'll go back to prison."

I held her to me and rocked her a few times. "That's great, sweetart. She's out of your lives. I'm relieved for all three of you. You get to move on now without the looming trial or threat of Darla being acquitted and staying in town."

"I'm so relieved," she said, her voice telling me just how much while her hand rubbed against my soft t-shirt. "You're still wet."

I laughed and kissed the top of her head again. "I was just finishing in the shower when you called out. I'm officially done with curriculum work for the summer. I still have work to do, but for the most part, I can do it here."

She looked up at me with her gorgeous hazel eyes shining. She was stunning, even on a Friday afternoon wearing nothing but a simple sundress and her hair thrown into a messy braid. I wanted every part of her from her beautiful eyes to her tortured and twisted leg. My hand ran along the length of her left thigh, watching her face for a reaction. I got none, which meant the skin wasn't bothering her much anymore.

"I finished most of my work today, too," she said, still watching my face. "I was wondering if maybe I could start working over here now? I know we said I'd use the apartment as my office, but now that I'm done with all the paperwork, all I need is my laptop. It's kind of silly to walk over the—"

My lips took hers to show her how she didn't need to explain to me why she wanted to work here. I wanted her here with me all the time. She mewled low in her throat and wrapped her arms around my neck, digging in for the deeper connection we always seemed to crave whenever our lips touched. My fingers found their way to her hair and pulled the hair tie from the braid, patiently unwinding her hair until it slid through my fingers like butter.

Her tongue was exploring mine, and I had to stop myself from rubbing my brutally hard dick against her leg. I didn't want to hurt that leg. I was already in enough pain from the desire coursing through me, and I didn't want her to be in pain, too. She was everything to me. That was a lightning-fast reaction to promising to love and cherish her until death does us part. Maybe to her, our vows were for show, but in my heart, they were real. I would stay married to this woman forever if she asked me to. I had so many plans to show her that. Starting this weekend, I was going to show her that a guy like me wanted everything to do with a girl like her.

I broke the kiss off, both of us panting with desire and unfulfilled need. "God, you're incredible, Amber," I whispered, her hair wound up in my hands.

"Is that your way of saying it's okay if I work over here during the day?" she asked on a sigh of contentment.

"I'll bring everything over here first thing Monday morning," I promised, kissing her again. When we broke apart, she was gripping my shirt tightly in her fist.

"There isn't a lot, but I'll need it to work on this weekend. I don't have anything else to do, so I might as well keep going on it."

"Wrong," I said, tapping her nose. "We have plans for the weekend."

"We do? Are we finishing the deck?"

"The deck is being finished this weekend, but not by us. Chris is going to work on it while we're gone."

"While we're gone. Where are we going?"

I untangled my fingers from her hair and sat her on the couch so I could turn to her. "On our honeymoon."

She sat silently for a heartbeat before answering. "Our honeymoon?"

"Yes, that thing you do where you go off as a newly married couple to cement your marriage."

She waved her hand in the air. "Bishop, we don't need a honeymoon. The marriage isn't real. You're going to divorce me as soon as that brace is paid for."

I didn't justify that with a response. I wound my hands back in Amber's hair and grasped her cheeks, caressing them with my thumbs. "Think of it as a short summer getaway if that makes you feel better, but we're going. I already cleared it with your bestie, so she knows you won't be available for the bakery until Monday."

"My bestie?"

I nodded, and I noticed her long, slender, smooth neck bob as she swallowed.

"Where are we going?"

"To the lake. We're going to have campfires, watch the waves, dip our toes in the wa—"

"No! I won't go camping!" she shouted, jumping up off the couch. She forgot she didn't have her crutches, and I caught her as she went down to the carpet, her right knee hitting the floor, which was better than her face.

"Amber!" I pulled her back to a standing position and held her there. "You gave me a heart attack," I said, my heart pounding. "The brace doesn't even hold you up anymore, does it?" She shook her head, a tear dripping down her cheek when I pulled her into me. "You're scared. This is the first time you've been this scared that the leg is never going to work again." Her head nodded on my shoulder, and I held her, rocking her gently. "I'm not going to stop taking care of you, Amber. We'll find a way through this. I know it won't be easy. I know that I'm not the one dealing with the pain and uncertainty every day, but I am going to be here to support you."

She grasped me desperately, her fear palpable against my skin. "Thank you, Bishop. I know you want to go camping, but I can't. I'm staying here. I'm sorry."

She lowered herself back to the couch, and I ran my finger over the spot on her knee that was red from falling. "I didn't mean to scare you. I wasn't taking you camping, my little tart. I'm not cruel. I understand your feelings about that, even if you think I don't. I would never do anything to make what you deal with even harder. Do you believe me?"

Her head nodded, but she shrugged. "Maybe not intentionally. I know that my reaction to the mere idea of camping is ridiculous, but I can't help that. I've tried, you don't know how many times I've tried. I decided if I was going to live a relatively normal life, I was going to have to stop trying. I was going to have to stop trying to please everyone else to the point that it crippled me. Summer is hard. I struggle with not obsessively checking the weather to make sure nothing is going to take me by surprise. I will always struggle with that. When it storms, even when I'm in the basement, I'm curled up in a ball sobbing while it rages overhead. If I'm at work, I hide in the cooler until it's over because I can't hear it in there. Hay-Hay never says a word, bless her heart."

I stroked my thumb down her cheek and leaned in for a soft kiss. "You weren't curled up in a ball sobbing in my basement that night."

"I was on the inside," she said, finally laughing a little bit. "You were good at distracting me from the fear. I guess when I'm alone, the thoughts that no one will know I was down there, or that I was hurt, just take over my mind. It's stupid when it's just a little summer storm, I get that, but I can't change it, either."

"It's not stupid. I don't know if anyone has told you this before, but I feel like I should. What you experience during storms is normal after the experience you lived through. It's normal, Amber. Has anyone ever said you're completely normal to be out of your mind afraid of something that once tried to kill you?"

She swung her head back and forth. "Never. I was told I needed to be stronger against the emotions taking over my mind. They gave me biofeedback techniques and ways to focus on other things, but that's hard to do when you're too scared to remember any of it. I need to be stronger, but I'm not. I'm too weak right now."

I took her shoulders and turned her to look at me. "You're wrong. You don't need to be stronger. Good God, what you've lived with and dealt with since the injury proves your strength. Fair warning, if I ever hear anyone tell you to be stronger, I will bitch slap them."

Her laughter filled the room, and she laughed for a good long time. "I'll remember that because I'd like to see it."

157

I caressed her cheek tenderly and smiled. "I would, but the point is, I know you feel weak right now. You're not. You're stronger than I am. You're beautiful to boot, and this weekend, you're mine."

"I don't want to go anywhere, Bishop. My leg isn't good. It's hard to travel, and the crutches make beaches nearly impossible to navigate."

I placed my finger on her lips. "I know. I have this all worked out. Do you trust me?" Her head nodded against my finger again. "Good. I'm going to get your crutches so you can clean up while I finish the plans I have, okay? Trust me? I've got you."

Her head nodded, and I grabbed her crutches from the floor of the foyer and carried them to her.

"Thanks," she said, propping them under her arms. "What should I put on?"

"Remember that sundress you wore the first night we were supposed to go to The Modern Goat?" She nodded, and I winked before I headed to my room for a change of clothes.

Twelve

"You were right, this is the way to do a honeymoon," I said, floating on the water with the sun beating down on me. My brace and crutches lay forgotten on the dock, and I was enjoying the freedom to just relax without being uncomfortable. Last night we had finally made it to The Modern Goat for dinner. We shared their surf and turf and talked about everything from our childhoods to our college days. I had never been more comfortable with another person in my life.

Bishop laughed from where he was sitting in an innertube and trailing his hands through the water. He wore nothing but a pair of swim trunks, and I couldn't take my eyes off his chiseled chest and glistening skin. "I'm glad you're enjoying our staycation."

"So much," I agreed. "Also, I'd just like to point out that you might be a dad, but you most certainly do not have a dad bod. I'm a little jealous of that innertube right now."

His laughter filled the air again, and he bowed at the waist without falling out of the tube. "I'll take that as a compliment. I believe that it's hard to teach kids to be physically fit if you aren't setting the same example."

"That's true," I agreed, "but there's physically fit, and then there's—" I motioned around his body, "you."

"Good genes. That's all—a little time in the weight room and some high-quality protein. I'm not constantly working out or anything. It's just how I'm built."

I glanced down at myself in the blow-up chair I was floating on. "And this is just how I'm built. No curves. No boobs. Scars everywhere."

He paddled the innertube closer to me and grasped my right ankle. "You have curves. They're just less pronounced than other women. I'm not a sucker for big boobs. I'm a sucker for the ones that fit in my palms and my mouth perfectly. The scars are just skin in a different configuration than the skin around it. Those scars tell the story of how strong you had to be. They aren't everywhere, either."

There he was using that word strong again. He managed to work it into almost every conversation we'd had since last night on the couch. I kind of loved him for it, to be honest. He was helping me see the strength in what I'd gone through rather than the weakness.

"They are everywhere. I have scars in places you haven't seen. When I said the entire left side of my body was mangled, that wasn't an exaggeration. I'm not wearing a tank top as a suit for no reason, Bishop."

"Regardless, Amber, I'm not going to let you use your lack of curves, boobs, or scarred skin to push me away. I won't allow it. I will bend over backward to protect you from storms and anything else that wants to hurt you, but I won't let your hurts ruin what could be the best thing that has ever happened to you."

"Wow," I said, laughing sarcastically. "Now you're the best thing that's ever happened to me. Someone thinks highly of himself."

"Never used to," he admitted, staring up at the sky as the sun dropped lower until it was nothing but red streaks across the clouds. "I used to think no woman would be interested in dating a single dad, so I didn't put myself out there."

"That's kind of silly, Bishop. Athena didn't even live with you."

He grasped my chair to hold it next to his. "That's true, but I was still heavily involved in her life. I had a few relationships, but in the end, they refused to bend when it came to the time I spent with Athena. That told me they weren't the right woman for me."

"I can't wrap my mind around that. Maybe it's because I grew up with Hay-Hay, but if I dated a single dad, their kids would be my kids. I would never ask them to spend less time with their children. I would do whatever I could to make sure he had the support he needed not only to see them but to make a difference in their lives. I wouldn't have felt any different if those kids lived with the guy I was dating. Asking someone else to be a shitty person just because you are isn't right."

He chuckled as he leaned over and kissed me in the gathering dusk, his lips warm against mine. "That's because you don't look at life the way most women do, my little tart. I think that's what attracted you to me in the beginning. You were so," he paused as if searching for the right word, "different, I guess."

"Different. There's a loaded word."

"But it's not a bad one," he promised. "You should wear it proudly. The fact that my exhausted, end of the year teacher's soul sensed you were different instantly should fill you with the knowledge that you are amazing. It takes someone special to stand out to me at the end of May. You were a bright spot in the storm, and rays spread from your being."

My hand smoothed its way across his soft beard. "I'll wear it proudly then," I promised. He jumped out of his innertube and tossed it on the sand, leaning over my chair and capturing my lips for a longer taste. I moaned, being careful not to rock the chair too much, so I didn't fall into the water. He was everything I'd come to understand over the last few days. "I want to feel close to you, Bishop," I sighed when his lips released mine for much-needed oxygen.

He pulled me from the chair and tossed it behind him, directing my legs around his waist as he sat down on the sandy bottom of the lake. "Let me hold you," he whispered, and I draped myself across his chest and over his shoulder, my lips kissing his neck gently

"I love how your beard tickles my lips when I kiss you," I sighed.

"How does it feel when I kiss your other lips?" he asked, his voice decidedly lower than usual.

I thrust against his belly and moaned softly. "Unlike anything I've ever experienced before," I whispered. "I love when it rasps against the inside of my thighs and raises goosebumps across my skin."

"Mmm," he hummed, his lips kissing their way down the back of my neck. "God, I love how innocent yet naughty you are, my beautiful tart. I want to have my head buried between your legs right now. In fact," he whispered, scooting me back until I was lying half in and half out of the water. "Stay right there, time for a new lesson."

He lowered himself under the water, moved my bikinis aside, and put that beard between my legs again. I grabbed for his hair, but the water made it float away just out of reach. He anchored me to the sand with two fingers inside me while his tongue stroked me. The sensation of being underwater while he did it just amplified the desire coursing through me. I moaned softly, knowing we were alone, but still afraid of being too loud. He lifted his head for air and was grinning as water trailed down his face in rivulets.

"I think the teacher is going to detention this time," I said, shaking my head on the sand. "He's very, very bad." The last word was said on a squeak as his fingers buried themselves a bit deeper to tease me. "Downright evil," I sighed.

He took another breath of air and disappeared under the dark water again, and then his tongue flicked in and out rhythmically. My hips thrust into the air, and my whole soul yearned for his throbbing manhood to fill me right there. I was so near release when he lifted his head, his gaze locking with mine. "Don't stop," I begged, pressing my pelvis into his hand. "I'm so close to coming."

He leaned over me and thrust his fingers in and out gently, his lips almost on mine. "I know. I want to see it happen. I want to watch your face as you soar up into that night sky and ride the moon," he whispered. I noticed his other hand was stroking his hardness, the rhythm matching what his fingers were doing inside me. He wanted us both to come at the same time while staying apart, I realized.

"God, what is happening to me?" I cried out, my hips bucking in the air as I watched him pleasure himself, his lips still near mine.

"You're learning to love yourself, sweetart," he promised, moving his fingers a fraction of an inch deeper until I cried out, the waves sweeping over his fingers the way the water lapped over his legs.

"Oh, God, Bishop," I sang until his lips captured mine, and he kissed me hard and deep, his hand brushing across my belly as he built up his release.

His moan was resounding inside my head as he tongue-fucked me so hard I was sure he was going to lose it down my throat. I pulled him to me and captured his dick between us, then entwined our hands. With our hands held above my head, he thrust against my stomach while his moans filled my head. "Amber," he cried, pushing forward one last time, and then his warmth covered me. I felt every last spasm until he shivered against me, and his swim trunks floated past my head to the sandy beach. "I'm never fucking giving you up," he hissed, grasping my hair in his hands and kissing my lips until I couldn't breathe and didn't care.

"This has been the greatest day in recent history, save for our wedding day, of course," I said as he strolled back into the living room after his shower. His hair was still damp, and he wore a t-shirt and boxers that left nothing to my imagination.

Dammit.

"Of course," he said, winking as he sat next to me on the couch.

"Dinner was wonderful. Someone must have had connections to get something like that done in this town."

After our beach-capade, he carried me up the hill to surprise me with a beautiful dinner by firelight. We sat at a table dressed in a white tablecloth, electric candles, and wine glasses. We dined on burgers and cheese curds from The Modern Goat, my absolute favorite dinner, while sipping wine.

"It was ridiculously romantic, too," I added, taking his hand.

"I thought it was going to be a lot harder to find a closet romantic than it was. It turns out she was just down the street."

I shook my head at him with laughter on my lips. "Hay-Hay has become one since she met Brady. She never used to be. She was always very determined to never trust a man or fall in love."

"Wow, I think I've heard that story before," he said, bopping my nose with his finger.

"For different reasons, though," I said defensively. "Look what happened with the last guy I dated."

"You need to put the last guy you dated out of your mind. He's not even worth the words you just said about him. That's over. You've got me now, right?"

If only it were that easy, I thought as he stood up. If only I didn't have to think about Rex whenever I looked at my leg.

"At least for a little while," I agreed.

"You control the timeline of this relationship, sweetart." He walked back into the room with a bottle and two glasses. "I thought we should toast to each other since we didn't on our wedding night." He sat and lowered the glasses to the table while he worked on the cork in the bottle of champagne.

"We didn't, did we? We did other stuff instead."

He snortled, and the cork popped at just that second. His quick thinking with a glass kept the carpet from drinking the champagne, too.

Tart

He handed me a glass and held it up. "Here's to us and new adventures."

I clinked glasses with him and drained mine in almost one swallow. He refilled it, and I leaned back on the couch where he pulled my legs up to rest over his. "Tell me what the real reason is that you want to start working over here." The sentence was said while sipping at his glass nonchalantly and his hand rubbing up and down my calf.

I almost choked on the swallow of champagne in my mouth. "There's no real reason," I said after swallowing. "It just makes sense."

"Really? Because the discussion we had the day after our wedding involved a lot of you insisting that we had to work separately and have time away from each other or you'd go crazy."

I shrugged and drank more from the glass, which he promptly refilled. "I changed my mind. I decided it's silly to walk over there every day when I don't have to."

His brow went down, and he eyed me with determination. "I don't believe you. You've been distracted since yesterday when you came running in here yelling my name. It has nothing to do with the trial either, so don't try to sell me that one. Something is going on."

I sighed, the champagne making me dizzy with bubbles. "If I tell you that I want to work here because I miss you, will you stop asking questions?"

Where I expected a grin, I got eyes that melted right in front of me. Bishop took my hand and held it to his chest. "You just answered every question I have, sweetart," he whispered.

We sat in silence, drinking our champagne and listening to the sounds of the crickets in the night as they sang us a love song. "It's so peaceful here," I sighed, scooting down to get more comfortable on the couch. "And this champagne is making me drunk in an instant."

He laughed and nodded, staring at his glass. "Me too, but it's good champagne. A gift from the school district for our nuptials."

165

"That was nice of them," I said, taking another large gulp. "We shouldn't let it go to waste."

"That would be a travesty," he agreed, finishing his glass and refilling both of ours. "How about another toast?"

I held my glass up to match his. "To the happiest four days of my life," he said, clinking glasses again.

He drank his down, but I held mine in the air without moving. "The happiest four days of your life?"

He lowered his flute and smiled at me with that smile he wears when he's unsure of himself. "At least in the last decade. Spending time with you is like my sunshine now. I didn't know how much of my life was spent under gray rainclouds before. I was living, but I wasn't happy. Since you came into my life, I'm finding happiness in things I would never have before."

"What kind of things?" I asked, drinking the bubbles down.

"All those little everyday things like sitting by a campfire with a beer and laughing with someone who understands you. It's sitting down at the breakfast table and sharing your bagel and newspaper with someone who has way too much energy at seven a.m."

I laughed then and rested my head back on the arm of the couch. "Sorry if that annoys you. Usually, by seven a.m., I've got half my day in."

He shook his head, and his face turned serious. "That's the thing. It doesn't annoy me. Not even a little bit. It's one of the things I love about you."

"One of the things you love about me," I said, sitting up. I was dizzy drunk and grabbed at Bishop to keep from toppling off the couch. "You can't love me, Bishop. That's a bad idea."

"Well, I can love you. It's not even hard. It's as natural as getting up in the morning if you want me to be honest."

"I mean, I mean," I was stuttering around looking for words when he took the glass from me and set it down on the coffee table. "I mean that you could do so much better, Bishop. Like, so much better. Not to sound like Darla McFinkle, but you could have any woman you want!"

Tart

"Stop. I don't want to hear you say that again. I warned you before. Don't make me spank you." His brow lowered, and I swallowed, a little bit afraid but also curious. Would he really spank me if I didn't hush up? "I don't know how Darla comes into play with that sentence, but if what you say is true, then the woman I want is you."

I hung my head until my chin hit my chest. "You know what I mean!" I exclaimed, pushing at him. It was like trying to move a brick wall. Impossible.

"First, tell me how Darla comes into the equation."

I waved my hand around in the air. "She always told Haylee that Brady could do so much better than her. She'd tell Brady the same thing. That was how Haylee got her kicked out as the beauty queen."

"She deserves to rot in prison. Haylee is a beautiful, bright, wickedly funny woman, and if I'm honest, and Brady knows it, too, she could do so much better than him. The thing is, she doesn't want to. She loves him. That guy. The one who would step in front of a bullet if it meant she lived. All of that atmospheric noise about doing better or marrying up is nonsense. We all have things that make us less than someone else when you compare apples to apples. I can lift weights, but I can't lift weights the way some guys can. I was a decent father, but I wasn't hands-on all the time like some fathers are. If we spend our days telling ourselves that we aren't good enough, eventually, it will be impossible to believe that we deserve to be happy."

"Except when everyone else is telling you that, too," I muttered, taking his glass from his fingers and drinking it back. "We should go to bed. You said you had more in store for us tomorrow."

He grasped my chin and turned it to face him. "Who else is telling you that you don't deserve to be happy or loved by a man who worships you the same way Brady worships Haylee. I know for sure it's not Haylee."

I lowered a brow and tried to concentrate on what he was saying. "Do you always use that teacher voice on people when you want them to answer a question? It's a tad bit annoying, not gonna lie."

167

His other brow went down, and he cleared his throat. "You can't distract me with teacher talk."

"Hmm, too bad. I'd admit I was hot for teacher if I could."

"Tart," he warned, his tongue coming out to lick his lips. I wanted to moan, but I could see he wasn't going to let this go, and that was a serious turn-off.

"My mom, okay? She always tells me to settle for whatever guy is willing to take me on."

"Take you on. Were those her actual words?"

I half-nodded and half-shrugged. "I mean, she's not that wrong. I'll be a handful for anyone, both physically and emotionally. There have been plenty of men who have run the opposite direction as fast as the women did when they found out you were a single father."

"I'm sorry," he whispered, his finger caressing my cheek. "She never should have said that once, much less multiple times. You don't need to settle, sweetart. You are a goddess who deserves to be worshiped, don't ever forget that. The right guy will do exactly that."

"I used to rage against the idea that I'm a handful, Bishop. Then it dawned on me that I am one. My disabilities, emotional and physical, will cause situations to arise that are unpredictable. Not even my parents want to deal with them anymore."

"And that means you suffer in silence."

"More like I just shut myself off, so I don't get hurt again. If I don't go out with anyone, then I don't get hurt," I explained, motioning at my leg.

"First of all, you are a handful. A handful for me when I cup your cheek, your breast, your hip, and that fucking beautiful apex that makes me so hard I want to come right now just thinking about it. You are not a handful in any other way. Despite your physical and emotional challenges, you are more successful than half this damn town. Do you even see that?" he asked, so worked up now he was tossing his hands around. "Do you even see all the things you've done since that accident nearly killed you seventeen years ago? Do you see that without you, Haylee and Brady don't have a bakery to sell their goods? How have you done that all these years, Amber?"

"I guess grit and determination," I said, sitting up on the couch and staring at my wedding band. I wasn't comfortable having this conversation, but it was easy to see he wasn't going to let it go.

"Grit and determination built one hell of a life for you, haven't they?" he asked, and I nodded, half shrugging a shoulder until he held it down. "Then why do you undercut everything you've done by coming up with all these excuses why you can't claim your success?"

"Psychological conditioning, I guess?"

He sighed and shook his head. "You've been told so many times that because you still live in your parents' basement or because your leg doesn't work the same way someone else's does, that your success isn't equal to everyone else's, right?"

"Among other things," I agreed. "I'm just tired, Bishop."

That statement was heavy. It was heavier than merely the current conversation we were having. That statement carried the weight of the world on it.

He stood and scooped me up again, shutting down the lights in the living room on his way to his bedroom. He laid me out on his king-sized bed and shut the lights off, leaving only the small lamp on in the corner. "I know you're tired, Amber. You have earned the right to be tired."

"Why am I in your bed?" I asked, my champagne-filled mind fuzzy and slow.

"You're in my bed so I can hold your burdens tonight, and you can sleep. I know you'll still be tired in the morning, but for a little while, you'll get to rest."

I grasped his hand and held it to my chest, tears fighting for real estate in my eyes. "No one has ever understood me before. Not the way you seem to. It scares me."

He stroked my forehead with his free hand as though I was a child that he had to soothe to sleep. "Why does it scare you?"

169

"Simple mathematics, Teacher Halla. When we go from two to one again, I'm back to having no one who understands me. I don't want to come to rely on you knowing that eventually, you will find someone else to hold who isn't tired."

"My sweetart, we are all tired in some way or another. Some of us carry heavier burdens than others, but the bigger picture is this. When you find the right person to carry yours, it's not hard to carry theirs in return."

"You just dumbed down what being in a relationship is for my drunken mind, didn't you?"

He laughed and kissed my temple, letting his lips linger for a moment and inhaling the scent of my shampoo. "No, I just dumbed down what love is, Amber. Love is carrying each other's burdens, even if sometimes it's not an even split of the weight. Sometimes, you'll carry more of it than they will and vice versa, but in the end, being able to shift the load between you is what love is all about."

"Shift the load," I said, nodding my head as my eyelids drooped. "Love is carrying each other when the load is too heavy."

"Exactly," he whispered in my hear. "Right now, I'm carrying the load, so sleep, my beautiful wife. I've got this."

Thirteen

God, she was unbelievable in so many different ways. What she'd gone through, what she'd done since, and doing it all with so little support. Finding out that Amber's parents weren't as supportive as I would have thought took me by surprise, until I started to think about it. As a parent, I can't imagine the guilt that would riddle me if Athena had been almost killed because of a decision I'd made. It wasn't their fault, but I knew they had to carry horrifying guilt regardless. They were probably too hard on her, but I could see both sides. If they coddled Amber too much, she might never find the determination she needed to make a life for herself. If they pushed her to keep moving forward, at least they felt like she'd eventually be okay. While a lot of what they've done I disagree with, I can see that they were probably equally traumatized by the events of that night. Parents aren't perfect, even if we wish we were. We're still humans, but now we have emotions that live outside our bodies.

Amber had been sleeping for a few hours, but I couldn't stop staring at her. I was memorizing every detail of her. Maybe it was knowing that eventually, she would leave my bed, and my house, and we'd live separate lives again. Maybe it was knowing I was in love with her and was desperate to spend as much time with her as I could before she left me. I wasn't sure why, but while she slept, I didn't. I mapped those scars on her leg down to the very last one, noting the coloring and size, so I would notice if something changed or the infection came back.

She shifted toward me to her right side, and her shirt bunched up in her sleep. I snuck my hand over to pull it down, but my hand froze halfway, and my breath caught in my chest. She wasn't kidding. The entire left side of her chest was mangled. I didn't see it the other night because my head was between her legs, but I saw it very clearly tonight.

"It's a skin graft," she said sleepily, her open eyes taking me by surprise.

I'd been focused on her side and didn't realize she was awake. "You weren't kidding about the scars."

She tried to tug the shirt down, but I wouldn't let her. "Stop. You don't have to hide it from me."

Her hand fell to the bed and her eyes, too. "No, I wasn't kidding. I kept it hidden the other night," she said, clearing her throat.

"What caused it?"

"The doctors aren't sure. It could have been sliding down the bark of a tree or some other debris that just ripped the skin away. All of my ribs were broken, and they had to wire them back together. The skin was too damaged after surgery to even try to repair it, so they used a skin graft. It was one of the only parts that healed decently well. My ribs don't bother me as far as pain goes, and as long as I keep the skin graft covered from the sun, it's fine." She pointed at her right thigh. "They took the skin from that leg, but thankfully, you don't notice the slight scar it left.

I pushed her shirt out of the way, exposing the bottom of her breast where the scarred flesh met pink, unscarred skin. "I'm so sorry, Amber. I didn't mean to downplay what you went through when we were on the lake yesterday. I truly didn't understand."

She shook her head with her lip captured between her teeth. "It's okay. You didn't know it was like this because I didn't show you. I wanted you to keep thinking I was beautiful. I knew if the leg didn't turn you off, this would."

Tart

My chin hit my chest, and I shook my head. "No, this doesn't turn me off, sweetart. It's horrifying to think about what did it or how much it had to have hurt, but that skin is still your skin. I don't think it's any different than the skin on your legs or belly, which by the way, is torturing me right now."

"You're not a leg man, and you aren't a boob man, so you're a belly man?"

I licked my lips and leaned in, pressing a kiss to her navel, dipping my tongue in until I felt her shiver. "You've discovered my secret. I'm a belly button man."

She grasped my hair, sliding her fingers through it to find purchase for her need. "I like your secret."

"And I like your soft, trim belly that leads down to that soft mound of curls I want to bury my nose in again," I promised, blowing across her belly until goosebumps rose across her skin. "But you haven't been sleeping very long, and you need more rest."

I tugged her shirt down and rested my hand on her belly, cuddling her into me and kissing her forehead. My dick was hard and pulsing against her hip, and she reached down, stroking it with a finger on each side, making me want to come with her name on my lips.

"You haven't slept at all, have you?" she asked, placing a kiss along the ridge of my collarbone.

I sucked in air while I warred to keep a cool head. Between her kisses and her tender stroking, I wanted to forget about everything else and just make love to this gorgeous woman in my arms. "N—no," I said, clearing my throat. "I was holding you and memorizing every little thing about you. I'm building you in my mind little by little because I never want to forget how beautiful you are, and how much you've changed my life." I thrust against her hand and moaned, her soft laughter filling the darkness of the room.

"If that wasn't so sweet, I might think you were a creeper, Mr. Halla."

"Not a creeper. Just saving up for when you disappear from my life, and I don't have you anymore. I will always want you, my little tart, always."

My lips came down on hers, and I kissed her until I knew she wanted me just as much as I wanted her. She arched under me, wanting me to move over her and frustrated by my refusal. I pinned her arms above her head and kissed her with enough tongue to show her who was boss, finally backing off when my chest started burning.

"I do believe you are kind of hot for teacher," I said, throwing her words back at her. "Only I think it's more like extremely hot for teacher."

"Even hotter for daddy," she whispered into my ear, taking a lick at the last second.

I grunted, thrusting against her leg without any self-control. "You are a little tease, aren't you? I might have to spank you if you keep up that kind of talk."

"But we don't have a yardstick," she said coyly, her eyes traveling to my boxers, which were tented with a footlong. "I suppose that would do, though."

I growled before my lips attacked hers again, my hands still holding her wrists to the bed. I thrust my tongue inside her mouth the same way I wanted to thrust inside her heat, and she shivered with anticipation. She was incredible in immeasurable ways, and I wasn't going to last much longer without having her. I could tell myself all I wanted that I could marry her and then walk away, but the second I sank inside her, that would be it. I would never fuck another woman. I hadn't even made love to her yet, and I already knew that much. She was going to bring me to my knees, but as long as I healed her with my love, I didn't even care.

"If you throw my tongue in the mix, it will more than do, little girl," I promised, rubbing my still clothed hardness against her hip. "Do we need a repeat performance from earlier to refresh your memory?"

She nodded her head coyly. "Yes, Mr. Halla. I can't remember if I come before or after you do."

I growled and grasped the hem of her shirt, my brow arced toward the sky. "I would prefer coming together, but first, I'm going to take this shirt off and quench my curiosity."

"What's that?" she asked, leaving her arms above her head while she waited for me to strip off the shirt.

"If your breasts are as small as you claim they are."

Slowly, I pulled the shirt up to reveal the sweetest nuggets I'd ever had the pleasure to see. "Mmmm, these look delicious," I said on a sigh, stripping the shirt off the rest of the way."

Her brow went up. "I told you they were pathetic little eggs."

"On the contrary, they're like that perfect bite-sized tart from the bakery. Sweet, savory, and a perfect mouthful." My finger trailed her dark nipple that beaded instantly at my touch. "This nipple is like a homing beacon for my lips," I hissed, my head lowering so I could grasp it in my teeth. "You're so fucking incredible, and you don't even know it." My words were cut off when I caught the tender flesh between my lips, my tongue stroking it lovingly while she moaned under me. My other hand found her right breast and cupped it, my moan filling the room and vibrating against the flesh in my mouth. That ripped another low moan from her, the sound vibrating in her chest and through my soul. I let her nipple go with a pop and blew a fissure of air across it until she was covered in goosebumps. I cupped both in my hands and grabbed her hot, needy gaze with mine. "Do you remember what I said about these?"

"That they would be the perfect handful," she squeaked, her breath heavy in her chest.

"And who was right?"

"You were, teacher," she moaned.

My lips tortured her right breast the same way they did the left, while my thumb stroked her belly, moving dangerously close to her curls each time it did. I desperately wanted to see if she was as wet as I wanted

175

her to be, but I also wanted this to last forever, so I forced myself to hold back and wait.

She plunged her fingers into my hair and grasped it, pulling me from her breast to her lips. Her tongue took possession of my mouth then, and she pressed her belly into my dick, rubbing so seductively I could have come without any further encouragement. I refused to, though. I had plans for this woman. She had things to learn.

I ended the kiss and hung over her, her eyes all pupil and her chest heaving from the kiss. "Are you wet for me, tart?" I asked, hooking my thumbs in the waistband of her shorts. "Tell me the truth. I'm going to find out anyway."

"Yes," she hissed, "so wet."

The shorts were gone, and I eyed her tiny mound of flesh and curls, my tongue coming out to lick my lips at the sight of her. "Incredible," I whispered, rubbing my dick with my hand.

She sat up and grasped the bottom of my shirt. "It would be more incredible if you wore fewer clothes."

I stilled her hands and pushed her back to the bed gently. "Don't be so impatient. I decide when my clothes come off."

Her brow went up again. "I never expected so much domination out of you, Mr. Halla."

"When it comes to how I make love to a woman, there's a right way and a wrong way," I said, going back to ogling her beautiful center. "You're glistening," I said on a breath, parting her gently with my thumb to peek at her center. I stroked my thumb across her, barely touching her, but the slickness covered my skin immediately.

"Oh, you are learning your lessons well," I hissed, bringing my thumb to my lips and suckling away the dew. I went back for more and then rubbed her wetness across the tip of my dick, the action nothing but painful pleasure. My pain didn't matter, though. The look on her face was worth all of the torture I was experiencing. There was so much anticipation in her eyes that she was drowning in it. She was dripping with desire for me now, and she allowed my tongue the pleasure of lapping up some of her heat.

Her hips came off the bed, and that was when I noticed how prominent the left one was compared to the right. I lowered them gently, stroking the left hip bone with tenderness from where it jutted from her pelvis. My lips fell to kiss the ridge of the bone as her breath hitched. I worked my way down to kiss each scar on her leg until I had covered her knee with kisses. When I glanced up, she was still holding her breath as tears ran down her cheeks.

"Breathe, baby," I whispered, rubbing her chest tenderly. "You are beautiful. I'm in awe of your strength when I see what you hide from the world every day."

Air filled her lungs then and I wiped away her tears patiently. She shook her head until finally, she could speak. "I'm ashamed and embarrassed by my body. How do you find it so desirable?"

"I find you desirable because you are desirable," I said, stripping my shirt off and throwing it to the floor by the bed. "I never want to hear you say you're ashamed or embarrassed by your body again, do you hear me?" Her head nodded, but I knew she was doing nothing more than agreeing for the sake of it. I slid my dick along the inside of her right leg. "This is the only tool you'll use to measure how fucking desirable you are from this point forward. Do you understand?" She didn't do anything but widen her eyes. "Do you understand, tart?"

"I understand, Mr. Halla," she said, her voice low and needy while I continued to rub my tip closer to her center. It was taking all the self-control I had not to sink inside her and end my pain, but I refused to rush the first time I made love to this woman.

"I think you should get a reward then, right?" Her head nodded greedily, and I stood, hooking my fingers in my boxers and letting them fall to the floor slowly. My dick strained into the night air, hard and hot, a drop of dew balanced perfectly at the tip just waiting for absolution. I crawled back onto the bed and straddled her, the tart knowing exactly what to do when she stole that drop of dew with her tongue and then swirled it around the tip, dragging a moan from my lips. I rose up on my knees when she sucked me in, my resolve to make this last weakening the longer she sucked, licked, and blew on me. When she cupped my balls and massaged gently, I moaned so loud I was sure the neighbors could hear me. Then I remembered I was fucking the neighbor, and she wouldn't care.

I grasped her chin and held her still. "Enough. I can't take much more," I groaned, extracting myself from between the pair of lips I loved, knowing I would soon be cradled by the pair that would take me to heaven.

Her hands came up to run across my abs and chest, tangling in the hair there while I teased her tiny buds with my thumbs, flicking across them until they were tight and pert. "Are you going to fuck me, Mr. Halla?" Her voice was nothing but dirty, and I growled low in my throat.

"I'm going to have to. You've been a naughty girl, Mrs. Halla. Detention is going to be required," I hissed, sliding down her body carefully until I sat on the bed between her knees again. "Look at the mess you've made of yourself," I said, my voice playful. "Now, I'm going to have to clean it up." My thumb found its way inside her and pressed down gently, holding her open for my tongue to sweep in and taste her sweetness. My tongue thrust in and out rhythmically to the sound of her moans, backing off when her thighs started to shake and going back in when they stopped.

"I fucking love detention," she cried, her hips pressing her center into my face, burying my nose inside her again, where I sucked wickedly. She grasped my head and clamped her thighs to my ears, forcing me to back off instantly. She noticed, sighing with frustration when I sat up and held her hips. "Are you sure you want this?" I asked, patiently waiting for her answer, but there was no hesitation in her nod.

"I've never wanted a man the way I want you, Bishop," she said, her voice softening with desire.

"That's because no man has ever accepted you for who you are, all of you," I said. Her nod was automatic like she didn't even have to think about if that statement was true. "I accept all of you, sweetart," I promised. "You were created and shaped just for me. You are mine now. I don't care what you say or how many times you try to push me away, that will always remain the truth. Do you understand?" Her eyes widened, but she said nothing. I fell across her and grasped her chin, kissing her hard and heavy, letting her taste herself on my tongue until we couldn't breathe through the fog of desire in our chests. "Do you understand?" I asked again, panting hard with my dick dangerously close to her opening. All she had to do was lift her hips, and she'd join us, so I moved back and waited for her to answer me. I stroked her sweet nub while I did it, just to sweeten the pot for her.

"I under—understand," she moaned.

"There will be a question on the test about that," I reminded her, sliding my thumb inside her. "Remember the answer."

"Yes, Mr. Halla," she said obediently.

I pulled the drawer open next to my bed for a condom, only to be greeted with emptiness. "Fuck," I groaned, my dick bobbing against her leg. "And not the good kind."

"What?" she asked, sitting up to check the drawer.

"I hadn't bought condoms in so long that I had to throw the old ones away. I never bought more. I guess we'll have to save that part of the test for another night."

"Like hell," she moaned, tossing her head side-to-side. "I've been on the pill for a decade. You don't have to worry about condoms anymore. Fuck me, Halla, now," she ordered, lifting her hips again, begging me to love her.

I stroked her engorged lips while I thought about it. I could trust her. I knew that. Part of me wanted to plunge inside her, but part of me was too scared of making another mistake in my life. "I've never had sex without a condom, Amber."

"Athena," she whispered, but I shook my head.

"I wore a condom that night. Do you see my point?"

She grasped my hand and pulled me down to her lips, and her hand came up to stroke my cheek while she

179

kissed me. "I can promise you that we are safe. The only way to fuck this up is not to fuck me."

I growled, attacking her lips again until they were red and swollen. I rested next to her and grasped her hips. "Let me do the work. I'm going to rest your left leg over my hip."

Her head nodded, and I positioned her in such a way I knew she'd be comfortable when I entered her. "I've never had sex without a condom. I don't know how long this will last," I whispered, stroking her breast in the low light of the moon. I grasped my dick and rubbed it across her wetness, wetting myself with her, so she would be comfortable. "It's now or nothing, tart. Do you still want me to fuck you?"

She growled and lowered her hips until she'd swallowed me whole and in one smooth motion. "Fuck, tart," I moaned, thrusting up to bury myself as deeply as I could. "Oh, my God. I've never felt this way before."

"Me either," she cried, squeezing me with her legs when I tried to pull out. "Don't," she begged. "I need to come."

I grasped her hips and held them still. "What are you doing?"

"Trying to come," she cried, clamping down even harder around me.

I stilled and cupped her cheek, my gaze holding hers. "That's not how this works, baby girl."

"It is in my world," she said, defeated.

I pulled out, and she cried out, grabbing for me until I grasped her hands and held them to the bed. "Listen to me, Mrs. Halla. That is not how you make love." I rolled her onto her back and released her hands, laying them out to her side. "Just let your pelvis relax into the bed," I instructed, stroking her belly tenderly.

"But," she sputtered.

I put my finger to her lips. "Don't interrupt the teacher during his lesson, tart."

She closed her lips, and while I stroked her belly, she slowly relaxed her bottom into the bed.

"Good girl," I whispered, stoking her fire again by trailing my finger up and down her slit, my dick aching to be back inside her again. "I'm going to teach you how to come when making love, but first, will I hurt you if I rest between your legs?"

Her head shook, and I leaned in, kissing her with enough tongue to take the look of fear out of her eyes and put the lust back in them. I nudged her legs further apart with mine, and without breaking the kiss, I pushed inside her again, moaning the full length until I was seated deeply, stopping so she could get used to the feel of me inside her.

"I just want you to know," I whispered, trailing kisses down her cheek to her neck. "This is the first time I've ever had sex without a condom. I had no idea what I was missing."

"Does the teacher like the student's homework?" she teased, trying to thrust her hips towards mine. I was holding them down, and she was frustrated. I could tell by the moan she let out when she was forced to wait for me to move inside her.

"He does, but he's about to teach the student a lesson she'll never forget. Are you ready?" I asked, and her head nodded as I thrust back inside her again. "Do you feel that?" I stroked her walls with the full length of me, using perfect precision each time, being careful to stay away from the places I knew would cause an immediate orgasm. "That's how a man makes love to a woman. Slow. Easy. Gentle. At least at first," I moaned, reveling in the sensation of her heat and wetness wrapped around me. "The goal isn't to orgasm because you force it. The goal is to orgasm from the pleasure of being together. Of pleasuring each other."

I lifted myself onto my toes and changed the angle just enough that I saw the immediate reaction on her face. "Oh, Bishop," she called, her hands grasping my shoulders tighter each time I pulled out until I pushed back inside her.

"Say my name, my little tart," I ordered, my thighs shaking with the willpower it took to hold back the eruption of my soul inside her.

"Bishop," she begged. "I want to come, please."

"Do you feel it starting to build? Is it spiraling inside your belly like a coil?" I asked, increasing the speed of my thrusts in and out.

"Yes, I feel it," she cried. "Harder!" she called. I laughed, burying my face in her neck and sucking while I pumped inside her, almost losing myself before I remembered the lesson I was supposed to be teaching.

I pushed myself up on my hands, my pelvis tight against hers, and sensed the beginning of her undoing. "It's time to come, sweetart," I warned her. "Here is the lesson. Don't get scared. Just let it carry you away."

"Okay, carry me away, Bishop!"

God, the way she said my name would ruin me for life now. I pushed forward, changing the angle of my tip to hit the spot so deep inside the bottom of her pelvis I suspected even she didn't know it was there. Not when she usually spent her time trying to force an orgasm every time. Not when her immediate orgasm hit her like a tidal wave. Her pelvis thrust up against mine, burying me even deeper and rocking around me until I couldn't stop the tidal wave from carrying me under the water with her.

"God, Amber!" I called, my seed spilling inside her in a way that didn't make me anxious as it would have with any other woman. I floated in a pool of water that stole my sight and my hearing while I spasmed against her. My breath was on hold until every last vestige of pleasure had been wrung from my exhausted body.

I remembered not to collapse on top of her. Instead, I rolled off and rolled her into me in one move, bringing the blankets up around us to ward off the chill while we caught our breath.

"Did I pass?" she asked, her body still quivering from the desire coursing through her.

I kissed her then, and my tongue was warm but sated on her lips. "With flying colors." I stroked her hair back and kissed her forehead, holding her to me in such a way I hoped she realized how much I cherished her. "Never, ever, in my thirty-four years have I ever experienced that kind of emotion, Amber. Did you feel it?"

Her head nodded against my shoulder, and her long hair brushed my bare chest. "It was so strong I couldn't tell where I ended and you began."

I kissed her again, longer this time with tongue, but still gentle and lazily. "That's because there was no beginning or end," I whispered. "There was just us."

Fourteen

I was sitting on the couch like a dutiful wife per the instructions from my husband. We had just arrived home after a Sunday drive, where we'd stopped for a picnic lunch at the state park and for ice cream at the cutest little shop on a country road. When we got back, he had the shades pulled to the patio doors and told me I couldn't peek at the surprise. I knew Chris had been working the last two days on the new deck, and I was dying to see it, but crutches didn't allow a girl to snoop and return to her seat quickly. Besides, after last night, or rather last night, early this morning, and later this morning, I was still exhausted.

To say he was a talented lover was an understatement. He was downright orgasmic. I snorted at my joke and rolled my eyes at my Instagram feed as I fed it pictures of cakes and bread. Even when a girl is on her honeymoon, she's still got to take care of business.

We took care of business last night. I had no idea that the G-spot was a real thing for women. I mean, sure, we all know it's supposed to be there, but finding it can be a lot like searching for Waldo in the dark. You just fake it and moan for a lot of unnecessary minutes. At least that's what I used to do. Not anymore. Not since unknown rebel, single dad, sexy as hell, teacher husband of mine showed up.

I rubbed my forehead and sighed at myself. I had to stop thinking of Bishop as my husband. That title was temporary, even if I wished his presence in my bed and my life wasn't. I was not going to pretend my life was anything other than a dumpster fire right now. Considering where he was in life, and after everything he'd gone through with

Athena, he deserved a little bit of stability and relaxation. He wasn't going to get that with me.

He seemed pretty relaxed this morning.

There was that voice again, and I growled at it while hashtagging Able Baker Brady does bread. It was ridiculous how many old ladies followed The Fluffy Cupcake account just to see pictures of Brady in his chef's coat mugging with a loaf of bread.

I leaned my head back on the couch and closed my eyes. After our night of mind-blowing sex, I was exhausted and needed a nap. I wasn't going to get one, though. I knew he had plans for the rest of the day. If I had to guess, I'd say he had plans for the rest of the night, too. Sacrifices would have to be made. A secret part of me wished I could do more in bed with him. My leg's inability to hold me up made it difficult to be in more than a couple of positions, and I was well aware that I was missing out on powerful experiences because of it. I grabbed my phone again and opened the browser, typing in every search term I could think of that would get me the desired results. Finally, a picture popped up that had potential. I clicked it, reading the page, clicking to several more, and eventually, I was taken to Amazon, where I could get what I needed with one-day delivery. I hit buy now just as Bishop strode through the front door. He stopped by the couch and leaned on the arm until I was finished.

"How does it look?" I asked after I shut my phone off.

He sat next to me and took my hand, kissing the back of it before he answered. "It's exactly what I wanted. It's beautiful and functional. I also wanted to make sure it was safe for you to use with your crutches. Chris did a great job. He said it helped that I bought the prefab deck. I guess it was like snapping together a Lego kit."

I frowned at his words. "I hope you didn't pay a lot extra for the safety factor," I said. "Eventually, this won't be my house anymore."

He stood and held out his hand, helping me up. "Don't worry about what I paid for it. It's a wedding gift."

"Wedding gift?"

He nodded. "Two, actually. They're outside. Come on."

I followed him out the patio door, which now had a gently sloping ramp from the doors to the first tier of the deck. I gasped when I took the whole thing in from the angle where I stood. "Bishop, this is beautiful."

"I'm glad you like it," he said grinning. "I tiered it so we could keep the grill separate from the eating area. Check this out," he said, holding up his finger for me to wait. He walked up the ramp to the larger seating area and grabbed a crank that opened a large umbrella and dropped it down over the table, creating lovely shade even during the hottest part of the day.

"We're going to use the heck out of that all summer," I said, leaning on my crutches. "Great forethought on your part."

"It breaks down in the winter, which means we can store it away, and it won't be damaged by snow and ice," he explained, walking back toward me.

"What's over there?" I asked, pointing to the last tier of the deck covered with a tarp.

He helped me up the ramp and across to the covered tier that looked out over the lake. "Close your eyes."

"Bishop," I said, exasperated, but he waited until I followed his orders. I heard rustling, and then he told me to open. When I did, I gasped, tears instantly filling my eyes. "This is so gorgeous."

He helped me up the ramp to the separated deck that was not only perfectly placed to gaze over the lake, but it had a brick fire pit in the center. New Adirondack chairs sat around the pit that was already set up with the wood for the next fire.

"Is this safe?" I asked in a whisper as I inspected the beautiful brick fireplace.

"Absolutely," he said, patting the inside of the firepit. "Chris purchased the kit to meet the standards. As you can see, it's sitting on a base, so it doesn't damage the new decking either."

"What possessed you to put the firepit up here?" I asked in surprise, running my hand over the brick.

Tart

"It's higher, so we can see the lake better over the crest of the hill, each corner of the deck has a spot for citronella candles to fight off the bugs, and since we aren't on the grass, they'll bother us less. It's also easier for you to navigate than the uneven terrain of the yard. I want you to find solace and happiness here without worrying about falling or hurting yourself on your crutches."

I dropped my crutches and put my arms around him, loving the way he picked me up around the waist and buried his nose in my neck. "Thank you," I whispered, my voice choked. "It's moments like these when I don't want to think about not being part of your life and your home. I know eventually, I will have to leave, but between last night and today, you've made that exponentially harder."

He laughed into my neck, raising goosebumps on my skin. "My evil plan is working then." He set me back on my feet, and before I could object, he captured my lips with his and suckled, teased, licked, and kissed until I was wet with desire and pressed against him to feel his own need between us.

"We should go take a nap," I murmured around his lips. "I'll give you a proper thank-you."

He laughed against my lips and then kissed my nose. "We aren't done with wedding gifts, and we have plans."

I shook my head a bit at him. "You shouldn't be buying me gifts, Bishop. I didn't know wedding gifts was a thing."

"Well, in your defense, you didn't have much notice that you were getting married, so you're exempt." He grinned and picked up my crutches, handing them back to me. "We'll have a fire later, but for now, we have somewhere to be."

"We do?" I asked, and he nodded, motioning me back to the house. I crutched up to the patio doors and inside. "The ramps make it much easier on the crutches," I said, lowering myself to the chair. "I don't know if I can do much more moving around, Bishop. My arm is sore from using the crutches again. Normally, I only use one under the right arm to avoid the pressure on my left one, but that's impossible right now."

He nodded and kissed my cheek. "I know and that brings me to your final wedding present. They came yesterday while we were gone, and I found them in the garage this morning. Hang tight."

He disappeared, and I wondered what on earth he was talking about now. I rubbed my forehead and sighed. I didn't want to go anywhere other than to bed. I was exhausted, and the idea of crutching around for another few hours was almost too much to bear. I could handle a night out around the campfire, but I wasn't sure I could force my body to move much further than that. I had a busy week coming up with work, interviews, and finishing the office at the bakery. I had to rest a little bit, and something told me I'd find myself in his bed again tonight.

My mind raced to the package being delivered from Amazon tomorrow, and I smiled. Maybe I had a wedding gift for him after all. Time would tell. I heard the door close again, and then he was walking back into the room with a long rectangular cardboard box. He set it on end and held it out for me to take.

"What's this?"

"Open it and find out," he said, holding the box, so I could stand up and balance while popping the tucked in flaps open. I peeked inside, but I still couldn't tell what they were as I pulled them out of the box. The white sticks were confusing until he pulled out the rest and put them together.

"What am I looking at?" I asked in confusion. "They look like forearm crutches, but they can't be."

"They aren't," he assured me, holding them out for me. "They're a new crutch designed out of the UK. They use your elbows and forearms to balance your weight rather than under your arms. Haylee told me you might have fewer problems with these since the injury to your arm ended above your elbow."

I nodded, biting my lip as I eyed the contraptions. "That's why I have so many problems with that arm," I said, clearing my throat.

He bought crutches for me. He sought out a solution to a problem I had and then checked with my best friend just to make sure he wouldn't make something worse. Part of me wanted to pinch myself and see if I was awake. Was he for real, or was he a dream?

He slid his arms inside the straps and grasped the handles that jutted upward like a video game joystick. "The crutches are fully adjustable, including the handgrips," he explained, flipping them down. "You can also move them out of the way and watch," he said, lifting his arms. The arm cups stayed on his arm but separated from the crutch on a swing-away motion. He put his arms around me and hugged me, then lowered the crutches to the floor and snapped them down again. "You can let go, and they don't fall off your arms, but they will break away if you fall."

"That's seriously sci-fi stuff, Bishop. Crutches have been the same since the Civil War. No one ever made them easier. These are a gamechanger."

He nodded and took one off his arm, flipping it over. "They are because the feet are completely different than most crutches. Instead of just a cap over a metal tube, these act more like those shoes you see kids hopping around on. They rock forward, squish down, and then pop back up on return to make walking with them more natural. They also have ones for ice and snow to keep you from falling."

He righted the crutch again and handed it to me, helping me adjust them, so they fit my height. He walked close to me while I tried them out, surprised by how easily they moved with my body rather than my body having to force them around. "Bishop, these are incredible."

He nodded, a satisfied smile on his face. "You walk completely different on them. You don't have to stop as often."

"No, because they aren't compressing the nerves in my damaged arm. I'm speechless."

He kissed my cheek and smiled. "From what I hear, that's nearly impossible, so I'll take it as a win."

Tears ran down my face, and he wiped them away. "Did I say something wrong?"

I shook my head and shrugged, looking to the ceiling to gather myself. "You're just too nice to me. No one is this nice to me. I don't know how I'm ever going to pay you back for everything you've done."

"You don't pay someone back for a gift, Amber," he said, wiping more tears until he finally had to get a napkin from the holder on the table.

"I'm not just talking about the crutches. You underplay everything you're doing to help me, but you know what I mean. Now we've consummated the marriage, too, so we'll have to pay for a divorce."

He chuckled and wiped my tears, resting the crutches against the table. He picked me up and carried me to his bed, still rumpled from this morning, and lowered me to it. "I'm not worried about paying for a divorce right now. I'm worried about making sure you get the care you need. As for consummating the marriage, I hadn't thought of that, but you're right, we did. We did it well, too, if I do say so myself."

He started taking my brace off until I grasped his hand. "I thought we had to go somewhere."

"We were supposed to meet Haylee and Brady at the lake. Brady is skiing in the waterski show tonight, but I think you need to get some rest. I did keep you up half the night making you come," he said, kissing me senseless while he took the brace off without even looking. I whimpered when he pulled away to set the brace off to the side of the bed.

"I don't want to upset them if they're expecting us."

"I'll text Haylee and tell her your arm is sore. She'll understand. Should I invite them to come over and christen the new patio with us tonight? I'll grill steaks, and we'll share a few drinks with them if you think you'll feel up to it."

"If I don't have to go any farther than the patio, I would love to see them. I just don't think I can do more than that, even with the new crutches, which are amazeballs, by the way. Unfortunately, it will be tomorrow before the pain from

190

the old set goes away enough to let me move around better."

He nodded and sat next to me on the bed, his fingers pushing the hair back behind my ears before his thumb rubbed my cheek gently. "I understand. I should have thought of that before I planned today's activities. You've been doing a lot of moving around on those crutches, and you're not used to that. Forgive me?"

I grasped his hand, bringing his palm to my lips to kiss. "Nothing to forgive. Are you kidding me? The last few days have been wonderful. I've loved getting to know you better and spending time alone with you. I wouldn't change any of it, a sore arm or not."

"Sleep or no sleep?"

"No sleep if it means I get another one of those rocking orgasms," I joked, his growling laughter satisfaction for my body and soul.

"I can arrange that," he promised. "Later. You rest while I call Haylee."

I nodded and rolled over onto my right side as he left the room. He was something else. Why couldn't I have met him a year ago before I had the misfortune of dating the biggest asshole in the state?

I was almost asleep, my tired mind, body, and soul finished thinking about all the what-ifs and what-could-have-beens. Especially when in a sleepy haze, I felt him wrapping an ice pack around my left arm and tucking it in under the blanket before he left the room again. My lips curled up in a smile, but my heart broke a little bit more inside my chest. Walking away from him would be more painful than anything that tornado ever did to me.

"You outdid yourself, Bishop," Haylee moaned, leaning back in her chair after dinner. "Those steaks were delicious. So tender and juicy."

"I'm glad," he said from where he sat next to me. "With the change in plans, they didn't get their usual marinade time, but it all worked out in the end. I should clean this up."

Brady stood and started gathering plates. "I'll help. Ladies, why don't you enjoy the fire now that it's going strong."

Haylee leaned over and kissed him. "That would be great, thanks, babe."

"Anything for my cupcake," he said, kissing her back while I made gagging noises, much to Bishop's delight. Bishop kissed my lips and then lifted me from my chair, where I startled, grabbing his shirt to hold on to him.

"What are you doing?" I asked as he carried me to the firepit.

"Giving your arm a break," he answered, lowering me to a chair and flipping the reclining part out so I would be more comfortable. "At least until tomorrow," he said on a wink.

He went back to the table while Haylee carried our drinks and my crutches over to the fire and sat down next to me. "Is he real, or is he an alien dropped here by accident?" she asked, handing me the bottle of cold beer.

"I double-checked last night. He only has one tentacle, so I'm not thinking he's an alien."

"Backup the cupcake cart, woman," she hissed, leaning in. "You slept with him?" I nodded, giving her the oops look while she waved her finger around my face. "I knew something was different about you. I just thought you were tired. It turns out you're all sexed up!"

"Shh, geez, tell the neighborhood why don't you," I groaned, looking behind me. I was relieved to see the guys were in the house, putting the food away. "I'm not all sexed up!" I whispered and then snorted at the look on her face.

She made the motion with her hand for me to spit it out. "Was it worth marrying him for?"

I shoved her in the shoulder with laughter on my lips. "More than worth it. It would be worth staying married to

Bishop for that perk." A shiver rolled through me, and she grinned with enthusiasm.

"Being compatible between the sheets is huge, Amber. I'm happy for you. Bishop will make a good husband."

I rolled my eyes to the darkening sky and sighed. "I'm not staying married to him, Hay-Hay. I'm just saying the sex alone would make it worth it."

"I don't know. It's easy to see how much Bishop loves you every time he looks at you," Haylee said, her brows in the air. "He hovers over you the way Brady hovers over me. It's obvious to everyone but you, I think."

"Do you believe in love at first sight?" I asked, rubbing my hands on my legs.

"I believe in what I call souls at first sight. Your soul knows it just met the one person they're supposed to be with forever. How long it takes those two souls to come together is varied."

"Like you and Brady taking six years to share your first kiss."

"And it only took you two weeks," she said on a wink.

I shoulder bumped her as the guys came out of the house. "That doesn't mean we're staying together."

We ate smores, drank wine, and laughed as we talked about our childhoods. Bishop introduced them to Athena as a proud dad, and I sat back, a smile on my face while he touted her accomplishments. It was nice to see him talking about her openly rather than hiding the fact that he was a father.

"We're almost all moved in now," Brady said, taking Haylee's hand. "We have a few things left at the apartment, and that's it. I can't wait until we don't have to do those stairs all winter."

"What are you going to do with the apartment?" I asked, suddenly realizing it would sit empty.

"We thought about using it for an office," Hay-Hay answered, "but then we remembered you couldn't get up all those stairs."

I grimaced and nodded. "Sorry, that would have been a good idea, too."

Brady shook his head. "No apologies necessary, we found a solution."

Haylee wore a smile on her face when she spoke. "As long as you're okay with it, we thought we'd rent it to Taylor and Sara."

"Yes! I'm totally okay with it!" I said, nodding immediately. "Wait, how is that going to work? There's only one bedroom."

Brady nodded and tipped his head at me with his brows in the air.

"Oh my God, they're a couple?" I asked, stunned.

"Is that a problem?" Brady asked, his words tinged with a tone of an argument.

"Absolutely not!" I exclaimed. "It's perfect. They'll be working similar shifts, and they'll be close to the bakery now that they both work there."

Hay-Hay smiled and grasped Brady's arm to chill him out. He was always going to be the defender of humanity. Sometimes I wish he'd figure out I was already in his corner. "We thought so, too. They're so excited to make it their home. I'm happy that it will be rented and we won't have to worry about the upkeep. You're the books lady, but if we could figure out how to give them a break on the rent, or make the rent part of their compensation, the accountant says we can benefit from that tax-wise."

"I'll talk to him tomorrow," I promised, crossing my heart. "I have everything else done and ready to bring back as far as the paperwork goes. How is the office coming?"

Haylee was sheepish when she answered. "We hired it done," she said, glancing at Brady. "It was just too much on top of moving and all the baking."

I held up my hands to stem her explanation. "That's smart. I'm sure it took them way less time than it would have taken Brady."

Brady laughed, his head nodding as he finished his beer. "For the price of six dozen donuts, it was done in under four hours. I hired three teenagers from the ski team who are also part of a Boy Scout troop. All I had to do was

Tart

donate the donuts for their next couple of meetings, and the work was done. It was a win."

"I think you'll find it very comfortable now," Hay-Hay said. "I like that it keeps you in the bakery. I don't like the idea of you upstairs or offsite all the time. We miss not having you there."

"But not this week, right?" Bishop jumped in to ask. "She doesn't have to come in this week?"

I turned to face him. "I have to go in for interviews and to get the paperwork filed."

"I know, but I don't think it's smart to go back full-time until you know for sure the leg is healed from the infection. Right?"

"Listen, you don't get a say in what I do with my business or my body, Bishop. We might be married, but you don't control me. Considering our marriage isn't even real, your opinion doesn't matter. I'll be the judge of when I can do something and when I can't. Not you or anybody else," I ground out, my eyes blazing mad, and my fists clenched at my side.

He glanced at the lake for a moment and then pushed himself up. "Well, look at that. We forgot to cover the pontoon boat. I better do that. I hear storms are on the way tonight." The way he said it told me he was trying to hit me in the solar plexus. It worked. I watched him walk toward the dock, my heart picking up its pace as my eyes searched the sky. It was cloudy now where it wasn't just an hour ago.

Brady stood and interrupted my freak out. "I'll give him a hand," he said, kissing Haylee's cheek and throwing me a death glare of disappointment.

He strode away, and Haylee clucked her tongue. "Well, that was an effective way to clear a room."

I tossed up my hands and then clasped them behind my neck. "Why is Brady always going after me lately?" I asked angrily. "He's always jumping on me before I can finish my thought."

"He's worried about you and doesn't know how to help, but he knows you need it. He's always been like that. I'll tell him to back off and give you some space."

I nodded and motioned at the dock where the men were standing like dark sentries. "Bishop can't tell me what to do. He's not my real husband."

Hay-Hay shook her head back and forth slowly. "Which you so tactfully reminded him. For the record, he wasn't telling you what to do. He was concerned you were going to risk the improvement you've managed to eke out of that leg if you went back to work. You're still working. What the fuck does it matter where you do it? Honestly, sometimes, for someone so smart, you sure are stupid."

"Great, now my best friend is going to verbally attack me, too. I think it's time to go to bed." I wanted to get inside the house and downstairs before the storm hit. I searched for my crutches around the chair, hating that once again my life was falling apart.

Hay-Hay held out her hands. "I'm sorry, I didn't mean to insult you. I was trying to say that sometimes you dig your heels in when it's unnecessary. He loves you, and you're going to end up pushing him away if you aren't careful. Is that what you want?"

I shrugged, my shoulder going up as a tear fell. "I don't know what I want, Hay. I think that's the problem. I know that I want to come back to work. I feel like I'm letting everyone down."

She helped me stand and then encapsulated me in her arms. "You're not. The work you're doing is far more skilled and beneficial to the business than if you were working the counter. The customers are being taken care of, the product is going out, and you're putting into order the business we've been neglecting. In reality, that's your strong suit, Amber. Your skills are wasted standing up front all day. And if your leg heals a little bit just because you're not on it for hours on end, then that's an added benefit, right?"

"It is, but I can work at a desk in the bakery the same way I can work at one here," I said adamantly. "It's like he thinks I'm Athena or something."

"No," she said, hooking her arm in mine to keep me upright. "It's like he thinks you're his wife and he doesn't want to see you in pain or something. I know you don't love him, but if you look at it from his point of view, the point of view of love, he just wants what's best for you."

"The truth is, Hay-Hay, I think I do love him. I think that's why I want my life to go back to the way it was before."

She tipped her head, but there was a broad smile on her face. "Because your life the way it was before was safe? You didn't have to worry about someone breaking your heart or walking away when you needed them?"

I wiped my eyes again and sighed. "You sound like you know all the excuses I can come up with off the top of my head."

Her laughter filled the night, and she nodded, her eyes smiling, too. "I ran through them all for years. At least you came to a conclusion much sooner than I did. You have to make this right with him," she said, a brow down. "He meant well."

I opened my mouth to speak when a rumble of thunder filled the sky. My heart started ticking away, and I froze, unable to move.

She grabbed my crutches and handed them to me, helping me up the ramps and sliding open the patio doors. "Go. Get yourself downstairs where you'll be safe. Do you need help?" I shook my head, unable to talk. She knew exactly why and didn't question it.

"I'll clean up the patio and tell Bishop where you are. It sounds like you have about twenty minutes before the storms get here. Be careful going down the stairs. I love you," she said, hugging me for a moment and then pointing toward the house."

"I love you, too," I was finally able to say as I crutched away, my heartbreaking that I would be sitting this one out alone.

Fifteen

A crack of thunder louder than the devil's damnation roared overhead, and I curled into a smaller ball, the blankets over me. I had my earplugs in, but even that wasn't helping tonight. I rocked under the blankets, counting the seconds before the next boom. It took longer this time, which meant it was moving away. Relief flooded my adrenaline-filled heart, and I sighed.

Bishop had been right. Storms were coming, and not just the ones that were raging outside. The doom sat heavily on my chest. Then again, maybe that was regret. I regretted the way I treated him, and I regretted the turn my life had taken. I didn't want to drag him into this, yet here I was, cowering in his basement under the covers of his guest bed.

I had come down here immediately, guilt filling me as I sat on the lift-chair he'd had installed just for me. I let it carry me to safety, but away from him. I didn't even tell him goodnight. I couldn't face him, or see the disappointment in his eyes. I washed up in the bathroom down here and crawled under the covers when the first boom hit.

The bed depressed behind me, and I rolled over, the sudden intrusion taking me by surprise. It was Bishop. He was wearing a t-shirt and shorts, his hair wet and sleep in his eyes. "Are you okay, Amber?"

I nodded as another crack of thunder filled the air at the same time. I jumped, and Bishop grabbed me, pulling me into him and resting us both back on the pillows. He pulled the covers up to ward off the chill of the basement and held me while I shook in his arms. It was ridiculous that I still shook with fear over a simple thunderstorm, but I'd learned years ago I could fight against it and be a nervous wreck for the entire summer, or I could let it flow over me while I was safe and away from everyone else, and be fine the next day. That was the only option that let me keep my sanity and live my life. It was also the reason I never went to Florida with my parents. Storms happen year-round down there. You can forget about it.

He rubbed my back soothingly and stroked my hair, holding me against his chest in silence until the storm slowed, and the claps of thunder became farther apart and with less intensity. Slowly and with more confidence, my exhausted body relaxed against him, and my heart slowed. I pulled an earplug out and gazed up at him from where I rested on his warm chest.

"I thought you were mad at me," I said, relieved that the fogginess of my brain when the storms hit was already starting to recede. Maybe it was because someone was there to share the burden with me.

"Being upset," he said, stressing the word, "doesn't erase or overrule the rest of my emotions, tart. I can be upset and still have empathy. I can be upset and still love someone enough not to let them suffer alone."

My hand came up to stroke his soft beard, the whiskers tickling my skin and keeping me calm as I gazed into his beautiful, but aggrieved, green eyes. "You're a good man, Bishop Halla," I whispered, dropping my hand from his cheek to his chest. "I owe you an apology."

He shifted uncomfortably on the bed, and I realized he was almost falling off it. I sat up and let him move closer and then rested on the pillow, face-to-face. I was secretly relieved when he kept his hand on my waist, especially when the thunder cracked overhead again. "The storms are heading out over the lake. I checked before I came down. Nothing severe. Just a few heat of the day thunderboomers. They're almost done."

I nodded my head slowly, knowing the look that was in my eye. "I'm sorry for being like this. I can't fight against it anymore, Bishop. It's too hard to be that anxious and worried all day every day. I tried the medications, but I hated feeling like a zombie all the time. If I hide away like a child when the storms arrive, at least I can function the rest of the time. Some things will always set me off, though. You can't blindside me with plans unexpectedly. I have to be involved in making any plans during the summer. If I hear people talking about storms or the news reporting about them, I have to leave. A loud motorcycle will make me cover my ears instantly. Fireworks are out forever. Those things will always be there. I can't change that part of my brain. I've tried it."

He grasped my waist, and his thumb trailed up and down my hipbone. "Don't," he said, shaking his head. "Don't defend yourself to me. You aren't a child, but you suffer because of what happened to you as a child. There is a difference. Hold your head high, Amber Halla. You are strong. You are resilient. You have overcome so many challenges, and protecting yourself down here, or anywhere, does not require an explanation—to me or anyone else. Do you understand?"

"You really don't understand how my life works, Bishop. I'm not strong and resilient. I'm just a scared, broken thirteen-year-old girl in a scared, broken thirty-year-old body. I wish it weren't true, but I can't lie to myself or you about the truth any longer."

His hand cupped my cheek, and his thumb strayed to my lips to stroke them tenderly. My lips puckered and kissed it without a conscious thought from me. He smiled and then spoke. "I'm just a scared sixteen-year-old boy finding out he's going to be a father in a scared thirty-four-year-old man's body, wondering if I did a good enough job. Now, that scared thirty-four-year-old wonders if he's doing right by the woman he would die for in the blink of an eye. He failed tonight, and fear spoke rather than love."

I tipped my head into his hand. "What do you mean you failed tonight?"

Tart

"I let the worry and fear I have about your leg make me stick my nose in where it didn't belong."

I let out a breath, and my chest collapsed on itself. "This is what I'm talking about, Bishop. You said what you said out of concern for me. My reaction to that was what didn't belong. I knew it as soon as you walked away. Brady shot me a look of total disappointment before he followed you. Hay-Hay told me I had better be careful, or I was going to push you away. She said she could see how much you love me every time you look at me."

His smile was soft, and when I gazed into his eyes, I realized she was right. The love was there, shining in those globes of green. "I try to hide it, but it never works. Maybe that's what gives this marriage validity to the rest of the town."

"That could be," I agreed, nodding. "It's possible I'm contributing as well. Hay-Hay also told me she could see how much I love you, even if I haven't come to accept that yet."

His eyes widened, and he coughed, clearing his throat. "She must think herself clairvoyant then," he said jokingly. "She's making all kinds of prophecies."

"She does think she's an expert on love now," I said, rolling my eyes playfully. "You get married once, and suddenly you know it all."

He winked, but shrugged his shoulder slightly. "Brady was equally as prophetic while we covered the boat. He said sometimes you have to dig in for the long haul when it comes to love."

I laughed and rolled to my back, staring at the ceiling. "And Brady would know about the long haul. It took a lot of years for him to convince Hay-Hay she could trust him."

"But he did, and now he's got the girl. I asked you for thirty days to prove that I want this marriage to be real. After talking to Brady, I realized I'd wait thirty years if that's what it takes to convince you that you're the woman I want to spend the rest of my life with. I know you don't want to hear this, but I love you, Amber Halla."

201

Tears sprung to my eyes instantly, and I swallowed, my lips shaking at the idea that he was that dedicated. That he was in *love* with *me*. As broken as I was, he was in love with me.

"Bishop, there's so much unknown about me. You shouldn't have to suffer those consequences, too. You deserve better than that."

He rolled me to him and grasped my face, his eyes boring into mine. "No. Stop. I told you I never wanted to hear you say that again, remember?"

"Sorry, teacher," I said jokingly, but he wasn't joking. I sighed when he didn't even crack a smile.

"Everything from this second to the next is unknown, tart. I could walk up those stairs and have a stroke at the top. I could wake up tomorrow morning and be injured mowing the lawn. We can't live our lives worrying about the consequences of living. Does that make sense?"

"I get that, Bishop, I do, but this situation speaks to a different place. While there is unknown, what we already know isn't good."

He held his finger to my lips. "This is what I know already. You're incredible. You're funny, kind, smart, beautiful, loving, devoted, and a million other adjectives that would test my English teacher skills." I smiled, and he moved his finger after I kissed it. "I know that you're a little tart in bed. When I think about sinking into you, my dick goes instantly hard, and when I do take you completely, there is this blooming, overwhelming, breath-stealing sensation in my chest that tells me you are the person I waited for all these years. Up until last night, I had never had sex without a condom because I didn't trust anyone enough not to lie to me about birth control. Once burned, twice shy, as they say. Last night, when you told me I didn't need to wear one, I just trusted you. That's what tells me what I already know is good. We are good, Amber. Love at first sight is real, and my love for you is good."

I wiped my eye on my shoulder and cleared my throat, grabbing his wrist, where he still held my face. "Is that what that feeling is in my chest when you do something incredibly sweet for me, and I'm overwhelmed? Or when you teach me how to come from pleasure rather than determination? Or how every time you sink into me, you pause with this look of total and utter spirituality on your face for a moment?"

"Is that what feeling?" he asked, his thumb stroking away the tears from my cheeks. "Love?" I nodded quickly, his lips tugging up into a smile. "It sounds like love to me, but I suppose it could also be gratitude."

"I asked Hay-Hay tonight if she thought love at first sight was real."

"What did she say?"

"She said she calls it souls at first sight. Your soul knows it just met the one person they're supposed to be with, even if we don't recognize it at the moment. Sometimes love at first sight is just our souls calling out for each other. Like Haylee, you might deny it because it's the wrong place, wrong time, or because we don't think we deserve it. Sometimes we deny it because we're scared. If that person keeps stepping back into our path, then we should stop and think about that first meeting in a different light."

"She's scary sometimes. Has she always been like this?" he asked, his thumb grasping my chin.

"No. Haylee used to be the exact opposite. That changed after someone tried to kill her. It was like the knock to her head turned her into an empath."

"Or she always was one, and the near-death experience gave her a way to tap into it."

"Probably that. Either way, what she said made sense to me more than anything else anyone has ever said. You kept stepping back into my path, and I had to look back at our first meeting in a new light. All I could picture was how kind your green eyes were when you immediately picked up on how afraid of the storms I was. I replayed opening my eyes in the van to see you reaching your hands out to me. That was the first time anyone reached out to me when I was vulnerable out of empathy and not obligation. Then you showed up in the bakery, and I agreed to meet you that night for dinner. I don't do that. I don't trust men. I've fought against it all this time, but the truth was there all along. I still fight against it because I'm not sure if my limited experience gives me enough knowledge to say what I'm feeling is love. The thing is, I don't have limited experience with myself, if that makes sense?" He nodded, and I smiled, letting out a sigh of frustration. "What I'm trying to say, while jacking it up royally, is that I love you, Bishop Halla. That screws with this whole fake marriage thing we've got going on, but pretending it isn't true is doing nothing but hurting the both of us."

He froze in place, other than the slight tremble of his hand on my chin. "You love me?" he asked as if he was clarifying what he heard.

Suddenly, I was unsure again. "I mean, I think it's love. I've never felt like this before, but when you got up and walked away tonight, I wanted to run after you. I wanted to beg you to forgive me. There was this feeling in my chest that my heart was being crushed. Even worse than when I fight with Haylee, and we're mad at each other. I always want to make it right with her because I love her. Tonight, the feeling in my chest was like ten times that."

He finally sucked in a deep breath of air, his lips coming down on mine in a hot, frenzied tangling of tongues. "God, I love you so much. Your words just tipped my world on its axis and then set it right again. Right for the first time in eighteen years." He pressed his palm to his chest and sucked in more air while I ran my fingers through his hair and across his soft beard.

"Are you okay?" I asked, worried when he kept his hand on his chest.

"I'm better than okay. I finally feel like I'm not going to be left carrying a heavy heart around forever when the woman I love leaves me. You're not going to leave me, right?" he asked, pulling me into him and kissing me again before I could answer. By the time he released me, I had to pant several times to get the oxygen in to form words.

"As I said, feelings complicate this fake marriage, but I don't plan on leaving you, Bishop Halla."

He balanced his forehead on mine and kissed my nose. "It's only a fake marriage if you keep referring to it that way, Mrs. Halla. If you stop calling it that, then we can make it a marriage from this day forward."

"To have and to hold?" I asked, teasing him a little by licking my lips.

"To have. To hold. To do lots of other naughty things until you can barely walk the next day."

"Well, that won't take much. I can barely walk on any given day."

He dropped his head and sighed. "I'm sorry, that's not what I meant."

"Don't be. I was teasing you. I know what you meant. You meant you were going to use this beard between my legs until my thighs were chapped from your whisker rubs," I said, stroking the hair on his face.

"True, but I also meant I was going to bury my yardstick in you over and over until you came with my name on your lips."

"Over and over," I said, rolling on top of him.

"Promises, promises," he whispered before he captured my lips again.

I helped her into the house, and she lowered herself to the couch, sighing heavily and with resignation. I went to the kitchen to get her a glass of water and, at the last second, grabbed a wine cooler, too. She might need something more substantial than water. When I got back to the couch, she was texting on her phone.

"Water or wine?" I asked, holding them up.

She looked up at me and smiled. "Am I supposed to call you Jesus now?"

I snorted and handed her the wine, setting the water on the table for later. "No, but you can cry on my shoulder if you need to."

She held up her phone. "I was just texting Haylee that I'd be over later to see her. I haven't even seen their new house yet. I mean, sure, I'm familiar with it since old Mrs. Daniels lived there forever. Did I tell you that we once picked her petunias? I convinced Hay-Hay it would be okay, but man, did we get in trouble. I called her petunia ever si—"

I put my finger to her lips and gazed at her under my brow. "Amber, it's okay to be upset."

Her head swung back and forth while she screwed the cap off the wine cooler. I moved my hand, and she took a long drink of it before lowering it to her lap. "I'm not upset."

"You're not upset that the nerves in your leg don't work at all."

"Some work," she said defensively.

I held up my hand. "I stand corrected. You're not upset that the nerves from your knee down don't work?"

"It's more like I'm resigned," she sighed, leaning her head back. "Let's face facts. It wasn't exactly a surprise. I can only make it bend at my hip, and even when I do that, the rest of it just flops around. I was hoping there were more treatment options than there are, but all I can do is keep moving forward. Being upset or pissy won't change anything."

I tipped my head in acknowledgment of that. "I get what you're saying, but it's okay to grieve the loss for a moment. I hope you aren't just saying this because you think I don't want to deal with it."

"I don't want to deal with it!" she exclaimed before her shoulders sank. "Sorry, you know what I mean. I've been doing this so long that I know how to internalize it. Nobody likes a complainer or a Debbie Downer. I just have to move forward like I've done all the other times I got a shitty hand. That's life. Either you live it, or you don't, but you can't make other people miserable at the same time."

Tart

"You aren't making me miserable because you're upset that your leg is paralyzed, tart. In my opinion, that's a legitimate reason to let someone comfort you for five minutes without feeling weak."

She tipped her head to her shoulder and shrugged. "Thanks for going with me today. I know it was boring for you just sitting there."

I shook my head, and grasped her hand in mine. "I wasn't bored. I was focused on being there to support you. I know you normally do these things alone, but you don't have to anymore. You're not putting me out by asking me to be there to support you, okay?"

She set the bottle down and nodded, rubbing her face with her hands. "Okay."

I gathered her into me and held her, the resignation in her shoulder blades heartbreaking to me. She was trying so hard to be strong, but the news like she got today would change a person no matter how positive they tried to remain.

"I should go to Hay-Hay's," she whispered, grasping my shirt in her hand tightly. "I promised her."

My hand rubbed her shoulder, and I nodded against the top of her head. "Take some time first. Take some time to accept what happened before you have to tell someone else about it. I love you," I whispered, kissing the top of her head. "I know you're a strong woman, but even strong women need a little extra TLC sometimes."

"I'm angry," she whispered, the weight of her words pushing hard against me. "I'm angry that everyone else in my family walked away from that night uninjured. They all carry scars, but none of them were physically hurt the way I was. Then I get angry at myself because I lived while other families lost their loved ones. Maybe it would have been better if I hadn't survived—"

"No!" I grasped her shoulders and pushed her out away from me, finding her gaze and holding it. "God, sweetart, don't ever say that again."

"It's not untrue, Bishop. I've been a burden since the day it happened. First to my family, and now you. That's not fair!"

I loosened my hands on her shoulders but didn't move them. "No, none of this is fair, tart. But none of it is your fault, either. You aren't a burden."

Her sarcastic laughter filled the living room. "Shows what you know. I can't wait to tell my parents this one. There will be much sighing and moaning about how much it will impact their life again."

I grasped her chin and held it gently. "You are mine now. I told you that before, and you told me you understood. Since you clearly don't understand, you're going to have to repeat that assignment."

"Bishop…"

"Don't Bishop me. I will have to teach you that lesson again later, but for right now, let me tell you this. I don't care what your parents think about the news you got today. They're inconsequential to your health now that you have me. They don't get to act put out about it anymore, and if they do, I will set them straight."

"Not a good idea," she whispered, dropping her eyes. "I might have to live with them again someday."

I tipped her chin up until she made eye contact again. "Not unless it's your choice. I have already made you my beneficiary, and you will always have a place in this house, whether I'm alive or dead. That said, I am not giving up on you, Amber Halla. I don't care if your leg doesn't work the same way mine does. Take notes, because this is important. Fuck everything your parents ever made you think about yourself except this one thing. You have enough determination to make the life that you want for yourself, even if you have to work around a few things to do it."

"I thought you were going to say I was strong," she said on a fake laugh.

"You are," I said, stealing a kiss from her sweet lips. "But you don't have to be strong all the time. Sometimes, you get to feel weak and not feel bad about it. Your parents pushed you to be strong, but instead, they just pushed you into feeling like you could never be weak. That you could never just take an hour to let out a breath and grieve for what you lost that day, and they just added insult to injury by doing that. I'm not judging them. I can imagine the guilt they deal with as parents seeing their daughter so broken by the decisions they made. They're not here right now, though. We're here at this moment, right?" I asked, and her head nodded. "Then we're the only two who matter. It is okay to feel the loss you suffered today, tart. You can let it roll over you here where it's safe, and you don't have to respect my feelings. I'm here for you and your feelings."

"I don't know how to feel," she admitted, her eyes dropping to the buttons on my shirt. "I just want to go see Hay-Hay and forget about it for a little bit."

I stood up and took her hand, and she looked up at me in surprise. "Let me drive you down there, though. I'm sure your leg is sore from all the prodding they did."

She stood up and finally made eye contact. "You're not upset with me?"

My hand stroked her cheek, and I leaned in, kissing her softly. "No, sweetart, why would I be? Not knowing how to feel about this news is okay. When you do know how to feel, and if you do need comfort, then I'm here, and I'm ready to hold you. Okay?"

She nodded and wrapped her arms around me, allowing me to pick her up and cradle her against me while I carried her to the car. She was going to crash later, and I'd be there for her when it happened, but for now, I'd let her guide me through this journey.

Sixteen

"Hay-Hay, the house is beautiful," I whispered, standing in the sunroom of her new house.

"Thanks, Amber. I knew you'd appreciate the changes we made while keeping it honest to the century it was built in." She pointed at the club chair by the window. "Sit. I'll get us a drink."

Brady and Bishop were doing their own thing out in the garage. What do men do in garages? Drink beer? Probably.

I lowered myself to the seat and set my new crutches to the side on the floor. They had become lifesavers, and I was grateful to Bishop for ordering them. My arm didn't hurt anymore, which made moving around less arduous and fatiguing. When she reappeared, she had two glasses filled with iced tea.

"Be careful," she warned, "it's spiked."

"A woman after my own heart," I chuckled, taking a sip. "Oh, yeah," I moaned, loving the rich taste of spicy rum mixed into the sweet tea.

"I thought we deserved it," she said, sipping her tea. "You more than any of us, though."

"It's almost surreal," I admitted, leaning back in the chair. "New faces in the front are now bringing in new customers. Am I that ugly?" I asked, laughing at her face when she registered what I asked.

She gave me the har-har face. "No, you aren't ugly, but you're also not twenty-one. If you notice, the age of the new crowd is in that ballpark. Their friends are coming in to see them and staying for the cake. The new girls are professional, courteous, and helpful to all the customers, so I don't have a problem with it."

"Other than having to increase your cupcake tally every day."

"Which is okay because now I have time to do it," she said, tapping her glass on her leg. "Are you going to work the booth at the Strawberry Festival next week?"

I swallowed a large gulp of the iced tea and stared over her shoulder. If I met her eyes, I'd cry, and if I cried, I might never stop. "I don't think so, Hay-Hay," I said, keeping my voice steady. "I didn't get good news at the doctor today. I don't think I can handle all the sitting, standing, loading, and unloading that the event requires. I want to," I said, my voice cracking, "but I can't. Not this year."

Haylee set her iced tea down and knelt in front of me, taking my hand. "Sweetheart, I'm so sorry for even asking. Please, don't stress about it, okay? I'll have the girls do it. They need the experience, and I know they will love to work the booth since the bakery won't be open."

I nodded and swallowed back the tears in my voice. "I'll make sure all the marketing information is ready, and I'll go over all of it with them. I'll be on-call for any questions, issues, or help they need. The uneven ground out there just makes it hard and a little dangerous right now for me, you know?"

She nodded and grasped my hands tightly. "I know. What happened at the doctor, Amber? What did he tell you?"

I stared down at our hands resting on my lap rather than her empathetic face. "Exactly what I already suspected," I answered, my voice firm, which surprised me. "The nerves used to bend my knee and ankle, as well as give me any sensation in the leg, are denervated, which is a fancy word for no nerve supply or—"

"Paralyzed," she whispered.

211

I nodded, a tear dripping onto my lap. "Dammit," I whispered, angrily swiping at my face with my shoulder. "I said I wasn't going to cry. It's not like I didn't already know."

She wiped away a tear from my face. "Suspecting and getting confirmation are two different things, Amber. You get to cry. That's allowed in my house."

I chuckled and shook my head a little bit. "That's what Bishop said, too, but I don't want to be that person."

She rubbed my shoulder tenderly and paused for a beat. "What treatment options did the doctor give you?"

My shoulder went up under her hand. "There aren't many. The expensive brace would allow me to walk again, but that is the only thing that will. The brace I'm wearing now is just to keep the leg from flopping around. It's not helping me walk anymore. If I don't get the new brace, I'll end up in a wheelchair."

"But you're going to get the new brace, right?"

"We have a meeting with them in a couple of weeks. The doctor wants the arthritis in the knee to heal more before we do it. He says they need to measure everything when it's normal, which makes sense," I said on a laugh. "As if anything is normal. Nothing will be normal again."

Haylee pulled me over onto her shoulder to hug me. "Maybe not the normal you were used to, but there will be normal again. Will it look different from the last seventeen years? Yes, but that doesn't mean it will be worse. You have so many people who love you and just want to see you happy again. Brady and I will do anything at the bakery so you can keep working with us. We miss you when you aren't there, and we want you back. Bishop will move mountains to make sure you're happy again. He loves you and doesn't want to see you in pain."

I nodded, tears falling faster now that I was in my best friend's arms. I never had to be strong with her. She always let me fall apart so I could put myself back together again. "Thanks for always letting me cry on your shoulder," I said over my tears.

"Bishop would let you cry on his shoulder, too, babe," she whispered. "He's not going to leave you just because you show a moment of weakness."

"She's right," his deep voice said from behind us. I stiffened immediately, but there was no way to hide the tears. "Love is filled with little moments of weakness that are made strong again by the bond we share."

His strong arms captured me, and he sat, holding me on his lap and letting me tuck my nose into his neck. "It honestly didn't hit me how bad my leg had gotten until she asked me about the Strawberry Festival," I said, my voice tiny. "Last year, I could do it all, and this year, I can't do any of it."

"That's not true," Hay-Hay said from where she sat by Brady. "I know you'll have everything ready for those girls down to the most minute detail. What you have to learn to do is work smarter, not harder. You're the business manager, not the grunt work. Turn your mindset around to that, and you'll be a lot happier."

"That's our mindset," Brady said. "We utilize everyone's talents now where they are most effective. We don't need you sitting behind a table taking money for cupcakes. We need you sitting behind the desk planning the marketing campaigns, doing the interviews, organizing the sales, managing the employees, and doing the books. I think that's enough, don't you? I know how hard Haylee works, but she doesn't wear that many hats every day."

I wiped my eyes and nodded. "It's just...I guess I feel sad because I always look forward to Strawberry Fest. Maybe not all the work involved with it, but the atmosphere. I feel like it's just another thing this shitshow has stolen from me."

Bishop kissed my temple and wiped another tear from my face. "We can go and enjoy the atmosphere without you killing yourself with all the work. I bet I even know someone who would love to experience Strawberry Fest for the first time."

"You?" I asked chuckling. "I didn't even think about this being your first year."

"It's true. I'm a Strawberry Fest virgin, but I was thinking of someone else." He held up his phone, and I read a text on the screen.

I sat up instantly. "What? Athena is coming to visit?"

He nodded with a huge grin on his face. "She called me when we were in the garage. She's flying home for a visit tomorrow!"

I threw my arms around him and squeezed him tight. "I'm so happy for you. I know you've missed her."

He nodded his head over my shoulder before he leaned back. "I have, and I can't wait for you to meet her. Will you stay here with Haylee and Brady tonight? I have to drive to St. Paul to pick her up early tomorrow morning from the airport. You've been through so much today. I'm not going to make you get up at the crack of dawn to go with me."

I grasped his face in my hands. "Let's go now. Let's go. Let's just go. We'll get a room and be there in the morning when her flight arrives."

"I think that's a great idea," Haylee said, standing up. "A little getaway will do you a world of good right now. We'll man the bakery, and when you get back tomorrow, spend the day with Athena. We'll see you on Wednesday."

Bishop kissed my cheek before he handed me my crutches. "Let's do it. We'll take a little time out from life to just be with each other."

I stood and hugged Haylee, whispering thank you in her ear. She squeezed me tighter, and I knew, no matter what, I was going to be okay.

"Are you sure you're okay with this?" I asked Amber when she sat back down on the bed.

She leaned back on the pillow and smiled. "Bishop, I already told you thirty times that I am. I want to meet Athena. I'm thrilled she's coming home for a visit."

"I know, but you're so busy with the bakery that I hate to ask you to take more time away." I strolled over and set a bottle of water on the nightstand for her. I had helped her to the bathroom after she woke up from a long sleep, and now I hoped to snuggle up with her and sleep until morning.

"You heard what Haylee said. It will be fine, and when I head in to help them, you can catch up with Athena."

I was surprised to get the phone call from Athena saying she was flying in to see me tomorrow. I suspected she was homesick, but whatever the case, she assured me she was okay, healthy, and just wanted to see me for a few days before she went to Illinois. She knew I got married, so I was sure that was part of it, too. She had to check out dad's new wife to decide if she approved.

"I'm having a security system installed tomorrow while we're gone," I said to change the subject.

"Why? It's Lake Pendle. I can't remember the last time there was a burglary there."

"The system I bought has weather monitoring and will alert us immediately of any storm warnings or watches. Also, if you fall when you're alone, you can use voice commands to get help. I planned to install a system before fall, so I just moved it up on the timeline a little bit. A security system is smart, and the one I bought will give me peace of mind when you're there alone."

She tipped her head to the side, her hand coming up to stroke my beard. "You found a system that warns of bad weather and acts like Life Alert?"

I turned my head and kissed her palm tenderly. "Peace of mind for you when we're home. You'll never be taken by surprise if we're sleeping, either. It's like a weather radio on steroids."

She laughed, and the sound was sleepy and relaxed. "I guess you plan on keeping me around for a while."

"I was thinking forever," I whispered, kissing her lips. "And ever, and ever. I want to be known as the most ridiculously cute married couple in Lake Pendle."

That got a smile out of her, and she kissed my lips, her breath minty fresh. "I don't know, Haylee and Brady might try to take that title."

"Well, they can try," I whispered into her neck, "but they won't win."

"What time is it?" she asked, glancing at the clock on the nightstand. "It's only three a.m.? I must have slept like a rock."

"You had been asleep since eight o'clock last night. I did some work and then crawled in bed around eleven. You never stirred."

"Yesterday was stressful. I guess I needed the sleep."

It *had* been stressful and emotional for her, and I was glad she got to see Haylee for a few minutes. They have a bond that she and I will never have, and I accepted that for what it was. Sometimes you just need to cry on your sister's shoulder.

I brushed a piece of hair off her forehead. "I love you," I whispered, my hand sweeping into her hair to grasp the back of her neck. "We'll get through this together."

She smiled that smile that told me she believed something I said was true. "I love you, too. I keep telling myself we'll get through this stronger than before. I concluded that letting someone help me, look after me once in a while, isn't going to sink my boat of independence."

I leaned in nose-to-nose and kissed her lips. "It won't, you're right. It might even repair some of the holes, and over time you'll be able to float longer without help."

"I think you might be right, teacher. It's just hard because our relationship is new, and I don't want to scare you away. I'm usually not this big of a disaster."

I smiled, my lips finding hers again to tangle with them longer. "Oh, it's hard," I agreed on a moan when I ended the kiss. "And you aren't a disaster. We all struggle, tart. You never asked why I moved to a new job in the middle of the year, did you? You just assumed I chose to find a new job."

She tipped her head at the thought and then nodded. "I guess I did, yeah. Come to think of it that is an odd time to change jobs."

"I had been out of work since the summer before when my old school district didn't renew my contract."

"Why did they do that?" she asked curiously. "Budget cuts?"

I shook my head but refused to look away from her beautiful face. "No, the district was fine. It was me who needed help. I was sinking into depression, and it was starting to affect my work. I called in all the time, and when I was there, I was irritable or lethargic, I didn't take direction well from my supervisors, and I argued about every little thing."

"Seriously?" she asked, holding my hand. "I haven't known you that long, but I know for sure that's not you."

I winked and kissed her knuckles, the sweet smell of her hand lotion tantalizing to my senses. "It's not, that's for sure. I'm usually the complete opposite of the person I was back then. Something was wrong. I knew it, and everyone around me knew it."

"What did you do?"

"I sold my house and moved back to Illinois, where Athena and Sam live. It was Sam and Ken who helped me see what was happening."

"Sam and Ken? That sounds awkward to me."

"We're friends, so it wasn't. Ken dragged me to the gym every day and made me work out with him. Sam made me eat dinner with them every night and talk. After about two weeks of being there, I started to feel like my normal self again. I was laughing with Athena at the pool, jogging around the neighborhood while she rode her bike, and helping her plan the decorations for her dorm room. The feelings only came back when we talked about her going off to school."

"Ahhh," she said, nodding her head in understanding. "Empty nest syndrome."

I made the so-so hand. "In a way. She didn't live with me for long periods, so that wasn't going to make much of a difference in my day-to-day life. It was more like empty life syndrome. Athena was my purpose. She was the reason I went to work every day for the last eighteen years. I had to take care of her and make sure I sent Sam money every month to do that. Suddenly, Sam and Ken didn't need me anymore. Athena wasn't going to need me anymore." She held up her finger, and I grasped it. "I know I was wrong. I know they still need me, just in a different way. I had to spend the summer grappling with what I was going to do when my main focus wasn't on making sure that little girl I loved so much grew into a decent human being. I'd done that. We'd done that. It does take a village to raise a child. It was Ken who sat me down and told me it was time to stop sacrificing my happiness because of guilt. I was too afraid to live because I didn't want to make the same mistake I made with Sam. It was a hammer to the head, but he was right. That's exactly what I was doing. I was using guilt to keep people at bay for so long I didn't know how to face the loneliness I was feeling about being less needed by the only family I had left."

"But you aren't any less needed, Bishop. She still needs her daddy. I think us being in a hotel by the airport is proof of that. That's never going to change until the day you die."

I smiled, her beautiful eager face filling my heart with so much joy. "I know that now. Last summer changed everything I believed about myself and my life. It set me on a new course of finding happiness for myself, personally and professionally. To be honest, I hadn't been happy for at least a couple of years at my old job. The administration wasn't great, and the physical education curriculum was stale. I needed a change. I worked for Domino's delivering pizza while I looked for the right position. Sam was gracious enough to carry Athena on her insurance during that time, even though the court mandated that I do it."

"But knowing you, you made sure you covered the extra in the premiums for her."

I laughed and nodded, giving her the palms out. "I did, but it was only for a few months. I started teaching in Lake

Pendle right after Christmas. I felt like I was back on firm footing again, which was a relief. I'm still glad it happened. It set me on a new path that I needed to find, but couldn't when I was afraid to give up the stability I had."

"I'm glad you found your way to Lake Pendle, Bishop Halla," she whispered. "So very glad."

"Your face smiling back at me is the reason I did. You're the reason I went through all of that because if I hadn't, I wouldn't be sitting here tonight. When I say you're mine, what I mean is, I'm yours for as long as you'll have me. It's not to be possessive or creepy. It's because I know what it's like to be alone and scared. To feel like you don't mean anything to the people you should mean the most to in this world. When you're with me, you're the most important person to me. No one takes precedence over your safety or happiness. Do you understand?"

She stroked my face, her hand warm on my cheek. "That's not true, Bishop. There is one person who is more important than me. Athena is, and I would expect nothing less. If she calls and needs you, I'd help you pack to get to her, just like today. If she calls and needs money, I'll go to the bank to transfer it. I am always going to be second place to her—"

My head was shaking before she finished. "No."

"Yes," she said softly, her smile gentle. "I wouldn't accept it any other way, Bishop. If we're going to make this marriage last, then we have to agree on that. I don't care if she's eighteen or thirty-eight. If she needs you, you will go to her, no matter what. Do *you* understand *me*?" she asked, emphasizing the words to make her point.

"Yes, Mrs. Halla," I whispered, kissing her again, my tongue warring with hers to taste her strength and adamance for myself.

"Mmm," she moaned against my lips. "Speaking of being a bride, I got your wedding gift. You should open it."

"Oh, really, Mrs. Halla?" I asked, raising a brow. "It will have to wait now until we get home. I am madly curious, though."

She pointed at the box in the corner. "You don't have to wait. I brought it with us."

I stared at the giant box and tipped my head. "I wondered what that was when I brought it in. I thought it was something you needed for the bakery."

She grinned and motioned for me to open it. I slid the box over by the bed and ripped the tape off the top, letting the flaps fall open. I stared into the box with curiosity. "What is it?" I asked, lifting it out.

She patted for me to set it on the bed, so I laid it in the middle and sat by her. Her hand rested on it, and she swallowed. I could tell she was suddenly unsure of herself. "After we made love the first time, and I discovered your secret sexy side, I felt bad."

"Oh, sweetart, no," I said immediately. "You fucking blew my mind that night. I don't know what you'd have to feel bad about."

"My leg," she said, sweeping her hand at it. "It will keep us from doing more adventurous things in our sex life. One of us will always have to move it around, and I can't hold myself up on it. This was my solution."

"It's sex furniture," I said, the light finally coming on. "Absolutely brilliant. Why didn't I think of that?"

"You like it?" she asked, my approval important to her. "I was worried you wouldn't."

"I fucking love it," I growled, my lips on hers, pushing her back into the bed. "I fucking love you and love fucking you."

Her laughter rolled through me, and I loved every second of it. "You missed part of the gift. Check the box."

I buried my nose in her neck for a moment and nipped at it before I stood, my boxers tented with desire for her. "I'll check the box, but then we're using that pillow." I reached into the box and pulled out a cuff with a long strap on it. "What is this?"

"It's um, for moving my leg out of the way. You can either hold it or fix it to the bed, so it stays where you put it."

I gazed at the strap in my hand before I threw it back into the box, my head shaking. I dropped to my knees by the side of the bed and moved the sheet aside, stroking her tiny, abused, twisted limb. "I will never attach a device like that to this precious leg, tart. Do I like to fuck funky? Absolutely."

"That's why I bought it," she said, forcing the words out. "I want you to be happy, and I'll do whatever is necessary to assure that."

I climbed over her and positioned the ramp to the other side of me, then sat, my hand caressing her breast over her pajama top. "Listen to me, tart. I am happy, but I won't stay that way if you think you have to put yourself at risk to keep me that way. Your leg is far too fragile to do something that will make it worse. If we need to move your leg to accomplish something we want to do, I will cradle it with love and attention, the same way I cradle your apex. Hurting you would kill me slowly and render me impotent."

"I love the way you love me, Mr. Halla," she whispered. "Now, fuck me."

I wagged my finger at her and sat her up, pulling the sleep shirt over her head. "First, you need a few spankings for this afternoon."

She covered her breasts with fake shyness. "What did I do to deserve a spanking?"

"You dared to think I would leave you because of something beyond your control."

"I learned my lesson," she said right away, nodding quickly. "Love doesn't work that way. Love doesn't keep score."

I moaned and leaned in, pulling her over my lap to kiss her, cradling her head in my hands while I made love to her lips. "You passed the test, beautiful. I still haven't forgotten that you didn't trust me, though. Now I'm going to have to punish you."

I lifted her onto the pillow until her bottom was up in the air, and her head was down. "That okay on the leg?" I asked, holding it carefully, afraid to have her put too much pressure on it.

"I like this position," she said, wiggling her bottom. "It doesn't hurt my leg at all."

"If you keep wiggling that bottom like that, you aren't going to like that position."

She hooked one finger in the waistband of her shorts and tugged, an evil smile on her face the entire time. "Do you talk just to hear your voice, or do you have a point?" Her words were almost a purr, and I grasped the shorts from her hands, pulling them down and away until she was gloriously naked.

"Oh, I have a point," I said, going up on my knees to show her. "It's going to be inside you very soon, but first, your bottom and I have to have a little chat. I'll need you to be quiet."

"There you go again—"

The flesh of my palm connected with her bottom, and she hushed, the slap playful and gentle. I wasn't going to hurt her. I had no desire to do that. Playful naughtiness was okay, but pain was not part of the equation. She knew that. We'd talked about it. She was ready to explore, as evidence by the velvet pillow she'd bought.

My fingers skimmed the tender flesh of her bottom, rubbing at the slight red mark my hand had made the first time. "Someone's been naughty," I said, tapping her again lightly with my hand. "So naughty that I don't think a spanking with my hand is enough," I said, stripping off my clothes until I was hot and hard in front of her. My dick held a drop of precum, and she gazed up at me, licking her lips.

"Do I have permission?" she asked, waiting for me to nod once before she caught the glistening bead on her tongue.

I leaned down, grasping her chin and kissing her, my tongue pushed out of the way by hers while she showed me who the boss was. I might think I was, but we both knew the truth. I would fold like an accordion to keep from hurting her.

"Now, where was I?"

"Teaching my bottom a lesson," she answered for me, spreading her legs wider, making me moan instantly.

"Oh, god, you are the best present I've ever received."

"The gift that keeps on giving," she said seductively, and I laughed, slapping her ass, my dick twitching at her playful yelp.

"More like the gift that keeps on coming, and you will be soon," I promised, kissing the spot on her bottom that I'd reddened. "Oh, look, my tongue slipped," I said, sliding it down her lips to her clit where I teased her for a hot second. "Maybe I need a spanking. Good thing it's not my bottom hung over that pillow for the taking."

I stroked a hand down her back, letting the sensation raise goosebumps across her skin until I grasped her ass cheek and squeezed it, smacking her with my dick on the other one. She moaned, and this time, my dick twitched against her hard on its own.

"Oh, your dick likes me," she moaned, wiggling her bottom backward for me to smack again.

"It fucking loves you," I growled, grasping her waist and flipping her over. "But you know what else loves you more? My tongue. Your wedding gift to me is glorious. It spreads you wide open for me to see every last bit of your folds."

I rested on my belly, my head between her legs, while I traced her with my finger. Up, down, and around in a rhythm that had her writhing around on the pillow, begging for me to fuck her. I didn't. My tongue stroked her instead, building that pending implosion until her moans of pleasure were coming faster, and her head rocked back and forth. The new way I had spread her open gave me full access to her in a way that only heightened her pleasure.

"Come for me, tart," I ordered without taking my tongue off her quivering folds.

She did, grasping my hair and crying out my name while her walls spasmed around my fingers. Before she had come all the way down to earth, I turned her over again, resting her back on that pillow, bottom up, and entered her, my dick straining to find its release as hers never stopped. Her moans built again as I stroked her, finding an angle that was overpowering to me. I couldn't stop myself, and I leaned over her back, buried my lips near her ear, and moaned loudly. "Holy fuck, Amber," I cried, my dick filling her with heat at the same time she let go again, her bottom pushed into my pelvis. Slowly she relaxed back into the pillow on a sigh.

"I love you so much," I said, tugging on her earlobe and then biting down gently. "So fucking much that I don't know where you end and I begin."

"And that's the way I love it, Bishop," she sighed, her body going limp.

I sat up and lifted her from the uncomfortable pillow, straightening her out on the bed and covering us, still naked and wrapped in each other's arms. I would die a happy man as long as she was always by my side.

The sun was setting, and soon the moon would be up, but I didn't care as I floated around the lake on my chair float. The water was still warm, and the company was delightful. We'd picked Athena up at the airport yesterday, and when we got back home, we spent the rest of the day talking, laughing, and getting to know each other. We even went to The Fluffy Cupcake for some of Able Baker Brady's sourdough to make her favorite dinner. Grilled cheese.

Brady was pleased to introduce Athena to Lake Pendle by handing her a loaf of his famous bread. Haylee had smothered her with hugs, cupcakes, and happiness, as she always does. Something told me my best friend knew exactly why this girl had come home to see her daddy.

Athena was indeed the spitting image of Bishop. She was gorgeous with beautiful long golden-brown hair and green eyes like her daddy. She was a full head taller than me, not a surprise, since most people are, and bubbly to boot. Whatever her reason for coming home, she hadn't revealed it yet.

"Lake Pendle is a great place," she said from her innertube. "Quiet, peaceful, safe."

I nodded and paddled the chair around so I could face her. "My hometown is idyllic most of the time. There's the Sunday evening waterski show on the lake every week. In fact, Able Baker Brady is always on the top of the pyramid like the show off he is. Oh! We have Strawberry Fest, too! It's like a county fair, but better. There's baking competitions, parades, animal judging, and the midway."

"That does sound fun," she agreed, her eyes on the horizon. "Are you and daddy going this year?"

"We are, it's this coming weekend," I explained. "The Fluffy Cupcake has a booth there every year where we sell cupcakes and bread. Normally, I staff the booth, but this year, things are changing. I do hope you'll still be here. I'd love to introduce you and Bishop to the fair for the first time."

She rubbed her belly around and around. "The Fluffy Cupcake was the best part of this town. Those Berry Sinful cupcakes were better than anything I could get in California."

I chuckled and nodded. "We have no problem selling our wares in this town, that's for sure. If you're going to school to be a chef, you should sit down with Haylee and Brady. They're both master bakers, and Haylee is a trained chef as well. She might have some words of wisdom to share."

"I'd like that," she said, her lips trying to smile, but failing. "She was very sweet to me today. Sometimes, Daddy's friends don't know how to act around me, so they just ignore me. I think it's because he doesn't tell people he's a father. I know over the years he's been ashamed to admit it to his colleagues."

I jumped out of my lounger instantly and grabbed her innertube. "No! That is not why Bishop didn't tell people about you," I said, vibrating with sadness for this girl who thought her dad wanted to hide her away.

"Don't get me wrong," she said quickly, "I love him, and I get why he does it. It's hard to be barely thirty-four and have an eighteen-year-old kid to deal with."

My head swung wildly while I pushed her tube to shore. "Listen to me, Athena. He has never been ashamed of you a day in his life. God, he loves you so much that he'd die for you. I know you don't understand the nuances of being a teen parent, but it's a real thing. He was cautious because he didn't want you to get hurt. He had to trust people before he'd tell them."

"He told you right away, though," she pointed out.

"He did," I agreed.

"He must have trusted you then."

I smiled and winked, hoping my face was open and honest. "He did, but in Bishop's defense, it just slipped out. We started this relationship as friends, and he didn't have any reason to hide you from me. Now I can see that he just needed someone to talk to about it. He missed you terribly, even if he tried to hide it," I said, and she chuckled, nodding her head.

"He's always the stoic one."

I pointed at her and laughed. "Exactly. He tried to hide it, but I could tell that he was struggling with his little version of having an empty nest. He's fiercely proud of you, though, and he'd fight to the death against anyone who tried to hurt you."

"Dinner is ready," Bishop called, jogging down the hill.

Athena smiled to acknowledge what I said, but I could tell she only half believed me. She jumped out of her tube, tossing it up on shore along with my float. I made my way to shore on one leg, and Bishop wrapped me in a towel before he lifted me into his arms to carry me up the hill.

"I love you, Mrs. Halla," he whispered, kissing my lips once while he walked.

"Newlyweds," Athena said from behind us with fake sarcasm and disgust.

I chuckled with Bishop, stroking his bearded cheek until he set me in a seat at the table. It was piled high with burgers and brats, chips, and watermelon. I happened to know some raspberry tarts were waiting in the fridge, too. I bit into a brat while we talked about everything from Athena's internship at Disney to her school days in California. It was the first time she had mentioned school or work, which told us that she was struggling with something that had to do with them.

"That was delicious. Thanks, Bishop," I said, rubbing my belly, now full to the brim. "I think I'll have to wait on those tarts in the fridge. I'm stuffed."

"Me, too," Athena agreed. "The brats were addicting."

While Bishop cleaned up dinner, I explained to her where the brats came from and how we have a meat market and smokehouse right here in Lake Pendle. With the moon out, Bishop started a fire, and we got comfy around the new pit.

"It's so unbelievably beautiful and silent here," she said, staring up at the sky streaked with clouds. "I miss the silence of the Midwest."

"It does have a certain essence the big cities don't have," Bishop agreed.

"Big cities aren't all they're cracked up to be," she said, nodding as she stared into the fire. "I moved to San Diego because of the huge LGBTQ community there, but I may have let that be the driving power instead of everything else."

"What is everything else?" Bishop asked, leaning forward to see her better.

"Common sense," she finally answered with a shrug.

"Are you trying to say you miss home?" I asked, hoping she'd finally come clean about why she was here.

Her head nodded while her chin trembled for a moment. "Desperately. It's not like homesickness, either. I know the difference. It's just that everything feels wrong when I'm out there. I don't belong, even in this gigantic community of likeminded people. They've welcomed me into their fold, and they don't treat me like an outsider, but yet, I'm not them. If that makes sense."

I eyed Bishop for a moment who sat stunned in his chair. Finally, he reached out to grasp her hand. "Have you talked to your mom about it yet?" he asked, squeezing her hand.

"No," Athena said, shaking her head. "She'll give me the standard social worker answer. Have you ever noticed she always tries to play both sides of the fence with me? It's never helpful. That's why I came to you, Daddy. I need help figuring out what to do."

"I'm always here for you, baby. Amber, too. We'll help you work through this. I don't want you to be unhappy, and we can see that you are. If you take the physical place out of the equation, do you enjoy what you're learning in school?"

"Love it!" she said, laughter on her lips again. "I love culinary school and the challenges it offers me. I'm not unhappy doing what I'm doing."

"You're unhappy where you're doing it," I finished.

She nodded, pointing at me. "Does that make me..." She paused and motioned her hand around in the dark. "A child? Does it make me a quitter?"

"Absolutely not!" Bishop exclaimed, pulling her into his arms and rocking her. "You are not the first, nor will you be the last, eighteen-year-old, who discovers who they are by learning who they aren't."

She leaned back on the chair and wiped a tear from her face discreetly. "You mean it's not a bad thing to feel this way?"

Bishop smiled and gripped her cheeks in his hands. "A bad thing? No, I think it's a good thing. You spent a year away from home and learned that big cities aren't for you. That's growth, and growth is never a bad thing."

I stayed quiet during the exchange between them because I knew he was right. Sometimes we have to do new things to grow, even if we learn they aren't for us. Look at me. I had to move out of my parents' house to figure out that I didn't have to live under their thumb any more. It sounds stupid, but sometimes we can't see the forest when we're among all the trees.

"Did you just take a break from Disney, or did you quit?" Bishop asked in the most non-confrontational way possible.

"I didn't quit, but I told them I might be gone for two weeks. They're okay with it. I'm not a flaky teenager, but I also couldn't wait until August to talk to someone about this."

"You have decisions to make about school," Bishop said, and she nodded.

"I've been here for forty-eight hours, and I already don't want to go back to the smog, heat, crowds, and noise. It's just not for me."

"There's nothing wrong with being a small-town girl, Athena," I said firmly. "I've lived here my entire life, and this town has taken care of me. Never underestimate the power of a small town."

She nodded and bit her lip. "I know, but the problem is, there aren't any culinary schools in small towns. They're all in big cities."

"Okay, so you find the smallest big city you can," Bishop said to drag a laugh from Athena.

"You do know that St. Paul College has a culinary school, right?" I asked, leaning forward. "I mean, it's not San Diego, but they've turned out some very successful chefs, including the incredibly talented Haylee Pearson."

"They do?" Athena asked, and I nodded. "I didn't know that, but it's still a big city."

"It's a big city that's a twenty-minute drive from here," Bishop added. "You wouldn't have to live there. You could live here and drive there."

"If you want, I'd be happy to take you to the bakery tomorrow to talk to Haylee about it. She'd love to tell you stories about her days at the school. The good news is, she's not too old to remember them or for them to still be relevant."

Athena laughed then, resting her head back on the chair with a smile. "I'd like that. I need to figure something out before I talk to Mom. She doesn't do well without a plan."

"Which is my fault," Bishop said softly. "When you came along, her plan suddenly changed, and she was without one. She didn't pivot well, and it twisted her into this regimented person who doesn't roll well with the punches. It's not her fault, sweetheart. It's mine."

Athena blinked twice and shook her head. "I know you've always felt that way, Daddy, and I might only be an eighteen-year-old kid, but I did have sex education. I'm worldly enough to know that it takes two to tango, and Mom was a willing participant in my creation. You have to let some of that guilt go for what happened when you were a kid. God, Daddy. It's been eighteen years. Mom's been married for ten of them. Just forgive yourself for whatever you think you did wrong. When things went wrong," she said, emphasizing went, "you stepped up to the plate and faced your responsibility. Everything you did was in my best interest, even when it cost you the most. I know Mom doesn't hold you responsible for her being a teen parent. She wishes you'd stop carrying the guilt as much as I do. Hell, even Ken thinks you punish yourself too hard and too long. Live a little. Laugh a little. Take chances. I'm all grown up now. You've done your job. Stop acting like it didn't all work out in the end."

Bishop sat back as if he'd been slapped, his back rigid. "I need to take a walk," he said, clearing his throat as he stood. Before I could stop him, he was gone down the hill and out of sight.

Athena moaned, shaking her head on the chair. "I screwed up, didn't I?"

I leaned back on the seat and sighed. Bishop was a big boy, and he just needed time. I'd give it to him. "No, you didn't screw up. You were honest. Honesty hurts sometimes. I've learned that over the last few months being married to your dad. What you just said freed him of a lot of shit he's carried around for years. I've tried to tell him the same things, but it's going to be harder to ignore coming from you. Your absolution of the crime he thinks he committed now requires him to end the sentence he gave himself. He can't claim his decision that day was a failure.

He didn't fail. You're a bright, beautiful, sweet soul who doesn't blame him for what happened. He's going to struggle with making that change in his mindset. He will get there, though. I promise."

"I hope so," she whispered with her eyes on the fire. "I don't want it to mess up your marriage. Daddy's done that for a lot of years."

"Done what?" I asked, confused.

"Pushed women away. Pretended like my existence in the world was the reason he couldn't stay with any of the women he dated. He claimed none of them wanted to deal with a single dad. I'm sure some didn't, but I don't buy that every woman he dated ran for the hills when they learned of my mere existence. I don't want that to happen to you."

"He can try, but he won't succeed," I promised, giving her a wink.

It was at that moment that I realized I was in this marriage for the long haul, whether he liked it or not.

Seventeen

"Bishop?" Amber called from the top of the hill, her voice questioning as she moved toward me. "Are you down here."

She knew I was down here. She watched me walk down here an hour ago. I sat down here until I noticed the fire die out and hoped they'd gone to bed. I planned to sleep in the basement tonight, so I had a little time to myself.

I heard her on the dock, her crutches thumping on the wood as she made her way toward me. "Athena went to bed."

"Good enough. I'm glad you hit it off with my daughter so well," I said, my surly mood making my words sarcastic and tight.

"Well, I'm sorry. I'll try harder to hate the sweet girl you raised," she said, her words as sarcastic as mine. "She was only trying to help." This time her words were soft, but they were like bullets to my back.

"By being disrespectful of everything I gave up to make sure she had a future."

"Is that what you got out of that?" she asked, her words shocked and surprised. "Or is that what you wanted to hear?"

I turned and stared her down, my eyes filled with an emotion I wanted to pretend was anger but was probably closer to grief. "I heard what I heard. She's eighteen and thinks she knows everything now. She doesn't."

"No, she doesn't, and she admitted that in her advice to you. She does know you, though. She grew up seeing the things you did, both healthy and unhealthy, and she recognizes them now as an adult. Even if she's only eighteen, all she wants is for you to stop feeling guilty because it hurts her, too. Have you ever thought of that?"

"What the hell are you talking about, Amber? That girl has had nothing but a good upbringing with parents who loved her and did everything in her best interest!"

"Agreed, but that doesn't mean you dying on the sword all these years to do it didn't hurt her. She understood more than you gave her credit for over the years. And before you say she heard that stuff from her mother, let me stop you because I will kick your ass with this crutch."

I sighed and shook my head. "I didn't die on any damn sword, Amber. I made choices that I thought were best at the time. I was seventeen-fucking-years-old. What was I supposed to do?"

"Maybe you were then, but you aren't seventeen anymore. You're thirty-four, and you raised that beautiful, smart, sweet girl to be a contributing member of society. What the fuck do you think you have to feel guilty about, Bishop? The fact that your condom broke? Do you think that makes you special? Condoms break all the time. Unplanned pregnancies happen all the time. Did it suck? Yeah, I'm sure it did. You were forced to be an adult in the blink of an eye, but then again, you were doing adult things, so you accepted that responsibility the moment you rolled on that condom. Holding onto your guilt now is pathetic. It's a pointless emotion. Your condom broke, and you had a kid. Oh, the horrors," she said, her hands to her face like a shock. "My parents watched their broken child be patched back together with no promise that she would even live because of a decision they made. That's guilt, Bishop. I understand their guilt, even if I wish they'd let it go. I don't want them, or you, to carry around this misguided emotion like it's somehow going to change things. It's not fucking going to change anything! Can't you see that?" She held up her hand. "I'm wrong. Guilt will change things. It won't change the situation that happened, but it sure as hell will change the rest of your fucking life if you don't forgive yourself for it. You'll lose your daughter. My parents have slowly lost me over the years because of their guilt. You worked this hard to show Athena how much you love her and want her in your life. Why are you going to fuck it up now? She's given you absolution in hopes you'll give it to her in return. She didn't ask to be created, but she was, and she's tired of living with the constant message that she's your punishment."

"Are you fucking kidding me right now?" I asked, anger making me turn and clench my fists at my side. "Constant message that she's a punishment? That's the most ridiculous thing I've heard today, and I heard a lot of ridiculousness up there!"

Her head shook, and she braced her crutches on the dock. "No, what you didn't hear up there were the words of your child who wants to move on from the toxic way you treat yourself. You didn't hear that she wants to live here, with you, and be part of your life instead of living across the fucking country. What you didn't hear was that she loves you so much that she came to you first for reassurance because she trusts you above even her mother." She waved her hand on a sigh. "I'm going to sleep at my apartment tonight. You can have your space to decide if you want to continue to be the Bishop who can't see that the job he's done as a father more than negates how he became one, or if you want to continue to act like a martyr and send the message to his daughter that her hurt isn't as important as his guilt. Once you've decided that, you can decide if you want to continue this marriage or if you want out. All I want is good things for you, Bishop. If that means you'd rather be alone, I'll honor your wishes, even if it breaks my heart for the rest of my life. I love you."

She turned and crutched back down the dock, her form nothing but a shadow in the darkness of the night. I wanted to call out to her, but my pride wouldn't let me. Maybe she was a little bit too on the nose about a few things. If I admitted it, then I had to accept it. If I accepted it, then I had to change it. If I changed it, then I had to find a new purpose in my life.

She is that new purpose, you asshole, my inner voice said.

I watched her until she made it to the top of the hill, knowing I should have helped her, but also knowing she wouldn't have let me. I turned back to the lake and sighed. I had two choices. I could go to bed and sleep on it or go to a bar and drink the thoughts out of my mind.

I turned away from the water, ready to go back to the house when there was a scream. I watched as my wife tumbled down the hill, her cries of terror and pain tearing my guts out as I ran.

"Amber!" I screamed, my feet thudding on the wooden planks in desperation, but it was too late. She landed on the edge of the dock with a sickening thud before she sank below the dark water.

"Amber!" I screamed again, splashing into the water and searching for her below the surface.

My hand brushed against her braid, and I found her armpits, carefully dragging her back onto the beach and lying her flat on the sand. "Amber, talk to me," I said, slapping her face while I checked for a pulse. It was weak, but when I leaned down by her face, she wasn't breathing.

"Daddy?" Athena asked as she ran down the hill. "What happened?"

"Call an ambulance!" I screamed. "Oh my God, call an ambulance!"

Athena was already on the phone as I opened my wife's mouth, water pouring from it as I tried to press my lips to hers to offer her the only thing I could at that moment. Lifesaving air.

"Come on, my little tart," I begged, my lips back on hers to force air into her lungs. "You can't leave me now. Fight, Amber!"

She sputtered, water spurting from her lips like a fountain while she coughed and tried to catch her breath. I held her neck still, talking to her while I listened to the sirens draw closer. "I love you," I whispered. "God, never forget how much I love you."

The house was quiet when Bishop carried me in and lowered me to the couch. "Wow," I sighed, leaning back and taking in the room. "Did the flower shop explode in here?"

He turned me on the couch and propped my bad leg up on a pillow, the lower half of it now in a walking boot since I managed to break the one part of the leg that didn't have a rod in it. The doctor's said it would heal in about six weeks, and once the walking boot was off, they'd be able to fit me for the new brace. I was already marking off the days on the calendar.

Bishop chuckled when he sat on the coffee table by the couch. "There are a lot of people who love you in this town, but no one as much as me. Athena said I went overboard on the flowers."

I smiled and held his hand in mine, something I'd done the entire three days I was in the hospital because he never left my side. "Maybe just a smidgen. There has to be two dozen roses in each vase."

"It must be all the cupcake counting you do. You're spot on."

"Athena might have been right about going overboard since I count six vases, but only a smidgen. They are beautiful, thank you. Where is Athena?"

"She's with Sam and Ken at Strawberry Fest. I made her promise to go and have a good time for both of us."

I frowned while my hand came up to smooth down his beard. "I'm sorry you had to miss it. I'm sad about it, too. I've never missed Strawberry Fest before."

"I wish I could take you, but the doctor said no immediately when I asked. He said that even in a wheelchair, it's too dangerous with your skull fracture to go out there."

I sighed with fatigue. "Nor am I up to it, wheelchair or not. I just want to enjoy being home and not eating hospital food."

He leaned down and kissed my lips tenderly, his touch almost tentative rather than confident. "I'm going to take care of you, and I would guess when Athena gets home, she's bringing some treats with her. She did grill your bestie for five minutes about your favorite fair food."

I put my hand to my chest and grinned. "She's a girl after my own heart. You raised her right, Bishop Halla."

"I know," he said, clearing his throat before he could go on. "You made me see that, Amber. Those things you said to me on the dock—"

"I'm sorry about that," I jumped in immediately. "I shouldn't have said what I said that night. I just didn't like seeing two people I love beating themselves up."

His finger came down on my lips, and I stopped talking. "Don't apologize, tart. What I was going to say was, you were right. Those things Athena said, and the things you said, were so damn right. I apologized to Athena, and I need to apologize to you."

"You have, about once an hour every day for the last three days. None of this was your fault, Bishop."

"Maybe not the fall, but there was a lot I did wrong that night, baby. If I hadn't been down there, you wouldn't have been. If I had just put my anger aside and helped you up the hill, you wouldn't have a skull fracture and a broken ankle. I can't change any of that, but I can say everything I should have said then, now."

I squeezed his hand in mine. "I just want to be here and enjoy whatever time we have left in this marriage, Bishop. My brain is too sore to make sense of anything too complicated."

"Let me tell you how much time we have left in this marriage, tart. Forever. We have forever because what happened three nights ago will never happen to you again, at least when I can prevent it. Everything you said on that dock that night was right—everything Athena said on the deck before that was right. I was punishing myself, but what I didn't see was that I was also punishing her. I made her think that my life would have been better if I hadn't rolled that condom on that day. I did that," he said, poking himself in the chest. "When the truth was, Athena saved me. She made me grow up fast, sure. But that girl also saved me. Athena's very presence in my life forced me to pick a path early in life and stay on it. There was no time for fooling around or losing focus in college. I had a child to support financially and emotionally. Maybe, when I was younger, there was a little bit of resentment about that, but now I can see that she gave me a family. Athena was someone to hold onto when I had no one left. She made me a better man, and I made her feel like she was less than."

I couldn't shake my head too hard, so I blew him a kiss. "No, you're too hard on yourself. She didn't mean it like that."

He smiled, but it was weak and unsure. "Athena said the same thing, and I sure hope that's true, but I don't know how it can be. Regardless, she understands now that yes, she changed the course of my life, but for the better. Athena understands now that I love her so much that I would die for her. She knows that she was never a punishment but a gift. A beautiful, sweet, loving, once in a lifetime kind of gift. Now, I need to make you understand the same thing."

I tipped my head to the side. "Understand the same thing?"

He nodded and knelt next to the couch. "Yes, the same thing. You changed the course of my life for the better the first time I met you, Amber Halla. When I reached my hand out to you in that van, it was more significant than I realized. We were going to help each other find a new course in life, and all you had to do was take my hand. You did, and now I love you so much I would die for you. You will never be a punishment to me, which I know you still think you are when we're dealing with your leg," he said,

Tart

and I shrugged a bit, but he knew what that meant. I did and probably always would. "I need you to understand now that you are a once in a lifetime kind of gift, and you came along when I needed you the most. I had no one else to turn to when I was alone, and suddenly there you were. You were a beacon of hope and light in my world that was dark and lonely." He reached into his pocket and pulled something out. I gasped aloud when I saw what it was.

"Bishop, what are you doing?" I asked, my breath trapped in my chest.

"I'm holding up a ring to a girl the way I should have done the first time I asked her to marry me. I'm asking her if she will marry me again, but this time for real. For love. For life. For hope. For joy. With all of the flowers, cake, and friends that we can fit into the church to say the words we said before with a whole different view on what they mean. Amber, will you marry me again, for real and for good this time? Will you keep being my wife?"

I laughed then, the tears running down my face even as my lips wore a grin. "I will marry you again on one condition."

"Name it, anything," he said, nodding exaggeratedly.

"That we get married with all the flowers, cake, and those most important to us at The Fluffy Cupcake. We started our life together with cupcakes, and I think that's a perfect place to reaffirm our love for each other, don't you?"

He leaned down and kissed my lips, his trembling against mine. "I do."

"I think you're supposed to save that for our wedding day, Mr. Halla."

"Maybe I'm just practicing until the current and future Mrs. Halla lets me put this ring on her finger."

He held it up again and waited for me to lift my hand for him to put it on. When I did, he started to work the band off my finger until I grabbed his hand. "What are you doing?"

"Taking the band off. You have a real engagement ring now."

239

I shook my head carefully and pushed the band back on my finger. "The band stays. Maybe when we said our vows around those rings, we thought they weren't real, but the truth was, they were never more real. This band was blessed that night, and it will never leave my finger, no matter how many rings we add to the mix."

He ran his thumb across my cheek to steal away the tear that had fallen there. "Those are terms I can most definitely accept, my little tart." He slid the beautiful diamond solitaire over my finger to nestle against the band, and he sucked in a breath. "They look like they were made for each other," he whispered, his eyes on my finger.

"Just like us," I sighed when his lips found mine.

Epilogue

Bishop's arms went around my waist, and he tucked his face into my neck, his lips kissing the tender skin there. "Happy ten years of business, my beautiful tart," he whispered, his words almost stolen by the sounds of the partygoers around us.

"Thank you, my love," I answered, caressing his beard with my free hand. "Thanks for being here."

"Here is everything to you, and that makes it everything to me."

I smiled as I gazed at the scene before me. Here was The Fluffy Cupcake, and everything was the people filling it. Taylor and Sara were serving specialty coffee drinks from the new coffee bar we'd added this fall. It was a dream I'd had since we first opened the bakery, and after I almost died doing something as simple as walking up a hill, I decided it was time to stop putting it off. For our tenth anniversary, we were opening A Tea and A Tart. We lost a lot of table space to make it happen, but no one seemed to mind standing once they got a taste of our selection of coffee and teas to complement the treats in the bakery case each day. It had been so much fun to plan, implement, and market that I hardly noticed the massive amount of pain I was in from falling down a hill and smashing my head into a dock before nearly drowning.

"You should sit down," he said, leading me to a table, but I shook my head.

"I want to enjoy being able to stand up again," I said, resting my hand on his chest. "It's been so long since I've been without crutches."

"Okay, but don't overdo it. Remember, the doctor said you have to break the brace in slowly."

"Maybe for some people, yes," I agreed, a smile on my face as I gazed at the miracle of modern medicine that now allowed me to stand and walk with only a cane. "But some people haven't spent seventeen years in a brace. I got this, Mr. Halla."

He laughed that laugh I loved of his. The one that didn't harbor pain, guilt, or unhappiness. "I'm going to go check on Athena."

I pointed at the counter where she was chatting with Taylor and Sara. "Honestly, I think she found her tribe," I said on a wink.

He kissed my cheek and whispered, *I hope so*, in my ear before he headed over to see her. Athena had found her tribe, both in Lake Pendle and The Fluffy Cupcake. She worked here baking part-time now while going to school in St. Paul. She'd graduate in the spring with her culinary degree and planned to apprentice here as the new master baker. Sam and Ken had arrived here within twelve hours of hearing about my accident. They hadn't even met me, but Athena's frantic voice on the phone was all they had to hear to know they were needed.

And they showed up. They were there for Athena, and they had given her their blessing to transfer to St. Paul and continue her education there. They weren't sad she'd no longer be across the country. They often came up to visit Athena in her new apartment, which happened to be right next door to her Daddy's house. When she decided to stay, she refused to live in the house with a bunch of newlyweds, as she put it, and I couldn't blame her for wanting her own place. When my parents arrived back in Lake Pendle after hearing about my accident from my bestie, they had the perfect answer. My old apartment was empty, but now it's not, and I was pleased Athena found a place to call her own. I was more pleased that Bishop had her so close to him now.

Unfortunately, I didn't get to spend a lot of time with them in the first few weeks. If it hadn't been for Bishop's quick thinking, I might not have made it to the hospital alive. Even taking the cracked skull and broken ankle into account, I was lucky. His new crutches had saved both of my arms from breaking because, as soon as I went down, they fell away, allowing me to roll without my arms snapping. I shuddered. It was an awful thought, but I was so grateful he'd had the forethought to get them for me. After six weeks of healing, and another four weeks of physical therapy, I finally got the brace that would change my life. I was mobile again, active, and back working in the business I loved so much. Unfortunately, the accident required us to postpone our tenth-anniversary celebration at The Fluffy Cupcake. Haylee said as long as we did it this year, it didn't matter that we couldn't do it on the exact date of our opening. Instead, we ran specials and added new surprises every week since August to keep our customers coming back to celebrate with us.

"Hey, bestie," Hay-Hay said as she approached. "You're standing over here all by yourself, and I mean that literally and figuratively."

My eyes creased at the corners with joy. "Pretty awesome, right? It might have cost the price of a small house, but it's worth every penny."

"I couldn't agree more. Considering what we have going on, we're going to need you here."

I laid my hand on her six-month-along baby bump. It turned out that the first test she took all those months ago had been wrong. It wasn't a scare, it was real, and now, they were going to make me an auntie. "And I'm going to be here taking care of the place while you and Brady raise your little able bakers."

Her laughter filled the room, and I stored it in my heart for when she wasn't here as much. "I can picture this tiny Able Baker Brady following his daddy around carrying baguettes bigger than he is."

"Or a little Able Baker Haylee with ringlets in her hair and cupcake frosting on her face."

She nodded, but her chin trembled a little. "I heard there's a good chance this little cupcake will be sporting those ringlets in her hair after all. Can't confirm, but we'll know for sure in a few weeks."

My hand went to my chest and my own chin trembled. "My heart just melted," I whispered. "I can't wait to hold her in my arms. She's going to be the sweetest baby this side of St. Paul. I love you, sis. I know you're going to be a wonderful mother because you know what it's like to not have one."

"I had one, and she's wonderful. Come to think of it. I had two. It's just that one happened to be my age." She hugged me again, her arms tightening when she spoke. "Happy anniversary to my partner, bestie, sister, mother, auntie, and everything you are to this community. I know The Fluffy Cupcake is going to be okay when everything changes again because you're here to make sure of it."

"Darling," I whispered, "it's going to be better than okay. It's going to be the legacy for our little ones—a place to grow up in and to make memories in that they someday tell their children. The Fluffy Cupcake isn't a building or a business. It's our life. It's our dream of building a community to support our community. We've done that. We've supported our community, and they, in turn, support us. It takes a village to raise a child, and this is our village."

She had her arm around my shoulder as she gazed out at the family we'd built over the years. "It sure is. We've taken our dream of having a little place to sell cupcakes and turned it into a business that is about to witness a new generation. I don't know how that happened, but I do know I can't wait to have our little ones under our feet, sneaking cookies out of the case, and chasing each other around the same way we used to."

"Our little ones?" I asked, feigning shock and surprise.

"Yes, our little ones. I might be going first, but I know you and Bishop will follow close behind. I sure hope so, anyway. We've done everything else together, and I can't imagine not raising our little cupcakes together, too."

"That would be a berry sinful thing to do," I said, laughter on my lips.

"What are you two whispering about over here?" Bishop asked, walking over to us with a drink in his hand. "Thirty years old and still whispering like schoolgirls."

"I was just telling Amber how I was looking forward to us raising our little cupcakes together."

He shook his finger at my bestie. "One teeny tiny cupcake and one even tinier tart."

Haylee laughed with abandon and pointed at him. "You got me, Mr. Halla. I'm so happy that you're here to celebrate with us this year, Bishop, and that you saved my best friend's life so she could be here, too. I love you both."

She pulled us in for a group hug, and I rubbed her back, knowing her pregnancy hormones were leading her emotional responses, but loving every minute of it. "We're building a wonderful family," I whispered, "Now, go find that man of yours before he sends out the police. You know he will, too."

Hay-Hay laughed and waved as she weaved her way to the side of the bakery where Brady was engaged with my dad and old Mr. Martinson.

"She's glowing with happiness," Bishop said, his eyes on her protruding belly. "I can't wait until you glow that way."

I huffed and put my hand on my hip. "Excuse me, Mr. Halla? Are you implying that I don't glow?"

His gaze drew me in while his lips captured mine in a short kiss that made me glad no one had noticed us. "Absolutely not. I said to glow in that way, which means your belly round with our child. I missed most of Sam's pregnancy. I want to be there for every step of the next one."

I leaned into him and nodded, my arm around his waist. "If my belly gets too round with our child, I might tip over. Oh!" I said, grabbing his hand. "I left part of our celebration in the back."

He followed me to the back of the bakery, and I was glad no one followed us to see what we were up to back here. Still considered newlyweds, they probably figured we were sneaking off for a little nookie. I held up my hand by the cooler and stepped inside, grabbing a box off the shelf. His head was tipped in curiosity when I held it out.

245

"A special Fluffy Cupcake anniversary gift for you, Mr. Halla," I whispered.

He took the box but held my eye. "What is it that you had to keep it in the cooler."

"It's an experiment," I said. "It's more like a work in progress. I haven't quite decided what it will be yet. Open it."

He set the box on the baker's bench and untied the ribbon, parting the bakery paper and lifting out his surprise. "It's a tart."

"The teeniest tiniest," I agreed, a smile on my lips.

He set it on the baker's bench. "Raspberry and blueberry together?" he asked, his brows furrowed in confusion.

"Yep. I couldn't decide. It will take a few more months for me to know which tart it will be, but it's most definitely a tart."

He froze, his breath held in his chest for a moment. "Do you mean a teeny tiny tart for us?"

I nodded, a smile on my lips and a tear in my eye. "I know we didn't plan for it to happen this soon, but I didn't think you'd be too upset about it."

His hand was shaking when he picked up mine. "Sometimes, the unplanned moments in life are what mean the most. You taught me that, and I can't wait to see all the wonderful things you're going to teach our tiny tart. Oh, God, I can hardly breathe from the joy and wonder of this gift. You are more than I deserve, Amber Halla."

My hand caressed his cheek while the joy of his love and the joy of this tiny seed growing inside me filled my heart to overflowing. "No, Bishop. We deserve each other, and all the wonderful things that are happening to us. Don't ever lose sight of that. You, my sweet teacher, taught me that. I love you."

He gathered me into his arms and rocked me soothingly, kissing my forehead. "And I love you, my sweetart."

Then his lips were on mine with the promise of being his today, tomorrow, and forever.

Tart

About the Author

Katie Mettner writes small-town romantic tales filled with epic love stories and happily-ever-afters. She proudly wears the title of *'the only person to lose her leg after falling down the bunny hill'* and loves decorating her prosthetic with the latest fashion trends. She lives in Northern Wisconsin with her own happily-ever-after and three mini-mes. Katie has a massive addiction to coffee and Twitter, and a lessening aversion to Pinterest — now that she's quit trying to make the things she pins.

You can find Katie on her website at www.Katiemettner.com

Tart
Other Books by Katie Mettner

The Fluffy Cupcake Series (2)

The Kontakt Series (2)

The Sugar Series (5)

The Northern Lights Series (4)

The Snowberry Series (7)

The Kupid's Cove Series (4)

The Magnificent Series (2)

The Bells Pass Series (4)

The Dalton Sibling Series (3)

The Raven Ranch Series (2)

Someone in the Water (Paranormal)

White Sheets & Rosy Cheeks (Paranormal)

The Secrets Between Us

After Summer Ends (Lesbian Romance)

Finding Susan (Lesbian Romance)

Torched

Find all of Katie's Books on Amazon!

Printed in Great Britain
by Amazon

31161771R00139